Malambo

Malambo

Lucía Charún-Illescas

TRANSLATED BY EMMANUEL HARRIS II

SWAN ISLE PRESS

CHICAGO

Swan Isle Press, Chicago 60640-8790

Malambo was previously published in the
original Spanish, ©2001 by Universidad Nacional
Federico Villarreal; and published in an Italian
translation by Giunti Gruppo Editoriale, ©1999
by Lucía Charún-Illescas. Chapter 1 of *Malambo*,
translated by Emmanuel Harris II, previously
appeared in a slightly different form in the *Afro-
Hispanic Review*, 22, no. 3 (fall, 2003).

Printed in the United States of America
First Edition
ISBN 0-9748881-0-9

Library of Congress Cataloging-in-Publication Data
Charún-Illescas, Lucía.
    [Malambo. English]
    Malambo / Lucía Charún-Illescas ; translated by
Emmanuel Harris II.
        p. cm.
    Includes bibliographical references.
    ISBN 0-9748881-0-9 (alk. paper)
    1. Blacks—Peru--History--Fiction. I. Harris,
Emmanuel. II. Title

PQ8498. 13.H295M3513 2004
863'.7—dc22   2004059013

Swan Isle Press is funded in part by a generous
grant from the Illinois Arts Council, a State of
Illinois Agency

www.swanislepress.com

Para que Nana
Malú,
Cae,
Mateo
y Ñaño
no se les olvide el rumor
que trae el Rio Hablador

So that Nana
Malú,
Cae,
Mateo
and Ñaño
don't forget the murmur
carried by the Talking River

Contents

Malambo 1

Translator's Note 223

Glossary 228

Malambo

Chapter I

The events of this story flow from the tropic of the mangrove and the orchids that are borne in the air, to the cold, transparent blue of the Strait of Magellan. Its concentric sides meet in the Ciudad de los Reyes under the coat of arms of a blue shield with three crowns and a flaming star, planted in the dunes of the coast facing the Southern Sea.

On the wrong bank, close to the herd's stables and the cultivated lands and to the skirt of the hill of San Cristóbal, spring the shacks of the miserable outskirts of San Lázaro. The waters of the Rímac repeat to the reeds those tales of the wind that meanders through the nearby corn and cotton fields. It is a subtle murmuring that reaches the fields of *lúcumas* and that echoes between the custard apple trees and the *pacayar* palms. Though these waters have a tame appearance, they also know how to aggressively overflow. In the high tides of summer, they enter, dragging mud and the rocky ground of the leper colony. They drain confused, tinged in blood, between the cadavers of the sacrificed animals of the slaughterhouse of Malambo, the corner where many of the Negroes from Lima live: seat and protection of the *taitas* Minas, the Mandiga and Angola elders and the *cofradías* of Congos and Mondongos. In Malambo, the Rímac proudly rubs elbows with the freedmen, the cimarrons, and the smuggled slaves who listen to it with suspicion but learn to understand its knack of speech. Because at times the river pretends to be slack. Lazy, it detains itself, conversing in the ditches and the puddles, in passing the dusty crevices and the tortuous and salty alleys of San Lázaro.

On the other bank, that of the Palace of the Viceroy and of the big houses with stone facades and great windows with silk curtains, the river begins to appear slimmer by orderly channels through the clay pipes. It runs united to the subterranean springs underneath Blanket Street and Weavers Lane and under Jewish Street, Silversmith's, Marketer's and Swordmaker's Lanes. It leaves behind the licentious tapping of the covered women in Blue Dust Street until encountering the fountain of the Plaza Mayor. He who stops to contemplate its bubbling cannot evade the gossiping of the Talking River.

〰〰〰

Almost in unison, the bells of the Cathedral began the six o'-clock ring in the Church of Santa Ana, in Santo Domingo, San Sebastián and Santa Clara and in the six convents and the six monasteries of the city. Tomasón Valleumbroso noted that in the church of San Lázaro time lengthened in silent tolls. They were the last to ring, as if the hours were in no hurry to arrive at the mud and reed houses of Malambo. A neighboring voice prayed the *angelus*. Tomasón cleared his throat. The voice pronounced "Amen" and Tomasón "Caraaá." He always had at the tip of his tongue a lethargic *carajo*, to be drawn out or cut short when he did not have much or anything to add. This time it could well have been: "Caraaá, it's already getting dark!" or "Caraaá, I'm tired and I'm not working any more!" or simply "Caraaá, the bell tower is not in time with the others."

Rubbing the steel and flint, he lit a candle of animal fat, and illuminated by the trembling flame, he gave the last penciling to the canvas. He stood back a few steps, scratched his head of nappy, gray hair and contemplated the image. In America, artists invented variations of the religious paintings brought by European masters. Tomasón dominated these like no one else. He painted the oils without giving perspective to the figures. With few chiaroscuros, "without a bunch of nit-picking or *mariconeo* caraaá," as he would say, he would adorn them in a way that satisfied his vision and made him plenty happy. In the midst of golden strokes, the archangel Gabriel suited in steel armor carried a sword of justice in his right hand. The archangel was suspended in the clouds of a twilight pink sky. Over his reddish hair flew four hummingbirds with wings joined by a wave of garlands and a vine shoot in their beaks.

"Thank goodness I'm done," he said, used to thinking out loud. "Master can't complain about the way it turned out, because I made it with the leftovers of the paint, not to mention the tattered and hairless brushes like the tail of a mangy dog. And his eyes are from what's-his-name, and his face has I don't know what, but it turned out good. The same for the feathers of his wings that I gave just enough shadow to, like master wants. If he's not careful, haa, Don Gabriel is going to fly away."

He finished cleaning the brushes while he passed a tired look over the hut. His room ten yards deep was not a plain house like that of other people. He lived crowded by broken frames, purple dyes, dried ochre, damaged clothes, and junk covered with a fine dark dust that, tinged with a splendor of shiny, crumbled velvet, saturated the air and followed him everywhere. One could barely walk through the room without bumping into one of the mountains of broken-down furniture and the clothesline that ran the length of the roof from which hung his pathetic jacket. The bundle of his spare pants was surrounded by pieces of sausage, two scraps of fresh meat slovenly covered in flies, half a bunch of ripe plantains, and two strings of pearl onions. And more rags. Along the wall, boards were set aside to dry to make a fire or to be painted and then set afire.

Tomasón delighted in covering the walls with the same persistence with which he colored his canvases and boards. The tight images, delineated with patience from pieces of coal, interwoven without beginning or recognizable end.

"But sometimes they fade away as if time robbed them," he thought.

And it could be true: they would disappear. When he least expected, they were no longer there. Perhaps they were protected below a stain of soot or humidity or they became part of the dark dust. God only knows!

If Tomasón had someplace to live and if this was living, it was because of Don Jacinto Mina, his *cumpa* Jaci, brother in spirit and corporal of the *cofradía* of Negroes from Angola. One week with no end, at the approach of evening, he appeared with three master builders whom Tomasón did not know and who nonetheless wanted to construct the dwelling without charging him a cent. The fame of the painter was a mysterious fountain of admiration and respect.

Don Jacinto Mina and the master builders chose a plot that was beside the slaughterhouse, situated in front of a row of trees that only bloom in Malambo. There were six of them. Since no one knew their surname, they were called by their first name: Malambo trees. When were they planted there and by whom?

For what reason? No one knew. On certain evenings, the leaves of these noble trees released a sweet aroma with hints of molasses. Jaci quickly tied the bamboo to put up the walls while Tomasón did not cease to distract him.

"Don't forget about the window, *cumpa* Mina. I want it to be big."

Intent on his task, Jacinto Mina pretended not to hear him. Tired of the deafness of his buddy, Tomasón moved to the helpers.

"And with mangrove wood of course, real big caraaá. I want to comfortably see the Rímac."

Finally the master builders gave in and the huge window opened its mangrove eye, a tremendous surprise from the flaming hovel. Before a week passed, the painter looked for Jaci.

"*Cumpa*, please make that window smaller. The wind seeps through. Between the air with its chill and the river with its chatter, they won't let me sleep, caraaá."

Jaci Mina treated him with care. He was one of the few Angolans who still lived in that group of shacks in the area of Pachacamilla, not far from the warehouses of the Ciudad de los Reyes. In spite of having to cross Stone Bridge daily to visit his friends, and having to go through a village hacienda, he preferred to settle there. People said that he was more noble than communion bread. That his look possessed powers of enchantment, that his eyes were capable of making others sleep, but that he himself never slept. At least that is what the pebbles under the water of the Talking River swear.

"It's fine, Tomasón. One of these days I'll shrink your window," Jaci promised.

And because that day never came, Tomasón had to get accustomed to the whims and the bad moods of the window. He remembered that the Indians from Cercado covered the entryways of their houses with llama skin. So in the opening of the hut, he hung an ox hide that was given to him by the butchers; he did not know why. Temporarily—though never taking it down—he fastened it with a few half-entered nails. Whenever he wanted to check on the gossip of the Rímac, he moved his little wooden bench, lifted up the hide, and put his ear to the wind. On its hard skin that nevertheless flapped like a flag, he painted, with a few strokes, a red bull—an exorcism of the beast with light hooves and yellow horns that always charged him in his dreams ever since his first night in Malambo!

If Jaci did not come for him, it was Venancio. He quickly recognized him from a distance since Venancio arrived preceded by the dense odor of shrimp and crabs covered in his fisherman's basket.

Tomasón placed the painting to the side and began to look at him, intrigued by the skill with which Venancio lit the small stove and threaded the shrimp on the wire stick, after having soaked them in a marinade of lard, garlic, and hot pepper. He sautéed them over a coal flame and for a long enough time so that they turned out crisp on the outside and juicy inside.

Venancio Martín's was a happy voice, about seven points high.

"Your color is as bright as the monkey bird." Tomasón picked on him alluding to those thrushes with hints of blue in their feathers. He felt a great deal of pride in Venancio's black skin, but an aversion for his reddish and messy hair. "Maybe that's respectable hair? No! It's the color of a cockroach, that's what it is!"

And while shaking his head, the fisherman continued smiling as if he did not hear him.

Venancio Martín was born on the bank of the river, from the free womb of a washerwoman. As soon as she had rinsed him off, she buried the afterbirth, digging deep between the rocks so that the dogs would not find it and eat it, because if they do, the child will grow up healthy but become a thief. She laid him on a wrap made of rags and placed him at the bottom of a bassinet. She returned to scrubbing clothes with soapbark seed, which leaves them better than new. She waited until the sheets had enough time to air out, but before the sun escaped, and she left pleased and annoyed at the cries of her new born. Venancio, without knowing it, began his memories with the lather, the mud, and the bamboo that bordered the Rímac. He grew up swimming from bank to bank. As if he were playing, he learned how to master a hook and the shrimp traps according to the instruction of the many fraternal and savvy Negro kids that populated Malambo. By twelve, without realizing it, he had already become a fisherman. When his mother died, his only known relative was called Altagracia Maravillas.

〰〰〰

The hands of Tomasón scared away invisible flies. It was his way of asking them to let him eat in peace. Without teeth and only with a few molars, he had to chew very slowly. Like the oldest folks, he had the habit of eating with his eyes closed, squeezing his eyelids tightly to take the last flavor from the food in spite of Venancio's chatter.

"This hut needs another room. We've already made an agreement with Jaci to raise another one on this side so that you have one to paint in and one to sleep in. Huh, Tomasón?"

Tomasón wiped away the red shrimp juice with his sleeve, "Why don't you grab four sticks and build a hut for yourself. With so many wasted fields around here looking for an owner, why do you have to get into my business? You're already too old, Venancio. You've been living unmarried for so many years now. Tramp! You leave it alone the way it is. You're the one who needs more room than I do. Go find yourself a woman, so that maybe you'll look like somebody and stop dressing like a scarecrow all riffraffy, eating nothing but catfish and shrimp."

"If you want *familia*, I won't come back anymore," responded Venancio feigning discontent.

"Enough already! Caraaá. Bother me with whatever you want and just keep bringing shrimp and crab. Or would you prefer that I lock the door and not let you leave?" Tomasón responded knowing that the fisherman would not let himself be so easily intimidated.

"What's it cost you? Another room that's all, a little bigger than this one so that people admire that bed properly," insisted Venancio, pointing at the extravagance of a bed with bronze corner brackets, a canopy draped with damask that matched the flowered bedspread, and the elegant bed skirt. Not in Pachacamilla nor in Cercado and even less in San Lázaro, had Venancio ever seen anything resembling that "viceroy's barbecue" that Tomasón protected under this mess of rotten wood.

From now on, I'll sleep softly, Tomasón promised himself on the day they brought it to him. But each time that sleep overcame him, or he woke up early on his work bench, or his unstable steps led him to the same old boards, he would sleep curled up without remembering the baldachin.

When Gertrudis Melgarejo wanted to buy it from him, Tomasón cleared his throat. The miller's wife offered him twenty pesos. He looked away. Forty, then. Nothing. The offer got up to a hundred.

"What am I going to do with so much money Doña Gertrudis?"

"You can buy your freedom. You can save, pay your price and that's it."

"And who told you I have an owner? Ever since I've had this pain in my chest, I have plenty of freedom."

"Ahh, you must be a fool! What about a hundred pesos, huh?"

Tomasón stayed quiet.

"Well, then. Because of my good nature, let's say a hundred fifty. Will you sell me the bed or not?"

"Absolutely not."

"Look, I'm not going to make you another offer."

"I hope not."

"I could ask for it from your master. Think about it."

Tomasón never spoke to her again. He erased her.

Just like the rest of the furniture and the excess of plates and goods that he lived with, including the food tin that hung on the line and the tobacco leaves, the bed came from the barters he made using the virgins and saints he painted. The clients of his master, the marquis of Valle Umbroso, bought the paintings to decorate their chapels, and so they came to Tomasón bringing different prizes. They would ask him for a painting of St. James so that the saint would help them tame their wild horses. A St. Anthony in order to find something lost in the house or to find a suitor for the daughter who was heading towards being an aunt.

Poor folks know. For the most stubborn tooth ache, two prayers to St. Apolonia settles it down and just one to St. Jacob de Sales in order to stop choking. Tomasón knew every saint and miracle since he turned ten and was entrusted as an apprentice to Simón Rivero, the painter at the Jesuit monastery in the Chinca valley. Tomasón would get misty eyed remembering that southern town, forty leagues from Lima. There he learned how to write. Even in old age, Tomasón did not forget the exact traits of any letter, and he knew how to rope them better than any colt to form the names of everything that existed on the earth or suspected in heaven. Nor did he forget the vice of the monks.

"Ay caraaá! Don't talk to me about unspeakable sins. *Mariconada* that's what it was, *cumpa*!" he told Jaci Mina. "But before they could spoil me, I saved myself learning the faces of

all the Christs, the color of all the virgins and the entire collection of saints, and if they asked me, I could paint them, even
a naked angel. And from then on my fortune took another face.
I escaped with some cimarrons that weren't going anywhere.
They came. They were more than enough: old, children, women,
infants. They told me that for them the important thing was
to leave as far behind as possible the place of the merciless. Trap,
whip, and torture, nothing more than that. They themselves did
not know if they had escaped two nights ago, twenty or maybe
hundreds of years ago, but for my luck or greater disgrace I found
them in that trance. The destiny of their travels carried them,
without plan or thought, directly through the valley of the
Rímac. Some of these folks were white, and in height they were
as tall as this ceiling. Others had their eyes gouged. The ma-
jority were Negroes or copper-colored. All of them had been captured against their will since forever and taken to remote places
that hadn't been reached yet. They had been robbed of their
names with church water thrown in its memory. And because
there were so many, how could they go unnoticed by the dogs
and the tracking foremen? Truly, I don't know how. I only saw
that they would put underneath their tongues three of the leaves
from a lima bean, the ones that sprout on the head of I don't
know which birds, and this makes invisible the person that
knows the trick to using them. At first they were suspicious of
me, and I'm not sure if there was a complaint or a new obsta-
cle, because I heard grumbling in the darkness. They didn't go
against the grace of a lady who appealed on my part.

   "'Don't give in to fear, *misangre*,' she said. She gathered the
oldest women of the caravan and they decided to take me in.
None of the men dared to dispute them. Seeing that I didn't even
have a little leaf of field grass, the lady taught me the Prayer of
the Fair Judge, which doesn't make you invisible but it helps. I
prayed it as many times as we were aware of being close to the

danger of the country houses. Ay caraaá! the forty leagues of the trip seemed more like eighty."

There are three lions that are coming towards me! Stop in your tracks like my Lord Jesus Christ with the Domine Deo. *I'll repeat it three times, Fair Judge. Let his eyes not see me, let his hands not touch me, let his mouth not speak to me, let his foot not reach me. With two I look at him, with three I speak to him, the blood I drink from him and his heart I break.*

〰〰〰

In the height of the scaffold where he finds himself raised, Tomasón recalls the prayer of the Fair Judge. Soon he is overwhelmed by a sudden excitation that, try as he might, he cannot figure out. He feels a dizziness that he wants to attribute to hunger, but it is too intense. He begins to sweat, chills shake him, he coughs ugly, caraaá. A hot, gooey band climbs up his throat. He does not need to spit on the palm of his hand to know that it is blood. He accepts that his existence would not leave enough time to wear out the leather shoes that the ambitious marquis had used to try to bribe him into doubling the speed of his paintings and etchings.

"But more than anything, Tomasón, given the agreement that I have with the Nuncio, once and for all finish retouching the mural!"

"I'll finish it when I finish it, no sooner or later, master."

"But when, for God's sake!"

"At the latest, any day now."

Holding his soul he came down from the platform. He went out on the street for a breath of fresh air and convinced himself not to think about what he would do with the rest of his life. Hearing everything at the same time, he greedily took in the racket of the evening carts, the desperation of the turkey buzzards over the market trash and the murmur of water in the fountain of the Plaza Mayor. Gaining control over the blotches that bewildered him, he observed that one of the freed Negroes from the guild of the water sellers had dismounted from his donkey and was filling his jugs. "Hey, *familia*!" he felt the Negro's greeting, far away, melting in his ear.

"Hey, hey *misangre*. For a while now, I've been trying to ask you a favor, without disrespecting the master painter whose beautiful works please his master and earns him a lot of money. Don't you think that you've already painted enough white gods and saints? Is it that you don't know anything else? With so many good saints and honest gods in Guinea that we have enough to give away! Ever since they brought us to these strange parts, we Negroes should be united. Don't you think it would be good to pray to Elegguá so that he gives us courage and patience, with fire for the journey, and that Ogún replenish our strength against so much abuse."

Tomasón recovered his clarity and looked at him suspiciously.

"I think I know you but from where I'm not sure."

"That's natural, *familia*, because I'm a name that's not mine. They call me Juanillo Alarcón."

Tomasón opened his eyes. The person that was in front of him could not be the same person that was in front of him.

"Juanillo Alarcón was killed by a mule three days ago, in case you didn't know."

The deceased sighed.

"Humm, no wonder I felt so strange but I didn't realize what it was. I should have sold that evil donkey. It's his fault I'm filling and filling this water jug because I'm burning with thirst. But the more I fill it, the emptier it stays. And the plaza is covered in so much fog that I don't know how I was able to make you out."

"Fog? Is that how the dead see things?"

"All of us? I'm not so sure. I'm new to this side."

Without interest in the topic, he continued.

"When are you going to paint me a saint that's not on the opposing side? My guild always wanted to ask you to bring us a Changó that knew how to hear us and that spoke our language. And what about if you begin with a good Yemayá, heavenly, shining, even if it's only on wood or cardboard."

"I'll do it Juanillo, I promise, but stop carrying that water."

And almost begging.

"Let it rest."

With his sleeve he wiped his feverish forehead. The reflection of his fatigue in the fountain returned the heavy look of the waterman disappearing in the ripples precisely in the middle of an increasingly black blackness. He gradually disappeared. Tomasón waited until he could no longer see him, although he would continue to see him as he remembered the day that Juanillo Alarcón changed the path of his life.

He turned around and headed towards the marquis' residence. He passed through the backyard, scorned the miseries of his dwelling, made a knapsack from rags, packed his brushes and paints along with the bowl and the wooden spoon, absolutely determined never ever to return for anything in this world, caraaá.

If he remembered correctly, it was on October 18, the day of St. Luke according to the calendar of saint's days. Even though it was spring, the sun heated up as never before. Shining like that is how Tomasón painfully remembered it. The panting tam-tam of his chest drew him away towards another one far away that he carried tucked way deep inside, bent with harshness, encouraging him. He began to walk with large strides, almost, almost measuring the steps that were left for the Grim Reaper to catch up with him. He crossed Stone Bridge; he wandered through the streets of San Lázaro and turned into Malambo.

Venancio was the first to greet him—a bent stick, curved by the weight of his pack that hung on his back. He came asking about a relative of his. Today I haven't seen him, but he always comes, Venancio told him, saddened to observe the painter in such misery. And trying to disguise his worry.

"What really brings you here, *mitierra*?"

"Don't you see that I'm dying? Caraaá!"

His legs give way, he slides slowly to the ground. He lies down, making an effort to keep his eyes wide open under the leaves of a Malambo tree. He is comforted by its fragrance and he waits.

Venancio feels sympathy for the painter. He figures that something serious has happened with his friend and that nevertheless the worst has not happened to him. He sees his ribs protruding, lined with unflagging sweat, and those stalks that he carries for legs, so long, thin, and tired. He grieves in seeing his sunken face. Venancio pokes to the bottom of his huge fish basket and takes out the gourd of cane liquor and offers him the well-known drink of comfort.

The lips of Tomasón recognize the sweet *guarapo*. With each sip his congested cough is tamed. The liquor bites and singes while slowly relieving him of the burning spit. Little by little it unknots his chest and for a moment he breathes freely again. He dries his mouth with the back of his hand. A sticky thread stains his fingers. Once again he remembers the promise that he made to the late Juanillo Alarcón.

It was already a year since Tomasón dissolved that frozen knife encrusted in his body. Jaci and Venancio intuit he will die of a chest ailment when it is least expected, but Tomasón Valleumbroso is moved to debate them.

"Some die when they want, and others when the saints decide it. The only thing that I know is that not the king of Guinea himself, and maybe not even the very Obbatalá, will get me to abandon Malambo."

And always thinking out loud:

"Because you all ought to know that the marquis also wanted to challenge me by threatening to report my escape. My escape, imagine that, as if I myself had not made it known to him where I was. And he wants to make me return to that pigsty in his house. And I tell him, well go ahead and report me, that I don't have anything else to lose except the air that still serves me. If you accuse me, I'll stop right there and I'll never even paint a puff of an angel feather."

With his gaze fixed on the canvas, he rests his wrinkled eyes. The fatigue of the journey floats lightly in the air and settles on his fragile body. Tomasón receives it, leaning his head against his chest and breathing deeply, he surrenders to the pleasure of the drowsiness that allows him to sleep.

Six, six-thirty, he hears what the bells say, growing distant. Six, six-thirty, they say again. It's not possible, for he thinks that he has just lain down. He does not need to lift his head: he opens his eyes and distinguishes brightly colored mud. Excited, he closes them again. He can't figure out where, caraaá, that gleefulness comes from and a vague terror hounds him. He imagines the mixtures that he will have to make on his palette to obtain the same shade of the mud. This thought entertains him until he becomes aware that his feet are buried in that same yellow, uneven, warm mud that he is contemplating. What's that bog looking for here!

He separates his feet and the color spreads and finally yields. The painter tries to determine the circumstances in which he fell asleep in the middle of this swamp and immediately he dismisses the idea of being in a marsh.

"This is a mudslide! It came from the river, caraaá!" He hoped to convince himself, but his shout was drowned out. The hoarse voice caught in his throat, and the idea of the Rímac disturbing his slumber in order to drag him away with the boulders from the rainy season makes him shiver even more. He looks around without being able to orient himself and a voice that is not his own calls him. No, no he's not dreaming. The last hint of drowsiness vanishes.

"Tomasón," someone says shaking him by the shoulders vigorously, "you shouldn't talk in your sleep. The *Carcancha* can get inside your mouth."

Tomasón's eyes adjust to his surroundings and he sees an Indian in shirtsleeves.

〰〰〰〰

"Yáwar Inka!"

"It's not good to sleep with the door open either. If I had not arrived to cover you with my poncho, you might have died."

Tomasón caresses the vicuna skin blanket covering him. In the brown hair of the poncho he thinks he recognizes the ripples of the swamp.

"Take it off me. It's just given me a nightmare."

"I wanted to leave it for you as a gift. You're not going to refuse it."

"It's accepted, but throw it over there where it won't be in sight."

Satisfied, his bad mood passes, his legs tingle. They have fallen asleep. Between yawns he lights another tallow candle.

"It's taken you a while to come, Inka,"

"I didn't want daylight to give me away. How have you been?"

"The same or worse. At least the marquis decided to leave me alone. The miller collects the work that I paint and he makes money the same as before."

"As sick as you are, it's double the abuse that he keeps taking advantage of you."

"He won't let me rest not even after I'm dead. But let's not talk about what won't change. I've got your order ready."

"Already?" Inka's voice gets happy.

"Right here it is."

He bends down in a corner of the room, removes some junk, sets aside deteriorating frames, and returns with a roll of plantain leaves. He meticulously unfolds it. Yáwar Inka brings it close to the warmth of the candle and his smile widens.

"With this map, you'll never get lost," Tomasón confides in him. "I know all the locations of the churches as if they had grown from my fingers. One thing though, don't forget to burn it after . . ."

"First let me memorize it," mutters the Indian already deeply concentrating on the parchment. The painter finishes his evening routine lighting the stove and placing a clay pot on it. *Caraaá, finally Yáwar Inka has come to visit me in my own home.* With vanity and affection, he ponders the silhouette of the eagle appearing between the black, straight locks of hair, the massive body that without a doubt was barely able to come in through the door, the impeccable embroidered shirt, the vest encrusted with mother-of-pearl, and the pants made out of thick, dark cloth. Yáwar Inka sports an immense ring and a heavy gold chain with a medallion in the shape of a radiant sun. He uses the title of Inka as a paternal last name and the authorities do not dare to doubt the authenticity of his lineage.

"You say here that the San Francisco Convent is connected underneath the bridge with the Santa Catalina nuns?"

"Just as you see it there. Nor do the tunnels of the other churches or holy places have any errors in my drawing. Trust them."

"And the way stations?"

"I marked with an X the ones that are in service."

The Inca passes his right index finger over the map. Tomasón smiles with contentment. "You'll stay to eat with me, right? Because he who eats alone dies alone."

He takes great pains to attend to him, offering scraps from the slaughterhouse that for Tomasón are a feast—a stew made of beef tripe cooked with potatoes and a pinch of salt.

An old emotion delays his desire to eat. He is affectionately content thinking about Inka.

"How long have we known each other?"

"Since before time. You were the first Negro that I saw with my own eyes and you will always be."

"Look at you. And I thought you followed me from chapel to chapel because you liked my paintings!"

"That's true too, but I need to recover all those mountains of silver and the church artifacts of gold and precious stones. The land is reclaiming them. Pachamama demands these payments from us."

"As for me, I'm not worried, Inka. On the contrary, I'm happy. If these riches are to be returned to who they belong, take them."

"That I'll do, you can be sure. And before I leave indebted, one more bother. Do you still smoke?"

"Now more than ever."

"Then I will send you plenty of tobacco and coca leaves."

Chapter II

The painted bull shook three times. Yes, three soft knocks grazed the window frame. Tomasón lifted only a corner of the ox hide and saw them. A light-skinned Negro man with nappy hair—a mix of a white man and a black and Indian woman, like those people who are known as *tentenelaire*—was cautiously looking up and down the side street, with his hand on the shoulder of an eleven-year-old girl. Maybe twelve at the most. By their half-calf pants and wool jackets, Tomasón assumed that they came from the country. Runaways, he said to himself, glancing at their bare feet.

The nervous stranger extended his neck, "Don Tomasón are you alone?"

The girl had the unmistakable air of those who do not ask permission to enter. Two dimples formed in her cheeks and her round and half opened mouth uncovered a tunnel between the two upper front teeth. He was amused by the way she had tied a red rag on her head. It slid down her forehead and covered an eye that she was trying to uncover with one hand, while with the other she held a blanket balanced on her shoulder.

Without bothering with questions or greetings, Tomasón moved to the side, and the man entered following the girl. He waited to get used to the brightness of the dark dust, scrutinized every corner and then seemed to calm down.

"Look *familia*, I am Francisco Parra and she is my daughter Pancha."

His callused, extended hand was missing both the index and the pinky finger. Tomasón held it, and through his fingers came the memory of guarango bark marked by countless grooves along with the scars down to his wrists. The shackles, caraaá. Subconsciously he remembered those delicate "look-but-don't-touch" hands of the saints that he painted.

"We come from the priest's hacienda in the Sierra, as you can imagine. We only need a little corner to stay in until to-morrow. We're sorry."

"My home is yours for as long as you want."

He filled two bowls to the rim and left them at peace so that they could eat calmly and in silence.

Outside, the sky took possession of the night. From afar the shouts of the street vendors and *mazamorreras* could be heard. In a little while there would begin a cry that could be heard only in Malambo. At the time when the workday in the neigh-boring towns ends, the laborers would whisper, covering their mouths with one hand so that the Rímac would not repeat what they were offering—*sweet melon, lady, ooorrranges, pears, little pears sweeter than honey, watermelon.* And in a low voice—*little lady, I have the best. Buy from me, nothing but fruit stolen from the hacien-das when the overseers weren't watching.*

Tomasón increases the flame in the oil lamp, which enlarges

Pancha's shadow on the walls and antiquated ceiling. The dark dust teases the girl from each corner, flirting with her nose which suddenly sparkles in front of the double smile of her surprised eyes. And Tomasón? He loves every minute of it! Thrilled and happy that the girl is pleased with the humble miracle that coats and covers every rag, every flake of wall, every dish and every painting of a prudish saint. At eight o'clock the bells call out for the prayers to save the souls in purgatory, and from the opposite bank, the rounded chants form a chorus with its litanies. With a dizzying ebb and flow, the monotonous *Our Fathers* and *mea culpas* die down on the bed of the river and a black voice like the midday answers them: *Ayé, Ayé sambagolé, sambagolé Ayé Ayé!* And now the cane plant and the reed and the Malambo trees begin to sing: *Ayé, Ayé sambagolé, sambagolé!* and the rush reed and the tangled tsacuaras—*Ayé*—and the sound of the clinking chains to the *Ayé sambagolé!*

Francisco Parra bites his molars to the ankle of the pipe, and smokes. His daughter fades from his sight. She is transfixed, anxiously in front of the painted walls, outlining silhouettes with her finger.

"Maybe they'll be erased by tomorrow," thought Tomasón, and he wakes up with a gentle nod of his head.

A flame sparks from the brazier on which he warmed the dinner, weak, but it lights and attracts. Francisco Parra avoids being looked at. Tomasón prefers to watch Pancha.

Whenever he gives shelter to someone, he fears hearing about some misfortune that happens to them. This is the first time that he has seen a male cimarron with a girl. Women, yes, they do escape with their young ones. But infants, not their older children. Those that were Pancha's age were a bother, thought Tomasón, pleased that Francisco Parra would take such a risk.

"As I said to you before, in Malambo you're safe. My house is respectable, and if you need to cross the bridge to Lima, I myself will write you a pass, exactly like the ones that the masters make when they send us on a trip."

"We appreciate it, *misangre*, but we are just passing through. I've got things to do on the other side of the river and I'm going to take care of it alone. Pancha can stay under your care, if it's alright with you, and tomorrow night we will continue the road to the South."

The girl figured the conversation had ended.

"You know how to draw letters too?"

And without taking her eyes off the chubby archangel that fluttered with his elbows peeling beside the flaming ox, "By the time my *taita* comes back, do you think you could teach me?"

"From now until the time he returns, you will have learned even to fly." Tomasón smiled at her and turned to Francisco, "Do you know anyone in the city?"

"Not any more. I used to have a relative who sent for me, but ah! Aunt Candelaria left us a few years ago."

"Candelaria Lobatón?"

"The same."

"I've heard of her. She used to cook for what's-their-names that returned to Castile and they sold her with the house, along with the coach driver and some furniture."

"I heard about that. Somebody must have told me."

"Then why are you going? It's not good that you wander around Lima. The Holy Brotherhood troops are out hunting people without owners."

"I know how to take care of myself."

Seated face to face, they smoked without looking at each other. Tomasón did not remember exactly when the girl took his hand, when she asked what she asked, and much less when he became attached to her forever.

"And what's that?" She pointed out a brilliant space of light on the wall, crossed by vertical shadows.

"It doesn't have a face, feet, or hands. What is it?"

The painter cleared the blue smoke from his throat. He got comfortable on the bench, and as if he were a guest, he asked the girl for some lime flower tea.

"The day that I get rid of this cold, I'll come across people I haven't seen for a long time. In the meantime don't worry; I only do my job and trust in the will of Obbatalá. Those that you're looking at are the saints that are with me when I sleep, pretty girl. I always had them inside me, but I could never dream about them because the master never let me sleep when I wanted.

. . . This splendor comes from deep within and it still doesn't have a face, in the moment that we see it clearly and head on, we will have gone with the light. Whenever it is that it has to happen, I hope that I too will light up along with the ancestors and have someone who dreams about me. This I ask and no more. The shadows are neither rays nor shadows. They are bars of a prison. That color of hot white light, golden like the sun in the morning, is our God Creator, Obbatalá, whom they unjustly have imprisoned, accused of stealing a horse. Yes sir. As if in this land stolen with blood, there was still a horse galloping free! Seven full years Obbatalá was enclosed in the middle of the filth, suffering more than anyone from hunger, pain, and misery. Know that because of this, in those seven years the world went astray. No longer was there more water to fall from the heavens. Widowed from their shadows, the molle *trees did not prosper. Up until this point the* tsacuaras *swayed hidden without fruit. The crops? Disaster! Before they suffocated in this life, the offspring preferred to die in the bellies of our mothers. And without children, without adolescents playing, everyone knows that the world turns upside down. Obbatalá suffered in seeing us, yet he could only bear it like the splendor that you see here until proving his innocence. And that's how it was. Once he was set free, the world has returned to almost what it once was, because Obbatalá does not hold a*

grudge. He does not despair. He does not lose faith. He does not die. Obbatalá never ever is going to end. Before there was time, he was already there and he will continue being until long after the end. Not for pleasure. Before everything was, he already was who he is, when the sun grew cold, smaller than a little ball, like this: tiny! A poor spark that wasn't good for heating or giving life to anything!

What's wise for you to know, I'll tell you that Obbatalá made us with a piece of clay and blowing whaaa whaaa whaaa gave the shape of a man or a woman. Through his teeth that's all, and there! Ready! another boy or girl began to run alive throughout the world.

There needs to be said what's true at least, that the gods also have their weaknesses and flings. At one point Obbatalá drank too much chicha and corn liquor, which is treacherous when it's fermented with bull's foot and it grabs sweetly without one realizing it. It was one of those times when Obbatalá got drunk. And, like all drunks, stubborn and not wanting to listen, the idea came to Obbatalá to keep making people. Every time he breathed whaaa whaaa! the creation that he made was born crippled. The next one that he breathed was missing an arm or had his eyes misplaced in his face. Another he forgot to put an eyebrow or a nose. He made ears of different sizes. Let me tell you! Nonetheless, he realized his guilt and ever since never permitted anyone to wrong the crippled, nor people who suffered those birth defects. This is seen still today.

"But Obbatalá comes from your dreams, or is he a god that can be touched like that angel or like you and my papa?"

"Too many questions for someone so young, pretty girl. The gods of my dreams are purely true. The same thing happened to our creators from Guinea, who, ever since I painted them, still visit us in Malambo. They never get tired of strolling around the gardens, and their huge steps dig those puddles that walk along the bank of the Rímac."

"When I see them, I'll believe them," smiled Pancha. "I

haven't had dreams like that," untying the red scarf on her head. "But herbs? That's what I know. Many herbs." And solemnly her long ponytail began showing the seeds and the splinters and the dried flowers that traveled hidden among her hair since their flight through the mountain range.

"Well *familia*, that's how my daughter is. If you don't send her to bed once and for all, you'll see the sun rise with her chatter. So I'm warning you and I'm following my own advice. See you soon, *misangre*."

His embrace left a worried feeling in the bony chest of Tomasón.

〰〰〰

On the other side of the city, the resonant cry of the mournful women was spreading. The wife of Jerónimo Cabrera Bobadilla y Mendoza, Count of Chinchón and fourteenth viceroy of Peru, rapidly slips away from this life, cooked by the fevers of the swamp. In Malambo the vigilant, devout women listen to her in the river's whisper.

Their simple sham does not find any other way to help her except to remain awake with her all night, praying for her. They arise quickly with the calm affection of those who feel like they are about to participate in an imminent tragedy. They are already dressed in mourning, pulling their woolen hose over their swollen, sore, cold knees. Their crooked legs join at their hips. They enter their tunics headfirst; they get stuck and then descend with a pull down over busts and spread out to the sides over their chests. It is always the same black iridescent style: a shroud frazzled from use. Almost a transparent sieve at the armpits, as shining in the elbows as in the back. The splashes of seasonings and greasy foods, which rather than diminishing with each washing, reinforce clear aureoles that crisscross the gown.

The church of San Lázaro is full of women. Kneeling on the hard benches, they begin the Lord's Prayer with zeal, and the *Hail Marys* and a *Glory to the Father.* Tempted by the smell of the adulterated incense or perhaps Satan himself, during the prayers of the joyful mysteries they drowse. They lose their train of thought fingering the sweaty, tortoiseshell rosary beads. They want to be there and don't want to be there, sleepy, yearning against their will for their rickety old beds and longing to feel snug against the bodies and the snores of their atheist husbands. They look at the growth of hair and wrinkles on their spouses' nape. Before that face turns over on the pillow and those arms raise them in the air, they close their eyes and exhale with the heavy breathing of pleasure. They pretend that they are sleeping when his strong hand slides down and finds their nightgown's edges, rolls them up and rubs between their legs until the blessed inferno of the flesh, without yielding, breaks them apart. Rubbing themselves they settle into the weightless sway of the *Our-Father-who-art-in-heaven* and horrified but satisfied, they continue the murmur of the prayers that clamor for the health of the vicereine.

The adjoining streets of the Plaza Mayor awakened more populated than normal, even though the daily racket seemed conspicuously absent. City vendors and clerks waited and waited. One thing, or another. Three florists whispered discreetly so that the breaths of the Rímac would not hear them. I hope she dies, they prayed to themselves in the shadow of the entryway to the cathedral. The recent fatigue visible in the bags under their eyes gives them away. They haven't slept either, only they did not spend the night praying, but rather hurry-quick-running between gardens that color the countryside of Piedras Gordas, until the plot owners agreed to sell them an entire week's worth of roses.

The perfumes from the nine full bags of flowers, three for

each of them, winds, converses with the stagnated wind from the early morning in the Plaza Mayor. The petals, impressive in complete burial honor, will rain over the coffin and cover the path of the carriage pulled by four horses.

In front of the engraved main door of Sagrario Cathedral, on the corner where each day the wood of the unending green balcony traces its tranquil route along Fish Market Street, Jerónimo Melgarejo leans below one of the gallows' pillars that the authorities forgot to dismantle after the last execution a few days ago. Indolent, the miller has a face like vinegar. A few moments ago he paid off two fines: one for selling wheat flour at the price of a pirate, and the other for taking advantage of the folks presumably stunned and saddened with the circumstances regarding the palace.

For Melgarejo and all the creoles from Lima, to run politics with the slogan of "for bigger problems, bigger taxes" is nothing more than complete snobbery and nothing less than another of the caprices of the viceroy.

The morning started off well and started off badly. The payment of the fines brought in its wake a heavy feeling like that of Judgment Day. The good news arrived while he was eating breakfast: the most recent Indian uprising left a disaster of deaths, among them the mayor of Potosí, who left for the other world believing that Melgarejo was his friend. Melgarejo cared little about the mayor's death. What was important to him was to run into someone he knew so that he could use it as a pretext to spread the news and find out about the critics of the colonial administration.

The sun bounced from the fountain in the center of the Plaza and fell flat on the heads of the talkative crowd.

"Have you already heard about the riot in Buenos Aires?"

"It happened exactly as you predicted it would happen."

"Didn't I tell you? In Cusco they assassinated a chief magistrate and right here in Lima now there are merchants that refuse to pay the four percent sales tax."

"In my opinion they're not wrong because we can't keep supporting the Court's squanderings."

Melgarejo is delighted but his malicious smile is cut short.

"It's not fatal any more," says a Jesuit at his side, dangling a glass bottle in front of his eyes that holds floating roots and bark.

"Can you believe it?" the constable that accompanies him chimes in.

"Yes, that fever doesn't kill people anymore. Doña Francisca Chinchón took ill the same day that she advised the viceroy to raise the price of wine and to prohibit women from using veils. 'There will be fewer drunks, and the women from Lima will learn that good girls don't go out in the streets with their faces covered. Not even if we were Moors!' They say that's what she said, although of course she doesn't deserve to die because of that mistake."

"Life and love are sent from above," Melgarejo intervenes in the discussion.

"This is what's going to cure the vicereine's fever: an extract from a plant the Indians call *cascarilla*."

And lowering his voice to the miller's ear, "And it has other herbs, of course, but now isn't a good time to tell them."

Melgarejo yawns. "Pardon me father, but I don't understand anything about those things."

The priest nevertheless amused him. It may have been his dusty attire like that of someone recently arrived from traveling, or some sparkle that his eyes betrayed. Now the priest had taken to chatting with the people gathered farther away. He thought of that concoction as a great medical discovery, and spoke of it with an altered voice and a sort of scientific fanaticism. If it were not for his cassock, Melgarejo would have mis taken him for a market showman, like one of those vendors of snake oil for broken bones. He was attracted to the priest, against his own disbelief. The brethren of the congregation of Ignacio de Loyola were known for their good judgment and clear reasoning. Finally he grew tired of snooping about and decided to return to his mill.

Three days later all the church bells rang, announcing the recovery of the vicereine. Melgarejo had to accept the virtue of the Jesuit's concoction. He said so to his wife.

"It's my confessor, Father José," boasted Doña Gertrudis.

※※※※

Venancio arrived at Malambo along with the latest ringing of the bells. But the fisherman brought bad news: in the dungheap, close to the river, they had found another dead person.

"He wouldn't be the father of that girl that you have here?" he whispered to Tomasón. "Because it's strange that he would have disappeared just like that."

"Be quiet, I don't want her to hear you. Are you sure?" replied the old man, not wanting to believe it, nor the stifling sensation that weighed him down with bad omens.

"No, but it sure looks like it is. Any more than that, I don't know."

He heard Pancha returning to the garden and he hurried behind Venancio.

"I'm just going a little way. I'll be right back," he said without turning around.

"I'm going too."

"No, sir! What a nosey child, caraá!"

And fearing that she might follow them he quickened his pace, almost running.

Francisco Parra was lying face to the sky. Quite some time had passed since his spirit had soared with the birds making circles between the hills. Nazario Briche and a very white woman studied him from afar with respect. Beside the body were people who knew how to look at death face to face as if they had always known her. Others were passing by, conversing, distracted. For the sake of gossip, they changed their route, and without ceasing their conversation, they lowered their heads to see him. They made sure it was a foreigner's death and continued on their way.

The turkey buzzards had punctured his eyes. His eye sockets did not even hold the memory of the clouds that paused in the light drizzle that was falling without end. Only his tongueless mouth still lived, making silent faces. Opening and closing his lips, a white nest of maggots smiled at them.

"When he comes back again, he will be born blind and mute," Tomasón grieved. He could find no reason to return him to the earth. With Venancio's help, he tied a rock to him and pushed him over the rounded songs so that he would finally sink or, better be borne away in its rumors, the current of the Rímac.

Chapter III

Altagracia Maravillas awoke happy as a lark. She put her duster on over her flowered skirt and began to sweep the big house. She heard the shouts of Antón Cocolí, called for him, bought a dozen eggs, but didn't stay to talk. She was never interested in the neighborhood gossip that the boy took charge of bringing and taking, much less so today when she was so happy. She had found an actual treasure in the hollow of the fulling mill, there where they store the scrubber used to clean the grinding stone.

"They'll be enough. Ten pesos will be enough. Or if not, I myself will have to make another miracle," Tomasón said to her when she asked him if, for that amount, he would paint a crucified Christ for the *cofradía* of the Angolans.

Today, she would pay it. She shook the broom with her hand and with it passed lightly over the office. She felt like playing. She went to the entryway balancing the broom upside down on the tip of her index finger. She cleaned the adobe bench on which the beggars were received. She tried to raise her left arm, which still hung inert at the side of her body, but she couldn't. She touched it, and in spite of the inflammation, she did not feel anything. She calmed down. Not even the end of the world would take away the happiness she felt that morning, she thought, as she lingered in organizing the office which was almost always locked.

The master preferred to spend the mornings in the ample, carpeted common room. Drawing the heavy curtain of blue-green damask, he would work shielded from the clipped light shining through the wrought iron grating that opened up to the patio, with its ornamental tile garden planted with honeysuckle, jasmine, geraniums, and *ñorbos* or passionflowers, as the foreigners called them.

Although badly maintained, it still seemed, with its stone facade, like an elegant, two story, big house. The previous owner had ordered that they paint on the threshold: "Praised be the Blessed Sacrament." The lower level, separated from the common room, opened into the dining room. In the center was a sideboard and an extended table with only three dark wooden chairs inlaid with mother-of-pearl, though very battered by time. At the end of the dining room, behind the service door, was the pantry. Although always in order, the kitchen was decidedly dismal, with the smells from stews and seasonings and smoke from firewood trapped by a low ceiling and a window that did not ventilate.

Ten copper saucepans of different sizes hung from iron shelving above a corner where they discarded the logs for the hearth and the brazier. In the opposite corner, the large earthen jars filtered drop by drop the drinking water. Next to these, the masses that made up the fulling mill: the small stone – a polished crescent moon, easy to handle and slippery — that swung against the large flat one lying on the floor. The infinite number of grains, herbs and substances that gave them work provided them both a dark green color.

In the center, round and exorbitant, was the table to prepare the combinations of soups and casseroles. Another one, less large and distanced sufficiently, was used for ironing. With a bit of malice and by ignoring the second table, one could distinguish towards the left the half-lit lintel with a hole like the mouth of a mine. To cross this frontier meant entering the alleyway that led to the untiled patio where the world ended and began, beside the stable dungheap and the shanty for the slaves. These were adjacent to the street cut by an irrigation channel, parallel to a river that was constantly clogged with human excrement contributed from both paths, and passed thanks to the painful cry of bladders and swollen bowels. Compact clouds of flies constantly clashed with two other armies no less frenzied and ravenous: rats and cockroaches.

The second floor of the big house was bright. It had two spacious bedrooms, with four airy and wide decorative windows, and a balcony covered by a flagrant barricade of well-worn slatted windows the height of prying eyes.

Irresistibly summoned by the chatter that bubbled from the parlor, Altagracia Maravillas put her head to the right, lower corner of the window, which allowed her to observe according to her whim without being seen. Her master was, as usual, with that friend of his.

Manuel De la Piedra was, to put it nicely, more indecisive than his body. He was tall and in his fifties. He seemed not to be bothered that his waist, in spite of his belt, began to unobstructedly devolve into an impressive, promiscuous and round gut, like a clay earthenware jar from Guadalajara. His curly hair, blond and red and graying, occasionally blew in the air, sometimes without reason. His face of incipient and onerous double chins still held the tacit arrogance of the affluent creoles. The deep circles under his eyes and his indiscrete fatigue did not impede him from anticipating—and always with certainty—the wishes of his surprised clientele.

If one pays attention to the rumors of the Rímac, ten years ago an anonymous De la Piedra strolled through the port of Callao general stores with no more luggage than a rolled bundle and three long jute sacks.

No one asked that he unpack the roll of silk pieces. They were only interested in what was assumed to be gall stones packed in the long sacks. The still unknown De la Piedra insisted that those calcareous hardenings, unlike those that were sold here and in New Granada, had not been extracted from the stomachs of llamas or alpacas but came from the now disappeared Berbers. Of those that listened to him, not even the most idiotic Chalacos or the Limeños believed the story of the African desert, or that that shabby seller was a legitimate creole and that in the past he traded honestly between Cabo Verde and Seville, as he repeatedly swore. Suspicious from past failures, or plain and simply in case it was true, they were convinced he was an adventuring peddler from no place in particular, worse than Portuguese. He was in for the disappointment of his life if he thought that he was going to con them with *guanaco* gall stones, in the best case scenario. But because of those motives, puzzling and irrational, even the skeptic Limeños, as much as the apprehensive Chalacos, fought hand to hand for the acquisition of the stones pieces, whatever their price. Not for their supposedly curative qualities, but because they heightened and strengthened the masculine drive. They had to believe something the Portuguese man said. He couldn't swindle them that much!

In fact, this was the way that he placed the first stone of his small capital. In a short time—God knows with what concoction of loans, sales, and interest accumulated—he was able to buy the big house, sold with the understanding that he would convert it into an inn, and that with it he would receive two slaves that no one would take, not even as a gift: Candelaria Lobatón, an aged and crippled cook who burned even the measliest broth; and Nazario Briche, a high risk coachman, perpetually dangerous and malicious, and on top of it all, half deaf, so as to not find himself forced to let loose his tongue, even in the confessional. His paralyzed silence was, in truth, a product of his general lack of volition.

To everyone's surprise and shock, especially the two aforementioned, the flamboyant master didn't even complain. Worse, he declared that he was quite content and gratified with Divine Providence.

Looking at it carefully, maybe he was right, because the gall stones initiated him into the business profession and he fell into such apostolic grace that one could even say, without speaking an untruth, that they baptized him. Though the universal ignorance that surrounded his familial and geographic origins was vox populi—none of the Limeños believed him in the least—few cared or paid much attention, much less went through the effort to expose him. However, at one time or another, solemnly, free of any affected pomp, and without batting an eye, he began to introduce himself as "Manuel De la Piedra" or simply "De la Piedra."

〰〰〰

Altagracia Maravillas saw how her master got up from the easy chair and remained still, like a hunter lying in wait, in front of the fiction bookshelf. She thought that he was about to be possessed by one of his absent moments that without warning left him empty, and that according to him was the lightning flash of a routine fatigue, an affliction unique to the genuine and true-blooded De la Piedras.

"If I buy the land from the widow Ronceros, I could plant wheat, which is selling at a great price now" said Melgarejo, "though with so many taxes, I'd have to think it over carefully. And more than anything, I'd need men. Would you be willing to sell them to me on credit?"

"Yes, but I'll give you two years maximum to pay it off."

"And since when have you given me those kind of terms, if I may know?"

"The business with the niggers, as a legally carried out business, my friend, isn't what it used to be, in spite of how it seems."

"With all due respect, I find it hard to believe you, now that Bartolomé de las Casas has come out in defense of the Indians before His Royal Highness in Spain, urging that rather than sacrificing so many native Americans in forced labor, the Crown commit instead to substituting them for Africans, who, according to the charitable Las Casas, are stronger and better able to handle the hardships. In other words, he's asked the King to increase his involvement in slave trafficking. The King will fill our coffers in the Americas, and naturally, later down the line, we will fill his royal coffers, based on taking advantage of the simple-minded happiness and fornication that's common to niggers as a race."

"That doesn't change one bit the fact that this business is suffering," snapped De la Piedra, having now completely recovered from his detachment.

The miller immediately readjusted his tone to the accustomed seriousness that characterized their morning business gatherings, which always gave way to swindling for their mutual benefit.

"You always complain about the same thing Manuel. But ever

since the Jews accused of being heretics filled the cells of the Holy Office, the truth is that you've been freed of any competition. That Juan Bautista, the one they call captain, was the most prestigious slave trader Lima has ever known. Now his clients have passed on to your control, but I suppose that you don't bring in the contraband niggers that made him so famous."

"Captain Bautista didn't work like that. At least as far as I know. The Jews are very proper in that respect."

"Don't be so sure because there are a lot of things yet to be known. They already have seventy-nine Jewish prisoners in jail. Heretics all of them, and the issue won't stop there because they keep accusing each other. Look at the case of Mencia de Luna. He wasn't very healthy; furthermore, his guilty conscience must have messed with his mind because he died from the torture, but not before giving the names of five of his own, accomplices to heresy. Why do you think the benefactors of the Holy Inquisition are so pigheaded in hurrying to build so many secret prisons? It's better this way, accept it. There are too many devils running loose in the streets, Manuel, believe me!"

"The real reason that they are jailing the Jews is quite another, my dear sir. The authorities fear that they will become absolute owners of all commerce, beginning with the viceroy's capital. Isn't it a public secret that they periodically send shipments of solid gold to Manaos, Río, Buenos Aires, and to Amsterdam via Catalonian and Andalucian bankers? This whole web of atheist conspiracy, or whatever you want to call it, has absolutely nothing to do with the idea of Christian faith. And don't be so sure, Jerónimo, at the fifth turn of the handvice or more likely with the first flame put to your feet, that you and I wouldn't confess to having always been a Hebrew follower. We would accuse our mothers of being heretics and confess to whatever barbarity the Dominicans decided to put in our mouths with their pious methods."

"Fine, that's fine. You can't deny that not only Jewish Street but also Marketer's Street were in the hands of those disciples of Satan. But naturally, that's not why they're imprisoned. And by the way, the Indians aren't left too far behind. They don't give up their pagan ways and they still worship even the stones on the road. I don't know if you remember that a few years ago the supposed treasures in the Merced, San Francisco, and Santo Domingo churches disappeared in just one night."

De la Piedra nodded, and Melgarejo continued.

"Father José keeps finding over and over the *wacas* and more *wacas* without end—those cemeteries that the Indians fill with offerings, because they keep burying their dead chiefs with their food and drink, but also with their dishes and little statues of their pagan gods. I've seen some of them made of silver and clay, three made of gold with emerald detailing! I know that Father José separates the most valuable pieces that he finds in those forbidden cemeteries so that they can be turned over to the authorities, sent to the King, or taken to his convent. I have evidence that he orders that they destroy the *waca* and erect a huge cross in its place."

De la Piedra is bored, his voice distant. "Yes, yes, I've heard about that."

"But since then, when our little father passes back by those same places of Incan paganism, he finds that the crosses have vanished. A couple of weeks ago, he told me that the earth had been dug up. Out of curiosity, he poked around and he was struck by the surprise of a new *waca*. Once again: a mummified Indian, wrapped in fine blankets threaded with gold, buried crouching and surrounded by offerings. He says it's the first time that something like that has happened, because the gold and silver pieces were recently made. Imagine that! Recently made! It seems hard to believe. He thinks that it's related to the robbery of the churches' crucifixes, candelabras and safekeepings."

De la Piedra emerges from his weariness. "Maybe not, maybe so. And what does that priest have to do with all this? I don't think that the Jesuits have stolen a single peso."

"No, but Father José has decided to look into it until he finds the thieves. He's very active about evangelical questions and works; and Gertrudis would make my life miserable if I don't help him. Anyway, I hope I can get a portion of the earnings from his religious devotion."

〰〰〰

Altagracia listened to them talk about utilities, the future of the kingdom, bundles of silk from China, the tapestry from Flanders, the swords from Germany, knives from Toledo and, above all, the days that remained to fulfill the required quarantine for the "pieces from Guinea" that the master had well secured in one of the Malambo slave storehouses.

He had bought her on one of those business mornings. According to what she would find out later, he did so more to rid himself of the prodding of Nazario Briche, who insisted that he needed a woman and that Candelaria alone wouldn't be enough for the big house to be converted into an inn.

Not the livery trimmed with braided gold, nor the large twenty-one carat ring that sparkled from his ear, would take away the coach driver's appearance of a bird of prey. His look was yellowish, treacherous. His wrinkled face was lined with transparent grays, the traces of innumerable sleepless nights, vigils, or celebrations. His steps kept secrets. The calendar had forgotten him sometime between thirty-five and forty-something. Perhaps from his inability to talk a lot or by his own decision to not speak at all, his throat would become agitated like a broken fountain and then quiet for weeks on end.

Nazario Briche had been a mine digger and small farm hand.

He was resold at prices considerably higher than his actual services. He had crossed the haciendas of the coast and was finally sold off cheap for his flaws. He was a chronic liar, thief, drunk, and inveterate gambler, in addition to being disobedient, with his nocturnal escapades and surprising returns. His bare spot showed green like a watermelon's shine. The poisoning caused by the mercury from Huancavelica robbed him of bluish facial hair. The whip drew a map of welts on his back, and on his chest a flower.

"But now I'm a tamed, working nigger and I need a woman's company," he would insist and since the nuns from the Incarnation did not ask a whole lot for Altagracia Maravillas, the master, to free himself of the coachman's requests, indulged him.

They soon forgot about the hotel pretense. Guests, what might be called guests, never arrived, except for one or another traveler who disappeared without paying. The only guest was, in truth not really a guest; he proclaimed himself honorary tenant-for-life of one of the side rooms near the back courtyard.

De la Piedra said goodbye to Melgarejo and went to the kitchen in search of wine. Altagracia followed him along the side of the courtyard and stopped at the window. The master approached the table and took large gulps directly from the mouth of the carafe as if it were running water.

"Just like the first time," thought Altagracia. At that time, she was practically a new arrival of only a couple of weeks and still used to iron the sheets with care. She would heat the iron on a makeshift stove. She tested the temperature with her index finger moistened with saliva. The precise crackle meant it was ready to smooth without leaving a golden or ashen trace on the white part of the clothes. But first, she made sure by cleaning it with a damp cloth. She scrubbed it hard and then immediately slid it along under the pressure of her inclined torso, hoping to erase the finest wrinkle.

"What can I do for you, sir?" asked Candelaria vigilantly that first time, when she noticed him standing in the doorway of the kitchen examining Altagracia Maravillas from toe to head, his glance stopping at her hips and breasts held by her bodice. He lifted the carafe in the air and drank straight from its discretely scalloped mouth, even after Candelaria offered him a crystal glass that seemed made on a whim out of a piece of ice so cold that it was never going to melt.

De la Piedra assessed her as if he were still at the auction of the pieces from Guinea. Knowing the products of the African nations, he recalculated, wondering if he had overpaid the nuns with his two hundred pesos. They told him that she was from Angola, but it seemed more likely that she was originally from Congo, judging from how small she was, yet mature, and with her hair cut flush to her head. He approached her.

Because of the suffocating heat from the ironing, Altagracia unmistakably smelled like the dense smoke of a wood fire, and like stews cooked slowly in a copper saucepan. The master gently passed his pinkish hand over her sweating cheek and then, very slowly, began to smell her fingers one by one. His tongue let him know the flavor of her face. Altagracia Maravillas was a tender chicken. Sweet-corn water. He recalled the aroma of cumin and garlic in the distance. She tasted like mouthfuls of impossible seasonings. It couldn't be true.

"How old are you, girl?"

"Twenty-two, sir."

"And what do they call you?"

"Altagracia Maravillas, sir."

He pronounced it to himself as if he were singing the syllables with pleasure, Al-ta-gra-cia-Ma-ra-vi-llas, to record it well. He made an unnecessary effort to hide his pleasure as he spoke to Candelaria.

"What about Nazario?"

"I sent him to bring alfalfa for the animals. I'm sure that he's going to take all afternoon."

De la Piedra laughed enthusiastically. His head moved in a trembling of red curls. His blue eyes squinted. He looked at the young woman again.

"Arrange it so that every evening, this girl . . . what's your name?"

"Altagracia Maravillas, sir."

" . . . Yes. That's it. Arrange it . . . that . . . she changes my sheets . . . every afternoon, so I can take a siesta."

"As you wish sir. But let me have some reales to buy soap from Castile and a small bunch of flowers." She blackmailed him agreeably.

"Why not, Candelaria!" he exclaimed raising his arms, laughing theatrically, "Now I understand why they sold you at a bargain price. Keep all my change." He took out some coins from a suede, sepia bundle and gave them to her. He drank one last swallow, this time from the crystal glass.

Candelaria opened the white handkerchief that she kept close to her breast.

Altagracia saw how she tightened her jaw knotting the coins and she wanted to continue smoothing the sheets for the siesta but the iron was already cold.

She must have been pretty, mused Altagracia seeing Candelaria seated serenely in front of her at the table. And this she thought, even though Candelaria winced as she got up to heat the water. She limped, bending to the side and dragging the joint of her hip.

"All this pain I owe to your husband. Nazario Briche left me like this," she told her the afternoon that Altagracia found her with her legs doubled, whining and unable to get up from the corner of the fulling mill. Candelaria had been grinding corn for the *tamales*, when a shot of pain pinned her where she was. "Bitterness, I don't have anymore. I keep it below the earth. And I've forgiven him because what's done is done. On the other hand, for Nazario, the remorse will always, always afflict him," she repeated and painfully repeated. Altagracia, however, did not believe the last part that Candelaria told her about Nazario. With regard to forgiving, her husband, just like the cook, seemed not to know about compassion.

The winter slipped through the holes in the thin roof, and a large clay frying pan in the cupboard broke without having been touched. Candelaria was seated once again in the chair, entertaining herself by counting her money. Altagracia jumped. "Don't be afraid girl, here things break just because. This old house is full of bad air and gusts of wind. You only have to ask Nazario to cover the holes in the roof with coal ash mixed with water. Anyway, he likes to walk at night along the roofs." She gave her a coin. "Guard it well," then, showing her the handkerchief, "all these pesos, my old master gave me. Look! There's a lot of them," she showed her gathering them in little mounds on the large table. "My master's wife knew that he liked to sleep in my quarters, though she pretended not to notice until the day she found the hiding place where I was guarding my five pesos."

"*You stole it,*" *she tried to accuse me.*

"*No ma'am, they're mine,*" *I said.*

"*Where'd you get them, if you don't work outside of this house? You stole my change when you were shopping for me. You don't think that I realize that you baptize the milk with water and bring less meat than what I ask you to buy?*" *And that's when I got so hot, I felt like I was chewing sand.*

"*No ma'am.*" *I said. "I earned those pesos fair and square. Master gave me five reales each time he climbed on me.*"

"*Shameless! Ungrateful! I'll make you stop wanting to charge my husband,*" *and keeping my pesos, she ordered Nazario to whip me.*

"Nazario has pure bitterness and not blood in his veins. It

can't be that he would punish me the way he did. I knew your husband before you were born. And he hit me from his soul with the same whip that they use on the horse when he gets wild or just like a mule. And afterwards, he followed word for word what that woman ordered. He locked me in the stocks. In the same shack where we sleep now there was this piece of wood with a big hole for your head and two other smaller ones for your feet and arms. And I was like that for fifteen days with bread and water, but the truth is, I had less water than bread and less bread than water. When I came out, I could no longer walk as God would have us. The stock and the beating ruined me for life. I became useless, but I don't care any more. Master gave me back my five pesos, money that I now take better care of, and no one, no one will ever know where I hide it."

〰〰〰

"Why are you looking at me like that, woman?" Candelaria reprimanded Altagracia. "Put down that iron and help me. Come on, get moving and start getting undressed so I can bathe you good." Altagracia now realized what was waiting for her in her master's bedroom. "Hurry up, before Nazario gets back! You don't want to cause another disgrace in this house." She began lathering her smooth body, scrubbing her with a grass scourer. Candelaria laughed again like before. "You're lucky that Don Manuel is single. Be happy that in this house there's no jealous or suspicious wife who would have them cut your ear or put red pepper in your private part," she said, rinsing her with fresh water. She dried her with a towel. It warmed her. "Be happy, woman! How many husbands have you had up until now?"

"Only Nazario."

"Oh girl! If it's true what you say, then you still have no idea what it is to take pleasure and make pleasure. But don't be silly, don't you worry that Nazario will notice."

Altagracia Maravillas changed the linen sheets, breathing in the lavender smell of the recently ironed clothes. She reshaped the soft pillows. With Candelaria's advice in mind, her heart jumped like a spring chicken playing in her chest. She felt light, like middays in February, resting under the sun reassuringly in the middle of the sky. She smoothed the embroidery and edging of Holland lace, and busied herself placing linen towels and starched napkins alongside the water stand, as when she attended to the recluses in the monastery. For those women, any of the summer aromas was enough to leave them sprawling in love with their divine beau. And Altagracia, the poor girl, longing to lose at some point the security of the ground in order to know that special something, didn't even feel dizzy. She wanted to disappear slowly, little by little or to fall all at once, completely crumbled. What things didn't she try! She motionlessly endured the torture of the sun, the burning, itching, that baked her body, without even wiping off a drop of sweat. She half closed her eyes in waiting and remained very still. But she barely achieved a light drowsiness, before a flame under her skin singed her soul and a tremendous thirst made her cease what she was doing.

Raised from a very young age by the women of the convent, she had not had the opportunity to know any other men than the ordained ones of the Sunday masses. As for a real man, she imagined him like a hungry cat that appeared in the kitchen feigning indifference. She would serve him leftovers of food in a porcelain plate along with a bowl of crumbs soaked in milk. She would wait for the cat to finish eating and would then rub his curved, surly back; the cat would begin to feel more comfortable with her. He would moisten his paws with saliva, clean his face and ears and between long yawns of a satisfied being would lift his head in her direction. He would have her within his range of vision but would not look directly at her, as if he wanted to give the impression that there was always something more important than she.

She played along with the game. The cat would comb his whiskers, throw furtive glances at her until the mischievous pretending was over, and he would begin to purr deeply, and do circles around her, rubbing against her legs. He'd coil his tail, climbing onto her lap, letting out a sigh, and at last give in to what she wanted to do with him.

It was satisfying to feel how his heat would pass through her apron and skirt. She knew that he could smoothly curl up or that she could bury her fingers in that fur and make the cat change positions. He recoiled and stretched, snuggling in on the side that she wanted so as to show her his claws. Then, he would release a protesting growl because of inopportune tickling that almost roused him from his pleasure. He'd awaken, stretch out to the full length of a meow, and leave where he had arrived, as if they had never met.

After that evening, Nazario adopted the habit of taking the mule to buy alfalfa. With the second ring of the two o'clock bell, he closed the front door and departed. As if by enchantment, De la Piedra lowered his auctioneer's voice. He would climb to the bedroom with careful steps balancing himself so as to avoid using the squeaky handrail. He tried not to make noise when he relieved himself of a long stream into the silver chamberpot, at least until nearly the end when the pressure lessened with the last loud drops. Once again quiet, his steps muzzled by the carpet and the discreet bubbling from the water in the wash stand. He is already waiting for Altagracia Maravillas when she enters the room, his arms extended so that she can dry his hands, finger by finger, fingernail by fingernail.

During the siesta, he was tepid, without any resistance and

ready for her to take him according to his will. Altagracia untied her bodice and offered him her breast as if to a suckling child. She then made room for him until she felt the contact of that soft pink body against hers. And in a brief second she turned to let him enter her, over and over again, to feel the intense sun that warmed her back and made her forget the security of the ground. She learned to lose consciousness, to fall while her master eased into his nap.

Candelaria, sitting in front of the oven, did not tire of tying in her immaculate handkerchiefs the coins that she received for her compliance. It was on one of those afternoons that death kept her from recounting her pesos.

She has them stashed someplace, and that's why she can't rest in peace, says Altagracia each time the boiling milk slips from her hand or the soup turns out salty or the overripe lentils end up in a sticky lump at the bottom of the saucepan. Nor was it for lack of attention or watering that the plants struggled in their flowerpots and that the recently washed clothes were dirtied with the coal iron. It was the late Candelaria.

A week ago, cleaning out the cobwebs, she saw the very end of a piece of cloth spying on her from below the big rock of the fulling mill. She pulled on it with all her strength. A handkerchief, wrinkled and tarnished from mildew, appeared, spilling coins. She counted ten pesos before the heavy grinding stone fell on her arm. That also was Candelaria, the cause for her own bruise.

〰〰〰

De la Piedra hurried to finish the remaining drafts of wine and Altagracia, smiling, greeted him from the window.

"Good morning, sir."

De la Piedra jumped.

"You scared me, woman! Maybe because I'm tired. I haven't slept. Last night figuring bills, the time got away from me. Where's Nazario?"

"He should be in the stable, sir. I think he's sleeping. It seems as though he didn't sleep last night either."

"Did he escape again? Until they put him in jail, and I'm the one that pays the fine."

De la Piedra started to think about her after their exchange. Who would have thought that that little pile of fear that he bought from the nuns would live without remorse going to bed with him and with his coachman.

"And your husband?"

"Yes sir?"

"Is happy or not about all this?"

"He knows that you care a lot about me, sir, and that you spoil me. Nothing more. And it's that trust he takes advantage of to leave at night."

"Must be, yes. But where does he go?"

"Maybe it's true what they say, sir."

"That he's looking for the bones of the dead and he buries them with a cross and all?" laughs De la Piedra.

"That's right, sir."

"Pure gossip. Sure, he's looking for something buried, but made of gold . . . How's your arm, girl?"

"Just the way it looks."

"Bad, very bad." The master is alarmed seeing that the skin has turned the shade of violets pulled days ago and that it has dried in a raised rash of flakes and bumps just like mosquito bites. And once again, he becomes distant with the same faraway smile that he has in bed. Spread out as full and wide as he is, below the slight body of Altagracia, as he tells her how to solve his clients' protests.

"It's better to have an injured nigger than a dead nigger. Remember Altagracia Maravillas," he repeats drowsily, making sure to close the blue silk so that the insects do not pester him. Later he mumbles: "Leave, leave me" and gently but firmly pushes her with one foot back to the kitchen. It is almost three o'clock. Now it's time for a real siesta. Once he marries the widow Ronceros he'll cease his adventures. He will miss the young girl, but he wouldn't be able to hide his involvement with her. Not that he's interested in the widow as a woman.

"It's never too much to stroll through the Plaza Mayor with a lady. If she's a widow and serious, even better. It instills more respect with your clients and gives us a certain formal air," he heard another merchant say who had recently arrived with next to nothing. At the wrong time, he decided to heed him without knowing that Catalina Ronceros would hatch the idea of marrying him. Maybe growing old together. Never separating, she told him, cheering him up, as if sharing a dream. But her words suggested a touch of reluctance. Most likely he imagined it. For at the moment, he did not even think about losing his overindulged bachelorhood with Altagracia Maravillas in exchange for the widow Catalina Ronceros. Who, to be honest, did not inspire him to share the siesta with her—not even in his grave.

Chapter IV

Pancha had left very early with herbs to sell. Upon returning she stopped to buy victuals in the flea market located behind the quarters of the Negroes from Mina. Already close to the house, she heard Tomasón conversing with Venancio. In order to listen to what they were talking about, she hurried, and the heavy basket that she wearily carried on her head slid to the ground. The onions, the yuccas, and the potatoes rolled. The sweet lemons and the custard apples rolled with pure delight too and gathered together as if to joke with Pancha. Annoyed, she picked them up. She strained to listen, but, with the exception of one or another lost syllable was unable to understand anything. She suspected they were talking about her father.

"No, Francisco Parra didn't abandon you, but good and dead he is and there's no more to be said, girl. They killed your father."

He had told her a thousand and one times. "He was dead when we found him on the banks of the river. If he weren't, he wouldn't be so stuck in my dreams, walking without making a shadow. As soon as I saw him, I recognized him. Best believe that I recognized him. It was he himself, Pancha."

〰〰〰

Four years ago he had told her the same thing. Nevertheless, it was difficult for Pancha to believe him. Maybe Tomasón had confused her father with someone else.

"But who would kill him and why?" she would ask.

"I don't know that either, girl." And he continued painting, sorrowful that she was suffering.

Pancha entered, greeted them, and left the basket with the mess on the table. The men did not venture to respond to her. Finally, looking up, Venancio broke the uncomfortable silence.

"You want to travel with me to Lima? I'm going to visit Altagracia."

"Well, first I have to make a quick trip around the garden."

"Go ahead then. I'll stay here." He made as if to organize Tomasón's brushes. As Pancha watered the plants that grew from the seeds that she hid in her braid, Venancio longed to be with her. True, Pancha could not see him with his arms crossed, thinking about her, and always sending her on some task. Like the morning when she had greeted him with the warning that the well was running dry.

"Venancio, the well is going to dry up. It barely has water as it is. Come help me dig another well. Just over there, right behind the house. I'll show you where." She pestered him until Tomasón, who was nodding off on his little bench, woke up.

"What well are you talking about? Not Brother Monkey,

huh?" Feverish, restless, and without fully waking from the slumber visible in the watery corners in his eyes, he scratched his head and began his story.

Brother Monkey passed close to a well and he heard that someone was complaining. Then he came close and asked "Whooo's theeere?"

"Iiit's meee, the puma, Brother Monkeeey. Pleeeeeaase Geeet me out of heeere!!"

"First prooomise meee thaaat you won't huurt meee."

"Iiit's a prooomise.

"Theeen graaab this braaanch and I'll tie it to my taaail so I caaan puuulll yoou out." No sooner said than done. He pulled him out. But as soon as the puma was out:

"Thank you, Brother Monkeeey, but you know just as well that a good deed is paid with a bad one."

"Don't tell me that you're going to eat me?"

"Yes, that's exactly what I'm going to do. Unless you can prove that what I've said isn't true."

"Ah Carambaá! If I had known that, I would have left you where I found you. Now I have to find a way to get out of this jam," said the monkey and he went looking for someone who could save him from the puma. Then he found the mule.

"Sala malecú, *Brother Monkey."*

He greeted the mule and after he had told his story, the mule commented, "The puma's right, a good deed is paid with a bad one. Here, just as you see me old and alone, I am waiting for death to come for me. My master kicked me off of the cattle ranch because I wasn't able to work for him anymore."

The monkey continued walking and encountered a hen in a corral, pecking some grain.

"Sala malecú, *Brother Monkey."*

And, after lending her ear to the tragedy: "The puma's right. I know already that when I can't lay any more eggs, they will ring my neck, just

*as they did to my mama. Let him eat you already, Brother Monkey.
That's life and there's nothing that can be done about it."*

*The monkey walked on and encountered a turtle and once again
told his story. The turtle thought and then: "I will go with you Brother
Monkey. I'll accompany you. Let's go to that well." And as soon as they
arrived they ran into the puma.*

"First of all, may you have a good day, puma."

*The puma greeted the turtle, who continued: "And allow me to say
that I also am in agreement with you. You are right to want to eat
Brother Monkey because a good deed is paid with a bad one."*

*And looking at the well, he added, "What I don't understand, puma,
is how you were able to get out of the well deep as it is."*

*"Well, I got this idea," said the monkey, and he again tied a branch
to his tail so that the puma could hoist himself up.*

*"Let's see. Get in the well again, puma, to see if Brother Monkey is
telling the truth."*

*Since the puma did not want to wait any longer to eat the monkey,
zooooom, he threw himself into the well to show that it was true. And
once again at the bottom, he hears Brother Monkey yelling to him.*

*"Puuuma, puuuma, you are right. A good deed is paid with a bad one,
and that's why I'm going to leave you down there untiiil you diiie."*

"And it was well deserved," commented Venancio, "but . . ."

" . . . but now you can grab the shovel and start digging the
well." Tomasón's story had not made Pancha forget that the well
was drying up.

"Look, Pancha, I got up to work before the three-in-the-
morning cry of the night watchman and I sold fish and shrimp
until around four o'clock in the afternoon. Today I am a tired
man. Sunday I'll dig all the wells you want, but for now leave
me at peace, Pancha."

"Then you're not going to help me?" asked Pancha angrily.

"No. Anyway, since when are you a water diviner? I once met

a Spanish-speaking Negro who just put his ear to the ground, like this, and he could tell if there was water running below or not because he learned how do it from a Moor. But where are you going to get that kind of knowledge, huh?"

"Boy, she knows about everything, even the things that one doesn't know with knowledge," intervened Tomasón who between yawns was coloring the wall with a monkey with a long tail and a turtle. "You go ahead, do what she asked you to do and quit complaining, caraaá."

"Pssst. Well, I'm not going to do anything. Until I see that this well is dry, I'm not digging any hole and I'm sticking to my word."

〰〰〰

Within a week the well was dry, and Venancio was pleased that Pancha came looking for him. He had been restless not seeing her. He was in love with all the Panchas that fit into Pancha. The bad-tempered Pancha, sweating blood as she cooked a stew. The caramel Pancha, frosted in dark dust, handing the paint jugs to Tomasón. The coy Pancha, unbraiding her hair, leaving his mouth watering with love. The pretty girl Pancha, caring for the vegetable garden and marking a circle with the tip of her clog, saying, "Come Venancio, dig from here to here, from heeere . . . to heeere."

He began the task after the cry of the milk vendor but before that of the ground maize seller's. By around two in the afternoon, he was up to his shoulders in the pit. From the muddy bottom a fine and crystalline trickle smelling like Pancha began to seep out.

Ñeque, yo ñiquiñaque
Acuricanduca

cova que cova
ñeque caracumbé
Give me your little water, to drink
ñeque ecolecuá
Bit of water, that now runs far.

Venancio improvised with everything he had, laughing and crying at the same time, but the bad-tempered Pancha made him be quiet. The fresh water launched onto his face, and with an apologetic gesture and reverence, he threw a small bundle of white flowers into the new well.

Pancha cared for the herbs just as her mother had taught her, and as she had been shown by the slavewomen in the hacienda where she spent her childhood. These women got her accustomed to getting up early, without making a sound, and to secretly running errands in the early morning. Crouched down amongst the plants, they would stop in the planted fields, hidden between the sugar-cane plantations. While they picked from the thickets, they showed her when such-and-such a plant was to be cut in order to have the *aché* that gives it the power to cure, when it was time to plant, and on which side of the plant one could harvest. For some are good on the right side for certain maladies; on the left side they might poison. If pulled up on Passover Thursday, they do well. On Fridays they are extremely bad, worse than the Friday rue. Many herbs work with the rising sun or are like the prickly pear that fills its *aché* from the full moon.

There are also sleeping ones that have no power. Not even on Resurrection Day, which is the best day in the year to collect herbs.

Remember Pancha, her mother would say, other dates are good—the 24th of June, the festival of Saint John, and in July the month of Santiago.

Pancha learned from the medicine women that the power enclosed in chicory lowers a fever; that valerian gives tranquillity; that quinine in tisane is the best against tertian; that the juice from cottonbud calms an earache, a poultice from its crushed seeds ripens a boil, and in tisane it rids one of the child growing in the belly, like artemisia and rue.

A juice made for cough is made with leaves from the carob tree and those from the *yerbaplata*. With the grains from beans, wrinkles are erased. Cooked potatoes heal an inflammation. Seeds from gourds, from parsley, and from rosemary get rid of lice and make hair grow. Hot lima beans cure a stye. Ground *huairuro* is good for a fever. *Sábila* and mint closes wounds, frees blocked urine, and scares away that which is harmful.

Chickpea makes one sleep and serves to terminate a pregnancy. Plantain poultice cures an ulcer. *Yerbaluisa,* camomile, and lemon balm tame stomach pains and give tranquillity.

"The two of you be careful in Lima, and you, Venancio, especially. With so many carts that break loose in the streets you can't go walking around in a daze. Go and come back quickly," Tomasón suggested as Pancha and Venancio left the hut.

Venancio took Pancha by the waist to help her jump over an irrigation channel. She lifted the hem of her skirt and allowed him to hold her without reproach. After jumping, she tightened her headscarf, let down her skirt, and slipped away from his arm.

Out of habit, she wore seven long skirts that came down to her ankles. She never lacked blue, yellow, or black ones, always embroidered and held to the waist with a black sash. She adorned them with gold trinkets, two coral amulets to guard against the evil eye, and some bracelets for bad air. The two went slowly along. Pancha was happy to go to the other side, to the city. For fear that someone would recognize her, she rarely crossed Stone Bridge.

Preoccupied, Tomasón watched them move away. He saw her

spruce herself up each day. Recently he had begun to think seriously about Pancha's future. Jaci Mina told him:

"Look, that girl is now of age where she's ready and it's best to give her to Venancio, who wants to marry her before another suitor comes after her. What do you think?"

It was true that Pancha, olive skinned, was no longer the child that Francisco Parra had left, but rather a woman, sixteen years of age, grim, scowling, and at times foulmouthed. Venancio yearned for her, but Pancha did not pay attention to love. After selling her herbs, she worked in the vegetable garden and she combed her long ponytail and listened to the river's conversation. Pancha did not sleep without braiding her hair. Then she formed a little ball with the hair entwined in her comb and threw it in the fire. It would sizzle until it turned to nothing.

When she turned fifteen, Jaci built her a room to sleep in. Venancio used lime to whiten the rushes and reed walls. Tomasón painted her an imitation of golden stucco, and the three of them placed the luxurious, canopy-covered cot as the centerpiece.

Of the neighbors from Malambo who saw the room, there were more than a few whose own envy was reflected in the bronze columns and handles polished with ashes from the hearth. They marveled at the damask of the canopy. Perhaps not even the vicereine sleeps in a bedroom its equal.

"Why don't we get married, Pancha?" They skirted the river.

"I won't marry until I know that it's true that my *taita* is dead and why they killed him."

"He's definitely dead, there's no doubt about it. Tomasón doesn't forget a face. The bad thing is he doesn't have anything to prove it to you. Neither of us know who killed him, much less why. If only we knew who he went to visit that night. Do you know?"

"How will I ever know? "

"Then promise me you'll marry me."

Pancha responded, but her words were drowned in the water without even making a wave.

They continued walking in silence. Venancio slowed the pace upon seeing a small mound of floating leaves, swimming with the drift. He spoke to them very gently, in the same manner that he did as a child. He guided them with his breath so they advanced with the current. So they would not drown. But they did not go very far. They got caught in the supports of the bridge.

"Pancha, what happens is, you don't love me."

"Of course I love you, although only at times. It's not like my father or Tomasón. I always love them."

"Don't get confused, Pancha. Keep those of us who are living separate from those who are already dead."

"Like that? Since when is this done?" asked Pancha, contemptuous. She quickened her pace.

Venancio did not know what to answer.

〰〰〰

At first, Yáwar Inka was not sure if his eyes saw Tomasón or his shadow painted on the walls. He waited to become acclimated to the shadow and to that shining flicker like a gunpowder castle slowly and quietly exploding.

"Is that you Inka? I thought it was that stubborn miller, come to pick up a painting for his master. Come in," he heard the silhouette say. "It's been a long time since you passed this way. Here, Inka, get closer so I can see you better. Where've you been?"

Yáwar took a seat in front of the table and allowed Tomasón to touch him with his fingers. The old man had not lost the custom of studying the hands of his people.

"Right here, that's all. I don't leave El Cercado. I'm busy with my own things. Regardless, I didn't forget to send you some coca and tobacco leaves."

"Yes, I always receive them. I'm never in need of smoke or chew." His hands had gone back to being wooden, cold. The lines of his palms were lost in unknown courses. Tomasón confirmed that he was no longer the Yáwar of before. "Tell me how things have been going."

"Good. Since I gave back to the earth part of the gold that had been in the churches, it's been going better. *Pachamama* likes it when things that are hers are given back to her. But I still have gold that I want to melt and sell."

Tomasón looked at him with concern.

"It's the priest José's fault, the one who goes after the Indians. It's his fault that I don't have an oven, and I can't do it myself." He complained.

"Be careful not to trust too much, Inka. I don't want to see your body hanging from a pole in the Plaza Mayor."

"You won't see that. But I came to Malambo for another reason. I'm passing through, nothing more. I brought you a gift," and he gave Tomasón a small statue the size of an egg.

"Hummmm. It's a little golden bull with horns and everything. It's very well made. It even looks like that bull that I always dream about." Tomasón examined what was in front of him. "I even painted it on that ox skin. Ay! I don't know why it is but I don't do well with that animal. Better not give it to me. It will bring me more nightmares. Take it with you."

"So you wouldn't be afraid of it is why I brought it! That bull likes water, you know? It's exactly like the one that lives at the bottom of Lake Titicaca, and only when it's mad does it lift its head and snarl and look to the sky. That's when the water turns into a whirlpool, but if you throw it in the river, you free yourself from all the wild bulls that there are on earth. You might even be cured of that sickness in your chest. Don't be stupid, Negro! Weak is what you are. Listen to me!"

"Don't disrespect me, because if you do, I won't keep calling you Inka." Joking this time Tomasón says, "Leave the charm on the table." The two of them are still laughing when Melgarejo knocks on the door and enters without waiting.

"I forgot that you were friends," the miller concludes, startled.

"Here a lot of people come and go to buy the paintings. I was already saying goodbye," responds Yáwar Inka recovering from the surprise.

"I see that he leaves without buying anything. At least let me offer you a ride in my cart. I take it wherever I go. Wait for me."

"Don't bother, I prefer to walk," he answers dryly, and leaves, making a gesture of departure to Tomasón.

For an instant Melgarejo wants to impede his passage, but he thinks better and lets him go. With an Indian, even if it's true about his lineage, he doesn't feel belittled as he does with the Castilians, who call him "Don," even while treating him like a second-class citizen. Only a creole.

He rubs his hand over his square face, which always has the shadow of a beard. Why doesn't the same amount of hair grow on your head? Gertrudis would ask him. Baldness had already arrived at his crown and made his thirty-eight years seem more like fifty. He remembers that he has to visit the French barber who makes wigs using the hair of the dead and dentures cut from wood.

Something shining on the table catches his eye.

"And that, Tomasón, what is it?" examining the little bull.

"Oh, that. It's not mine." He lies to reduce its importance. "It's a charm. I wanted to show it to Don Yáwar so that he could tell me how much it's worth. Doesn't it look beautiful?"

"It's an idol made of gold that the Indians bury in their *wacas*. Who gave it to you?"

"I came across it by accident in the stomach of a fish. One of those that Venancio brought me. I don't think it's made of gold. It seems more like copper."

"Are you telling me the truth?"

"Why wouldn't I? If you don't believe me, it's of no concern to me."

"Uh no? You don't fool me the way you do your master. Valle Umbroso believes your tall tales and that's just because you're sick and on the verge of dying. I know that niggers lie out of habit. Give me the painting that I came for before I loose my patience." He lifts his hand threateningly, even though he has never hit a slave. Superstitious to the extreme, he fears that the same fate would fall on him. Putting shackles on ankles or making them work for months at a time in the bakery kneading bread night and day seems less cruel to him. Furthermore, this gives slaves sufficient time to brood, he has always thought.

He holds the canvas that Tomasón gives to him, and the blood rushes to his face. The motif is openly obscene. Virgin Mary nude from the waist up, breastfeeding the child Jesus with one breast, and, with the other, Saint Joseph.

"I copied it from a painting. It's not my fault," Tomasón defended himself.

"You've done good." Flustered, he rolls the canvas, wondering who would have asked for a Virgin done that way. "I'll give it to your master. By the way, let him know if you need paint, brushes, cloth."

"I have everything. I only need the reales that he owes me for my wages."

"Ah, that's right. He gave them to me, but first tell me the truth. Where did you get that little bull? Think about it." He fondles the statue.

"Do what you want to with the reales, but give me that. It's not mine."

"Whose is it?"

"The water's. I have to return it to the river."

"You'd be a fool! Don't even think about it! I'll buy it from you." He throws some coins at his feet. He leaves, places the canvas in the cart, and goes away whistling a tune. The horse knows the way.

〰〰〰

The morning is quiet, and quiet are the clouds and the slaves. On the other side of the river the day grows. In the living quarters, the hours turn to nothing. They dissolve. Before a clear morning arrives, it darkens. Waiting for the end of the curfew, the slaves lie on the ground and remember the long voyage in that dark belly, tumbling with each wave in the storm that batters the wooden shell and expels them, mangled. Other bodies will be reborn. Only the memory will continue, swimming intact. Once again will come the calm, the landing, the clouds that do not move in the sky of the living quarters of Malambo.

Guararé Pizarro, a Panamanian slave, watches the firmament with confidence. He grows impatient counting the forty days: he wants to see Lima the beautiful, the city with filigree balconies hanging in the air. To wander her streets paved with bars of silver. To attend the theater and to wait for two o'clock bells in the summer afternoons, and in the winter, the ones at three o'clock that signal the beginning of the event. He wanted so badly to meet that actress with the mole painted on her cheek. Will all this be true?

Although his curly hair does not betray him, nor his dark skin, Guararé is mulatto. And if María de los Ángeles for a time saw him as white, it was because the clouds had already begun to grow in her eyes. Slowly, Guararé began again to darken as she considered him, until he turned back to being the youth that she cared for. Although not in all ways, he had lost for her that brilliant color that he had when he was a boy. She saw him faded, opaque, the color that silver becomes when it is burned, because of the sudden nights that began to cover her eyes, wandering and overflowing. When she least expected it, they were in front of her, and she fell into them without understanding why those dark waters did not get her wet.

"Guararé, my son, I just sold you to a merchant. I need the pesos to pay whoever can get this bad water out of my eyes. I can barely see."

"You'll never see me again." He said it calmly. He could not complain about what she had done. María de los Ángeles was not his mother and had waited almost twenty years to break the promise of not selling him.

"How much did they give you for me?"

"Little, actually. I sold you without papers. A hundred pesos they gave me, because you're going to go on a big ship. You're going to leave, my son. No?"

"Yes, yes I'm leaving. Don't worry. I'm upset, but it will pass."

"Then I'm going to give you a keepsake so that you don't forget me." From her ears, she took a pair of worn earring studs. "It's all I have. They're not even real silver, even though they have a very beautiful filigree."

"I'd rather have what my father gave you , if it's not too much to ask."

"Not that, no, my son. If I give it to you, how will I know that I had you with me and that it wasn't a dream? It will take away the pain of not having you." Feeling her way around the dark puddles, she opened an old trunk and showed him the gift. "But you can touch it again if you want."

It was a remnant of a transparent material, the size of a handkerchief. When he squeezed, it crumbled. Upon its release, it returned to being a piece of the morning sky. Guararé gave it back to her.

"Send me off by retelling my story, María de los Ángeles."

"Listen well, then, because it will be the last time." She passed the material in front of her, trying to catch its transparency. The moment she convinced herself that she could not see it, she enclosed it in her fist. She lay down on the hammock and waited for Guararé to rock her. Then she began her tale without changing a word.

She always began by asking herself how it was that the rowboat arrived in her town guiding two barges loaded with merchandise from the Orient. That is what she assumed. It probably got lost navigating the Chagres river. He carried you in his arms. You were still very small, you didn't know how to talk, the charge of a smuggler without a face or identity. The two of you were covered with mosquito bites, and he asked me:

"Do you have children?"

"Dead ones, I have several, sir."

"A husband?"

"A husband...? That, no I've never had."

"I'll give you ten yards of silk if you care for this boy until I return. I have to leave for El Callao. In six months, I'll be coming back. Agreed?"

"I'll take care of the child, sir, but why would I want something like silk? Better yet, leave me a little something to eat."

"It's all that I have, woman."

"Then I don't have any other choice but to sell it."

"Sell what you want, except the boy: he's my son."

"I wouldn't dare sell the boy. Mister, do you think that I have no heart? Anyway, he's still very little. No one would buy him."

"Take good care of him, and when I return, I'll give you another ten yards of any cloth you choose. Promise me."

"As you wish, sir."

〜〜〜〜

"I looked after you like you were my own son, but he never came back for you. Yes, Guararé. He told me that he was your father but you don't resemble him at all."

"You only saw him once?"

"He was white, you're not."

"Tall?"

"Not so much.

"Panamanian?"

"I don't know."

"Spanish?"

"Who knows!"

"What was his name?"

"He never told me, nor did he tell me your name."

"Then why am I Guararé?"

"Because that's the name that I gave you."

"And my mother? Is that right that he never said anything about my mother?"

"No."

"Is El Callao far, María de los Ángeles?"

"Very far. You'll never get there. It's in Peru."

When María de los Ángeles finished the story, a dark pool had already been long suspended in her eyelashes. It had made her fear the most subtle blink. She was silent, still, with her eyes very open, sensing his movements. But that did not stop Guararé, whose skin was the same matte black color that silver takes when it is burned, from tearing from her hands once and for all the fragment of silk that contained an entire life. He left.

※※※※

"Yes, it was very far, but I made it," he thought, seated on the ground of Malambo.

Chapter V

Before leaving his mansion, De la Piedra observes the city with the telescope. On clear days like today, the powerful lense draws him nearer to the blurred silhouette of a galleon anchored in the port, and to three deserted isles. On one of them he sees a brief sparkle. Maybe it is the sea's reflection. Hidden behind the balcony's lattice, he continues to take in the street activity.

He does not tire of closely watching the women, so slight in stature. Ever since he arrived to the city, the wealthy people's jewelry has captured his attention. Families that in Spain would be considered rich were here, with the same fortune, thought to be comfortable at most. Luxury was wasted and displayed. Women reserved the use of silver as the setting for their most valuable jewels. Incrusted with rubies, pearls, amethyst, or sapphires, silver was only there to make them stand out. Gold, on the other hand, being so shiny, made the stones less attractive, almost devalued them. For simple rings, for service dishes and cutlery, yes, it worked well.

De la Piedra observes "the veiled ones," the Lima women who, in spite of the prohibition, cover their heads and faces with a cloth tied to the waist, leaving only one eye visible. He tries to ascertain who that one might be who is crossing the street or who is walking below his balcony, swinging her exaggerated hips—the result of stuffing made of feather padding. She is walking with the gait of feet squeezed into hose, pulled tight, and with delicate slippers of satin and silk.

In the corner of Swordsmen Street, he makes out his tenant Chema Arosemena, a young student from Gijón who also passes his time observing his neighbors' every detail. He had participated in an expedition that drew documents and maps of various cities in the South Sea and he had decided to stay here. He was taking notes for a book that he was going to call *Notes on Travels and Customs in Lima, the Three Times Crowned City of Kings*. De la Piedra saw him write meticulously in his diary and guessed that his notes were prices and qualities of the polished steel of the swords, the daggers, and the unfinished and idle machetes in the shop windows.

A little farther away Father José is walking. The Jesuit had let his beard grow ever since he cured the vicereine with his medicinal powders. It was not strange to De la Piedra that the Jesuits maintained with such secrecy the formula of what the mixtures truly contained. What else was to be expected! They were worth gold. He would love to see someone rob them of their monopoly, he thinks. When he tires of watching the street, he leaves the telescope to one side and goes down the creaking and aged stairs that open into his office. Sprawling in the large leather chair, he waits for Nazario Briche to notify him that his coach is ready to depart for Malambo to visit the slaves.

Through the large window that faces the garden, he sees Chema and Venancio enter the mansion accompanied by a young girl. It was the colorful skirts that she wore—because at that distance he could not hear what they were saying—that made him remember the woman that he had been with such a long time ago. Her name did not mean anything to him, he realized after trying unsuccessfully to recall it.

What does it matter what her name was! The colors of her skirts still had not gone from his memory. He suffered increasing forgetfulness; he remedied this in business with annotations of the most minimal details. But in the end, not even wine calmed his restlessness. Memories of his life abandoned him, but their disappearance strangely left not a quiet space but a vivid sense that something had been lost forever. At times, with an effort, he was able to steal into that confusing web and rescue pieces of events in that pueblo. Perhaps a date, a name, the disjointed pain of a scar.

He met that woman at a time when his feet itched to continue traveling if he stayed for more than a month in one place. He was one of those small-time traders who buy and sell what they find along the way. Nonetheless, with that woman he did not have to negotiate. He won her in a game of dice.

He had rubbed his fingers with the charm stone before betting for the Abyssinian servant, a precious boy, the color of ebony with skin like silk. But luck did not befriend him.

"Neither one of them will serve you for work, much less for breeding," joked the other merchants when he won the consolation prizes: a mule with a bad back and an elusive, fragile Negro girl.

Before the first week had passed, the mule descending a hill stepped awkwardly, slid in the mud, and fell over the precipice. He thought the little woman might also fall, but no. She completed that trip and many more. She grew, got stronger, and learned to buy and sell as well as he. But she did not give herself over to the business. She wanted to be free, and being the slave that she was, she learned to escape.

The first time she fled was after a morning of storms that never seemed to end. He found her by having the dogs track her down. She herself told him that by following the route of the rainbow, one day she would return to the cost of Guinea.

Who was that woman with the multicolored skirts? De la Piedra wondered and went out that morning to meet Pancha.

"Good morning, Don Manuel," Chema greeted him.

"Good morning, sir" said the visitors, and Altagracia received them.

"Good. Good morning to you all. I don't see you often, Chema. Always traveling. Getting to know the city I imagine. Stop by my office one evening to talk."

He wanted to direct a word to Pancha, but Chema interceded and responded:

"I will Don Manuel. I need more testimonies from the people. I want to make it through the Indian town. I'll write about their customs and also I'd like to do the same with the Negroes. That's why you find me here, conversing with Altagracia, with her brother and his friend."

Chema is distracting his attention, and De la Piedra forgets the purpose for which he had gone out to the garden. "Do you think all that trouble is worth the work, Chema? I'd understand if you were writing about native plants and animals. But why write about the life of the slaves? Don't we also have them in Spain?"

"If I don't do it, my work will be incomplete. It's not just a guide for travelers, but rather a study about Lima society, an educational book that they'll read in Europe with pleasure because this city is incredible. I've already sent a few pages to my friends and they are anxious to read the entire piece."

"I confess that I don't believe much in reading. Here, as in Europe, it's still a privilege. I know many who don't know how to read or write, and it's not that they're common folk. If need be, they scribble a signature. With a book, one only reaches a few people who think they know everything. Come, let's leave that alone. Chema, my friend, along with seeing you, I came to say hello to this precious one. What do they call you, girl?"

"Francisca Parra, sir."

Chema interrupted them. "They say that tomorrow they will auction slaves. I'd like to be there."

"Don't worry about it. Bring your goose quill and take notes, you can go with me." And cutting off the conversation, he turns his back to Chema and separates Pancha from the others. He speaks to her with a certain intimate and lascivious tone.

Chema observes that, although De la Piedra makes an effort to be gallant, his words sound vulgar and crude. This custom results from daily practice in the streets of Lima. Chema had grown tired of witnessing it, how for many men it was a question of honor. They could not pass a woman who was not a relative or a friend without making an impudent remark. According to the social class, or clear skin tone, or if more or less silk and embroidery adorned the woman's dress, they elevated the tone of their praise of feminine attributes until arriving at a clear insult. This is what men from Lima call "flattery."

"How beautiful you are! How can it be that I haven't seen you around here, precious?"

"It's that she never leaves Malambo," offers Altagracia. "She lives with her grandfather."

De la Piedra ignores her. He inclines his head until it is the height of Pancha's chest and, covering his mouth, says to Chema, "Did you notice her great set of tits!"

Chema acts as if he does not understand him. "They tell me that there are two hundred Negroes to sell."

"Yes, that's my estimate."

With annoyance, almost without listening to him, he continues directing his words toward Pancha.

"Then you come from below the bridge. Do you have a husband?"

"No sir."

"Neither husband, nor master. Look what luck I have! Don't you want to work in the big house? Altagracia has a bad arm and needs help." He looks with interest at her olive skin and arched eyebrows. He so much wished that she were not Pancha but rather the other, the memory of whom is slipping away from him into nothing.

"How much do you want to earn? Eight, ten reales a day? It is that okay?" He rests his possessive hand on her shoulder. He feels her tense up and he shudders from nostalgia, thinking of the rainbow that her skirts hide.

"Let's go," Venancio states abruptly. "It's getting late, sir. We'll return another day, Altagracia." He takes hold of Pancha's waist and the two move towards the central walkway without stopping to wave goodbye at Chema, who is embarrassed to see them depart.

"Venancio is not the same as Nazario, be careful," De la Piedra says to himself pensively.

"The girl can work here when she wants. Tell her grandfather." He shouts to them before both are lost through the doorway. Then he remembers what Melgarejo told him about a certain Pancha.

"Is she the herbs woman from Malambo?" he asks Altagracia, who is sitting quietly.

"At least I could have given him the pesos so that Tomasón can begin to paint the Christ," she complains, and returns to the kitchen.

"That girl isn't going to let me have any peace!" thinks De la Piedra, and then he remembers the disapproving gesture of Chema and forces himself to recover his businessman's tone.

"Don't you want to note in your book how many slaves I have in quarantine?" And he responds himself, "A hundred and eighty-three. All of them entered legally, none are contraband. And of the best quality, believe you me. I have an associate who chooses niggers recently brought from the Guinea factories and a few from New Spain or the old continent: creole niggers. He buys them in the Cartagena de Indies market. He travels with them to Portobelo, some nine days of travel, and from there he crosses the Chagres river to get to Panama. From Panama to Callao they arrive to me in a month, if they don't have a lay-over in Paita or Guanchaco."

"You don't bring slaves from Buenos Aires or from Chile?"

"No, no one guarantees me their health. Tomorrow you can see for yourself. One thing, I warn you, if you want to go with me, you have to get up early."

"I'll do it," and he adds, "I've been making my calculations. The profits are very high."

"In all business there are losses and they too are very high, friend. Even though it cuts into my profits, I prefer to spend a few more pesos on shackles and chains, to keep the slaves well secured during the trip. And I pay an overseer to be quick with the whip."

"I imagine that you fear an insurrection, that they might take over the ship and escape."

"Yes, I demand that for the first nigger that gets daring, they give him ten lashes. If that doesn't teach him a lesson, then they throw him overboard. That's why they load extra 'pieces' with-out documents, understand. But the important thing is that the cargo arrives healthy to El Callao. With bubo or one of those shameful illnesses, I have to keep them for three months, not forty days. Niggers like that are lost, they only serve to be sold by the lot. That's why, as soon as they arrive, I send them to Malambo. I look for a doctor to check them over, and I begin to fatten them with a lot of *sango* and stewed potatoes. Just today I'm going to visit them. Don't you want to come with me?"

"No, I prefer to wait until tomorrow."

〰〰〰

Yáwar Inka steps away from the door, lets two men covered with lavish outfits and jewels pass. They are Juan de Soto, encomienda holder with an endowment of two hundred Indians, Gentleman of the Order of Santiago; and Diego de Esquivel y Jarava, who possesses the title of Marquis of Valle Umbroso, bought for thirty thousand pesos. The flamboyant nobles pass through a labyrinth of unsanitary alleyways. Since they have paid half a year in advance, they have the right to choose their slave before the day assigned for the official sale. Yáwar Inka appears to be waiting for someone. He busies himself amongst the storehouses, and if the door of one of them is open, he pokes his head in and looks around.

"But with us, the Indians, at least they treat us like the people that we are, but with the Negroes, they buy and sell them like beasts," he recalls telling Tomasón in amicable discussion.

"That's the disgrace that we suffer, but our situation isn't equal to the one that beasts suffer. The bull isn't aware that they have put a price on him, nor that they bring him to the slaughterhouse to sacrifice him, to slit his throat, to gut him and sell him in pieces, a leg here, there another, the head, the back . . . , even his tail is sold to whoever pays. They don't leave anything! As long as it's useful for a stew or a good casserole. The animal isn't capable of knowing! How would he? Who's going to tell him? The butchers aren't going to tell him, the bull can't understand! But we Negroes realize and there are those who rebel or ask the master, 'How much do you want for me? How many pesos?' They haggle over their price, they ask that it be lowered, they go to complain to the judge. There's others — like in my case — that don't want to pay nothing. There are those Negroes who escape, you know it. It's true what I'm telling you, Inka, the slave should know that there is a price on him and keep that in mind. Like that, said loudly, and to his face at the auction. Like that, with those huge numbers written in the big books they have. It's better than having them come and deceive you, saying that you aren't a slave but then working you to the point of breaking your back. They don't pay you what they should and they treat you worse than horrible. What's that freedom worth?"

Yáwar Inka avoids getting close to the overseers reclining in the entryways to the storehouses, who have little fear that the slaves might escape. The slaves have no idea where they are. It takes weeks — with bad luck, months — for the recently arrived to find someone who understands their native tongue. The traders go to great lengths to keep them separate. Even the "creole Negroes" who master Castilian have trouble, at first, understanding the Lima accent of the conversing river. What the overseers fear is that with the least negligence, their "good pieces" would be changed into "damaged pieces" by a neighboring storehouse. If that happened, they would be lost. How do you demand payment for the healthy men and women, who are very sound? They would not know how to recognize them. Their faces are not recorded. They do not have names. Their bodies are yet to wear the marks of the branding iron or the sign of their owner.

"Have you chosen your niggers already?" one of the nobles asks another.

"No. I haven't decided whether to buy a young one for the

hacienda or a boy who can learn the painting trade. Tomasón doesn't produce anymore. Ever since he moved to Malambo, I can't depend on him. Every once in a while he paints a portrait and sends word for someone to go and pick it up. Melgarejo or his woman always offers to do me the favor. They're receptive because I grind my wheat in their mill. I can't deny that Tomasón's paintings still sell well, but it's not a great enterprise. I really earned money when he used to restore oil paintings in convents or painted murals in chapels. The idea of painting saints I invented to keep him occupied at night and to keep him from leaving the house on Sunday. It's all the same. Tomasón is over for me." He stopped to listen to the murmur brought by the wild cane on the banks.

"Some help for the slaves, sir."

"Some help for the slave," whispers another voice close to them.

The two look at a mulatto standing in front of them. They had not seen him, nor paid attention to his request, because they were so involved in their discussion. The man wears the habit of the Dominican brothers. He is the doorman from the convent, a well-known layman who is famous for being as good as a saint.

"Say no more, say no more," they respond, upon recognizing the pious Martín de Porres.

"Here you go." Each one gives him a handful of coins, and they step away from his side, forgetting him. They continue to browse the stalls.

"But Tomasón paid for himself prior to going to live in Malambo?"

"No. That's what he would've wanted. He escaped from me, nothing more. He's a fugitive."

"And you reported him?"

"I wanted to but he threatened that he would quit painting

even the portraits of the saints. Anyway, he's very old now. Probably half crazy, I think. It's better that he stays where he is so that he doesn't die in my house and I have to pay for the burial."

"You're right. Say no more!"

~~~~~

De la Piedra finishes visiting the slaves and is about to leave the storehouse when he hears his name. Someone is calling him. He turns around.

It is Yáwar who approaches him.

"I was waiting for you." He speaks quietly. "I am Yáwar Inka."

"I don't believe that we have an appointment, if I remember correctly. What can I do for you?" He is surprised by the familiarity with which the other addresses him.

"Lower your voice," Yáwar tells him again, ignoring De la Piedra's status. "I come for a recommendation. I need a workshop that can smelt gold and silver discretely." He does not want to be heard by the river.

"I am only a merchant. Go to the silversmith's guild, they would know better how to direct you."

"I'm talking about a silversmith I can confide in, one who smelts out-of-use pieces, dishes, things that don't have a lot of value. Understand," he insists.

De la Piedra feels uncomfortable. He looks around and also lowers his voice, without knowing why he is doing so. "May I ask the name of the person who recommended me?"

"Again, I am Yáwar Inka, Moisés Pereira told me about you. Moisés knows you well."

De la Piedra searches his memory. He thinks for a moment. "The name doesn't mean anything to me. Pereira? I don't think I've met him. You could be mistaken? I'm sorry but . . . I can't help you. Believe me." He passes in front of Yáwar and heads towards his coach.

"I know that he knows you well, though it's all the same. I'll pay you like they pay that king of yours. How does a fifth seem to you?"

De la Piedra stops in his tracks. He waits to be persuaded to run the risk of smelting gold that surely is stolen. Or maybe extracted without permission from a clandestine mine, which amounts to the same thing.

"What do you need to smelt, Inka?"

Yáwar answers without hesitating a second. "Three gold candelabras, twenty pounds each."

De la Piedra makes a gesture of admiration.

"The church thief," he murmurs.

Later he tries to remember that Moisés Pereira. Pereira, he repeats to himself, Pereira . . . His memory plays tricks and translates the last name into another language and he remembers Moisés Birnbaum, the Portuguese Jew. It is probably him. He has changed his name, he imagines, and in that instant, without his knowing why, some senseless mechanism triggers the memory of Altagracia and Venancio's young friend. He tries to remember, but gives up—he has already forgotten the name of the herbs woman.

"Let me think about it, Inka. In less than a month, you'll have your answer." He walks away and climbs into his coach.

"Take me to Doña Catalina's house, Nazario," he orders, sitting down. He closes the window curtain, contemplating how, as they trot along, San Lázaro with its living quarters and slaves is already fading from memory, and how the imposing chiseled statue of Yáwar Inka is already losing its detail until it becomes just a rock that disappears the moment he turns and rounds San Cristóbal hill.

A fifth. A fifth. A fifth of the value of the stolen candelabras.

If Melgarejo knew. Tomorrow I'll talk with the silversmith Martínez, he thinks excitedly.

The coach proceeds north. On the road to the valley of Luringancho, two Negro women recognize Nazario and signal to him to stop the vehicle. The youngest one looks curiously towards the interior, while the other exchanges a few words in the language of Guinea with Nazario. De la Piedra returns her glance. Then, without moving from the soft seat, he takes up the sales contracts. He knows that Nazario will take leave when he and the women say, "*caimoco cuana mala.*" It means until we meet again, or we will see each other on another occasion. He always makes an effort to try to hear the phrase, at least that is what he believes he understands. There are a lot of intertwined languages that they speak. It does not make sense to try to learn them, he comments to his friends.

The coach travels smoothly as the skilled driver once again hurries the horse along. It is almost as if the reins get in the way of Nazario Briche's hands. He barely grazes them to guide the animal, and he knows how to stop immediately at the side streets to avoid useless confrontations, and is above racing other drivers to demonstrate which horse is faster. Furthermore, Nazario is as quiet as a tomb, and, aside from his bad habit of escaping during the night, he has no real vices. Of course, it bothers De la Piedra to see him carrying around that big sack, that rattle, that they say contains bones. But who knows if it's true!

On the other hand, he is not deceived by Nazario's ways. He knows that Nazario is not as passive as he pretends to be. He is sure that the coachman's body holds an enormous amount of energy, a terrible strength. Ever since that night that De la Piedra saw him crazed, he knows that there are moments when Nazario is incapable of stopping his violence. He did not ask him what had happened in the garden that night. He waited for a more prudent moment. There were no complaints from the neighborhood. He said nothing. Only it bothered him that he was not able to forget it. What a strange memory he had!

They were near the mill when, far away, he sees Catalina Ronceros and Gertrudis Melgarejo seated in the rocking chairs. The sound of the carriage makes them look up and they come out to receive them.

Catalina is tall and boney, with brilliant, black, almost crying eyes. She always dresses in dark colors, which makes her pallid whiteness stand out even more. Her skin is streaked with spots, freckles and blotches—if it isn't for the wind, it is the sun, the heat, the cold that harms her.

"The mosquitoes too," she says, nervously shaking the silk-edged fan. She slides the tortoiseshell latch, quickly opens it, and fans herself. It makes hissing sounds.

"You didn't tell me that you were coming."

"I didn't even know, darling. Good day, Gertrudis."

"Very good day, Manuel. Jerónimo told me that he went to talk with you, but you weren't at home."

"I go out a lot. I'm very busy with this issue of selling niggers. Just now I'm coming back from a trip to Malambo to check on things there."

"I'll bring you an almond drink," Catalina says.

"I would do better with a glass of wine."

"It's rare that I have wine in my home. I barely drink it. It would only turn into vinegar, and they charge a lot for it, too."

"Send one of your boys to me. I'll give them a demijohn of my best muscatel. It's good to have wine in your house. The doctors recommend a glass after meals." He is annoyed. "Where has Antón gone?"

"He still hasn't come back from selling the eggs." Catalina leaves them and enters the house.

"Jerónimo wants to talk to you about the farm. To close the business," Gertrudis tells him, once they are alone.

"Yes, I imagine. I'll tell Catalina to sell it, though the right moment hasn't arrived. Not yet. Our wedding won't be until next year. Before then I have to make some arrangements with my old house. Buy furniture, other service slaves. All that takes time, tell him." He wants to change the subject. "How is he? He wasn't very well."

"It's because of the cold that we're having. It will pass."

"I'm of the same opinion. It's nothing more," replies De la Piedra secretly joking to himself.

Simpleminded Melgarejo had confided to him the ailment that afflicted him.

"Believe me, Manuel. I'm not saying that the woman is a witch. Nevertheless, I swear it's true that she has the power to control water. Gertrudis says that it's because of the cold that we're having, and she suggests that I go see that Jesuit. That what I have is a weak bladder. But it's that herbs woman, not some sickness that I have stuck in me. I know it. It started after I had an altercation with her grandfather about some trinket. A little bronze statue of no value, which I paid a fair price for. After a couple of days I ran into her coming out of the general store. She ran right into me. She recognized me and wanted me to return that trinket to her grandfather and I said no. 'No, it's mine,' I tell her, and then to insult her I shouted, 'Scandalous!' How that herbs woman shines with her skirts. In this city, the niggers aren't discreet but dress any way they want. The vicereine should prohibit such crimes. Just as I finished talking with her I felt a warm stream running between my legs. I tried to hold it— I've never pissed on myself, not even in front of Gertrudis—but I couldn't. Oh, what a disgrace! Because I'm sure you know how difficult it is to stop peeing once you've started. I have witnesses to the fact that the herbs woman is responsible for it all."

"I heard that you postponed the wedding again."

Catalina serves the refreshment and awakens him from the memory.

"As silly as it might sound, I am set on this," says De la Piedra. "For a few months, no more. I want you to feel comfortable. The big house is very old. Seriously! Part of the roof in the kitchen is about to cave in. I will buy new furniture for the dining room and for the parlor."

"I don't doubt that you know how to arrange it with the best of taste."

"I'll do it. Be patient. If you go with Gertrudis to stroll among the shops, you won't feel as alone," he consoles her.

"I say the same thing," agrees Gertrudis. "We could even visit you. It would be a surprise!"

"That's it. You should spend more time together. However, the idea of visiting me, I don't recommend. I hardly stop in the big house. Business, . . . you understand," he states quickly, excusing himself.

"Why am I going to go to Lima, Manuel? I used to go often to buy flowers. Now they no longer interest me."

"She doesn't even go to church."

"No, not even to church," she confirms, fanning herself.

"Nor do you receive other visitors, except Manuel," observes Gertrudis. "You don't have other friends? Not even a relative, even some distant one?"

"My husband was my only relative, he was like my parents, and then he died from those swamp fevers which used to have no cure. And my husband's only relatives all died at the same time, though not from that sickness, nor by natural death. They perished in a terrible accident . . . a fire, to be exact. Isn't that true, Manuel?" She waits for him to confirm what she has said.

Getrudis notes this, then says, "How scary! To die in flames is probably the worst way to leave this world."

"That's why they burn the heretics and the Jews," adds Catalina Ronceros.

"That's true. I hope that one day you tell me how it happened. Was it here in Lima?" she asks her. "Poor thing! And Manuel—this is the first time I've heard of your knowing her relatives."

"No, not directly," clarifies De la Piedra. "I knew who they were, though I never had contact with them. I saw them at some occasion and that was from afar. It's not exactly as Catalina claims," he responds without much conviction. He allows himself to be distracted by the crowing of the hens pecking grains in the yard. He rises and says he needs to walk around to stretch his legs.

De la Piedra surveys the land that Catalina inherited from her husband. The house is very small and uncomfortable. It is not worth a peso. The farm has fallen into ruins of adobe and matting. Still, it makes sufficient profits with the sale of the eggs and the occasional broody hen. Thanks to the two slaves, Antón and his brother, Catalina has lived with decency and the farm was maintained. There were a few hectares of land, with streams giving parts of it value. There were subterranean veins of water and land along the river. Up to now there were six grain mills and one of gunpowder powered by the Rímac's waters. Melgarejo's was the smallest of all. There would need to be an infusion of thousands of pesos if it were to be profitable.

Yearning for a cup of wine, he returns to the two women. He notices that Catalina seems to be watching him, judging him—maybe he imagines this—so he decides to leave. "I still have to make other visits. I have a long evening ahead of me negotiating with clients," he excuses himself.

"You work a lot, Manuel." With consolation she takes his hands between hers.

"I need the money. I want to marry you as soon as possible."

He gently kisses her trembling eyelids, and thinks of her eyes that always seem wet.

He says goodbye and leaves to sleep the siesta with Altagracia Maravillas.

〰〰〰

That night, he searches for sleep but finds none between his sheets. He thought he heard a sound at the gate. It's Nazario escaping, he thinks. It was strange that he would have lost interest that quickly in his wife, after insisting so much that De la Piedra buy her. On the other hand, he wouldn't be surprised to find out that Nazario knew that he and Altagracia had been lovers since that first afternoon they spent together, and that Candelaria herself was the one who revealed it to him. You never know how niggers will react, he says to himself, ready now for sleep but bothered by the peculiar rhythm of a drum that begins to sound, probably from San Cristóbal hill.

〰〰〰

In Malambo, Pancha gives Tomasón the ten pesos from Altagracia.

"She couldn't tell you how she wants you to paint the Christ because a certain Chema arrived and then his master came and offered me work."

"Hummmm. Don't pay attention to him. I don't know that Manuel De la Piedra, but you're better off not going back there." All the masters are cut by the same scissors. When they see a pretty Negro, they take a fancy to her. Now, let me listen to that drum. I think I recognize it." He lifted the hide that covered the window and strained his ear. "I told you! It's Bernabé! How could I forget the way he plays?"

"Who is Bernabé?"

"Ah, Bernabé. Bernabé is a renowned Negro who plays the *makuta* well—that's what they call the talking drum. Listen! Listen to how his hands work the leather! Who would believe it!"

"What's so special about it? It doesn't sound like anything new to me."

"Of course. It's been a long time since Bernabé left. I remember like it was just today: it was a little before Saint John's festival. That year they lit a lot of bonfires under the pretext of the celebration, though all the Negroes knew it was to bid farewell to Bernabé. They accused him of killing his master. And it seemed like it was true, that every day he mixed a little poison in the food until one good day it did him in."

"He must have used some type of herb!"

"Maybe. I don't know, but I don't judge him. As far as I'm concerned, that master had it coming to him for taking his wife from him. Of course someone realized what had happened. When they went to capture him, Bernabé began to run. He escaped by the roofs. But it was a useless effort. The mounted officers brought him down with two shots and they put him in jail. Later, Bernabé repented and asked for a priest so he could confess his sins. Regardless, they still made him pay for his guilt. They dragged him through the city with a noose tied to the mule's tale and then hanged him in the Plaza Mayor. The judge ordered that they cut off his head and his hands. They impaled his head on a pike in the Plaza, and nailed his hands to the doorway of the house where he committed the crime. I saw those two hands. Afterwards I found out that the head dried in its place, but the hands disappeared."

"What do you mean they disappeared?"

"Yes, they escaped," responded Tomasón matter of factly. "Who would have thought that they would continue making the drum speak" he marveled. With his eyes half closed he looked inwards. He blinked rapidly, listening to the hands as they hit the drum sharply, until it vibrated a long time and the sound turned into a groan.

It was these groaning voices arising from the leather that the rounded songs of the Talking River repeated:

"Tomorrow, tomorrow, because it won't be today, there will be a Negro auction in Malambo. Macario Santos, Guararé Pizarro and Palito León: creole slaves they are."

"They're looking for their families, word has it they live in Lima," say the *tsacuaras* from shore to shore.

No one responds to them.

〜〜〜〜

After midnight, before going to sleep, Tomasón would paint one of the walls with a two mouth drum and below, in an even script, write:

For my frend vernave.

Chapter VI

Chema was punctual. He climbed drowsily into the coach. They proceeded through Milliners Street until they arrived at Indigo Street, normally called Blue Dust Street. From there they crossed Stone Bridge and continued into the San Lázaro vicinity, before entering Malambo. The slave-buyers are waiting in the four storehouses. Those that had paid money in advance set aside the youngest and strongest. They make sure that underneath the chocolate brown ones or the Negro from Guinea, there is not some mixture of Indian: a *zambo*. They order them to walk, to move, to lift their arms. They study them up close. And closely they themselves are studied, with astonishment, as they too walk, move, and lift their arms. The slave-buyers are judged ugly, but this judgment is not pronounced aloud.

They stink; both sides agree. It requires great tolerance to stand the foul stench that the other bodies disseminate. And as if that were not enough, they are completely shameless beings. The slaves note that these creatures do not have skin. They possess noses that are horribly pointed, and their ears let a pale sun's rays penetrate them.

Guararé had received orders to thoroughly coat himself with coco oil and to tame his hair with one of those combs made from the horn of a bull. He measured more than eight palms, and even though he was thin, almost weak, he was amongst the most valued slaves. The silversmith Juan Martínez opened Guararé's mouth with a stick that he carried in his hand for this type of function, and commented out loud:

"His wisdom teeth haven't come in yet."

De la Piedra encouraged them to verify that he only sold quality goods.

"Men made for hard work. They are free from disease. Look him over well," he told them ripping, away the loincloth. With both hands, Guararé grabbed his penis, thick and shining with oil. He showed them that he did not have disfigured balls, a rupture, or a shameful disease. A murmur of admiration and then awkward laughter surrounded him.

A buyer asks in a sarcastic tone: "You check them all out personally? Look at that, I thought that you only did that with women."

De la Piedra was in a bad mood. He does not know if it is the comment or the obscene gesture of the slave that makes him feel humiliated in front of the buyers.

Guararé realizes what has happened and he does not hide it. Lowering his eyes and tilting his head to one side, he responds, courteously, to those interested: "Yes sir, I'm creole. Yes, from Portobelo, sir. Yes, I worked with a silversmith. I also know how to melt gold. Jewels? Look at these studs," and he showed the earrings that María de los Angeles gave him. "They're not even silver, but I made the detailing," he lied with nerve.

"This is the slave that I was talking to you about," De la Piedra said to Martínez. "He's made for you. He still hasn't finished being an apprentice, but he worked in a goldsmith's shop for a year and learned a lot. I recommend him to you. In a little time, he will have earned double his price, and because it's work that doesn't abuse him, he'll last many years. It's a good investment. I'm asking eight hundred pesos. He's one of my best 'pieces.'"

"For eight hundred pesos I can buy three Negroes! Where am I going to get that kind of money! Forget it!"

"Pay me half and I'll give you a year for the rest. I have a special interest that he stays in Lima. The best silversmiths are taken to Potosí."

〰〰〰

Martínez thought about the offer that De la Piedra had made a few hours ago. He did not ask him for details. In the city there were plenty of clients who wanted to smelt gold obtained by illicit means. Most of them waited for a favorable occasion to send the gold to Europe without paying the necessary taxes. Judging from their weight, even the boxes of sweets and marzipan that the nuns from the Lima convent shipped for their abbesses in Spain were not filled only with blancmange, that delicious candy made from milk; there were also bits of gold.

"I've come to buy a barrow—that's not going to cost me too much—to keep the oven lit and carry coal. Nevertheless, I'll take you up on your offer and I'll buy that piece from you. In the long run, I know that it's worth it. But for now I owe you. You're a scoundrel!" He grips the other man's hand sealing the deal.

De la Piedra laughs. His gut rises and falls, his double chin shakes. Almost as an afterthought he asks: "Did you bring your iron?"

"Yes, I have it with me, but I'm not sure if I want to mark him. He's a creole Negro."

"I suggest that you do. He's a 'valuable piece' and I don't want him to escape from you — at least so that you don't cancel out on me — and the Holy Brotherhood can't recognize our transaction. The pain will pass. Besides, people will know who his owner is," answers De la Piedra, and he begins to dictate a letter of sale to the scribe.

"Don Manuel De la Piedra, sells to Don Juan Martínez, a creole Negro with all his faults, vices, and defects . . ."

Martínez hesitates a moment, then hands him the branding-iron.

〰〰〰

By mid-morning, Chema had already written in his notes that the storehouses were enclosed pampas without the slightest sanitary control. He wrote about the monotonous auction crier, the shouting of the buyers, the conversations in different languages, and the moaning. He noted that he enjoyed observing those from the caravels, with their serene manner and their tall and beautiful women. That it was true that the Mandingas were capable merchants. He had seen them exchange material and adornments with the Congos and Mondongos. But he had seen enough, had his fill and then some. The slave business repulsed him.

He went out to the street, between the buggies and coaches and looked for Nazario Briche so that he could return to Lima. But he did not find him. Two ragged men, with the onset of leprosy, approached him, extending their stumps and uncovering their sores. How different life was on the other side of the river! To avoid them, he once again entered the storehouses. In one of them, dark without windows, he found silence. He leaned against the wall, resting from the horror. He breathed deeply, and a nauseating pestilence rose to meet his nose: the smell of singed flesh. He would never forget it as long as he lived. Without realizing it, he was in the branding storehouse.

In the corner, a fire heated the irons red hot. He could distinguish silhouettes in the chiaroscuro of the fire's flames. He was repelled, but his curiosity got the better of him. He went closer. He observed several men holding some unfortunate soul, while another applied the red-hot iron to his cheeks. The skin squealed. Chema was startled by the stylized initials of Juan Martínez formed by the bloody shreds of skin.

They held the slave up as he collapsed.

"Talk, it eases the pain. Tell me how you arrived here." After a little while, Guararé began to speak. Chema moistened the quill and patiently wrote on the parchment until the pain subsided.

"That's all that I know about my life. Will you help me?" asked Guararé, sullen, without lifting his gaze from the ground.

Chema studied the section of silk in Guararé's hand. He felt sorry for the young man.

"It would be better if you forgot that story about the oarsman in Panama and you accepted your fate," he advised him. "The silversmith isn't a bad man. He'll treat you well. What you have in your hand doesn't do you any good," he added, pointing to the piece of material. "A lot of years have passed since it happened, assuming that it even happened the way that woman remembers."

"Then you won't do me the favor."

"No, that's not it. I know well what the stores sell and I don't remember seeing silk like that. It's very fine and the color sets it apart, but . . . I'll try. I promise you that I will. One thing though, it's going to take time. Don't get discouraged." He left quickly, wanting to abandon the place.

He will walk to Lima. He will cross the bridge and arrive at the big house by foot, he told himself. He was still dizzy from the horror of the branding. Without realizing it, he had advanced deep into one of the many alleyways of Malambo. When he noticed that he was lost, he continued walking. Almost strolling, he attempted to conceal the inquietude that comes with crossing into prohibited territory. He did not risk asking the people who live on the other side of the bridge where he really was. On the contrary, he slowed down and courteously yielded to them, as they crossed the stream on those insecure, improvised bridges of wooden slabs.

The people from Malambo wore rough trousers and flannel jackets. A belt on the waist held a sword, a rough, double-edged cutlass. Some sported necklaces with colored beads and even gold jewelry. They walked lightly, balancing on the head large baskets of fruit, firewood, jugs of milk, and huge bundles of alfalfa. There was always someone who stopped and openly stared at them, as if they were a strange species. Chema, who had acted similarly in the past, looked away from them. Finally he dared to approach two women and ask them for help. One of them, crouched in front of a log fire, was cooking pork rinds in the middle of the street. She was talking with the other woman, probably her daughter. They had set up a place to dry and air out clothes on cords strung between canes.

"Could you tell me how to get to Lima from here? I don't know where I am."

"You're a little ways outside San Lázaro. In Malambo. In Terranovas Alley to be specific," replied the younger woman. "You come from the auction, right?"

"Yes, yes. But I didn't come to buy slaves. I'm studying the local customs." He shifted nervously. "Where does the river run?" he asked them nervously.

"Go back the way you came and keep straight, that's all. Here in Malambo no one gets lost. On one side there's the hill, and on the other, the river."

The older woman looked at Chema. "But why are you in such a hurry. Stay and get to know Malambo. Besides, these pork rinds are almost done. Afterwards we'll take you where you want to go."

Chema did not refuse for fear of offending them. And besides, with them he felt protected from those Negroes with so much *ñeque*: brave and full of rage. In Malambo the blacks did not try to avoid the whip with practiced servility. Not being armed with at least a sword, Chema hoped to avoid a bad encounter with them.

With women he always felt safe. He tasted the maize liquor, and it lifted his spirits. Soon a group of ragged children passed by, chewing sugar cane. They stopped and commented familiarly on the quality of his cloak and his fine corduroy clothes and sheepskin stockings. Then they offered him a piece of sugar cane and sought out his conversation.

"Take me to Lima." Chema pulled away the sugarcane bark with his teeth. He chewed, grinding the juice from it, spitting out the pulp. A slice of fiber between his teeth scratched his mouth. It cut his lip. He sensed the salty taste of his blood and would have preferred to stop eating, but the children kept offering him more cane.

"Eat, then we'll take you to the other side," they said.

Chema noted that, in spite of all the prohibitions, decrees, and certificates of bloodlines, Lima already had a population of mulattoes, as well as light- and dark-skinned *zambos*. Mestizos with white skin and red skin, quadroons, quinteroons, eight percenters, yellow bones, black mulattoes, and as many mixtures of Negroes, Indians, and whites—children were taught to distinguish these. The third jug of *chicha* loosened his tongue, and he confessed to the women that he had just seen some poor soul branded. "It's a humiliating and atrocious act."

The women exchanged glances in silence, and then the older one replied: "I also bear a mark."

"Poor thing. Do you want to tell me your story? I'll include it in my studies as a testimony by a freedwoman." He wanted to add that he was against the system, but all of a sudden the words escaped him and he could not speak. The quill fell from his hand. He wanted at least to censure the system, to negate it with some noble gesture, shaking his head. He tried so hard that he fell on his face. He could not lift his head and keep it straight on his shoulders and he didn't know why.

He was drunk, he realized. He was not alarmed at his condition since he was beside two women who inspired trust. Furthermore, when he kept his head down this way, he began to discern the reed bank of the Rímac. Its whispering, conversing ways began to reach him.

This time, the echoing songs of the river resembled crackling logs.

A lot of water had run below the bridge before De la Piedra heard Chema tell the story of what happened with the women. And Chema did not exactly tell him, but rather told Melgarejo. The three of them had gathered in the sitting room, waiting for the streets to cool down from the early morning sun. Later, they would begin business and see clients.

Melgarejo listened attentively, and then said, "But I still don't understand why you've stopped writing."

"It's pointless to continue. It doesn't make any sense to . . . seeing me, you can understand why, Jerónimo."

"No, I really don't agree. But now, what do you plan to do?"

"I'll leave the city for a little while. Afterwards, we'll see. I'll look for a job. I can't live too long a time on my savings. Maybe I'll go back to Spain."

"Don't even think about it! Gertrudis just received news. Her family wrote saying that they can't see an end to the war. Zaragoza and Toledo are in ruins. Anyway, in Europe they still think that in these lands anyone can easily make a fortune. They don't know that here everything's not as it should be. The bonanza is over for whoever had it."

"You're exaggerating," said De la Piedra. "The situation isn't as bad as you say. Count on my help, Chema. You can keep your room all the time you need, without paying rent. Understand, this doesn't mean that I feel responsible for the mishap that happened in Malambo the day of the auction," he clarified, making a hand gesture of keeping his distance. "You were the one who asked that I take you to learn about the storehouses and the slaves. To return to Lima you only had to wait for Nazario. I agree that he wasn't where he should have been. For that, I have punished him and . . ."

" . . . and Nazario isn't at fault for what happened to me. Anyway, maybe it's because, like many people without money here in Lima, I'm turning into a fatalist. One thing that's true is that I think that what's going to happen is going to happen. Anyone could have been victim of this 'mishap' as you call it."

"I see it like this," said Melgarejo. "Those two women knew what they were doing, and if you weren't refusing to cooperate with the constable they would already be behind bars. They deserve a good punishment."

"We don't share the same opinion."

"Pancha wasn't one of them?" Melgarejo wanted to know.

"No, Jerónimo, please. Don't try to get Pancha involved in any trouble. She doesn't do any harm to anyone with those herbs that she knows so well. She's as good as a doctor. As for the other women, I'm telling you, I don't have any intention of punishing them. They are no more guilty than any of us. They taught me a lesson, that's all."

"But what a way to do it!"

"Chema's right about the herbs woman," said De la Piedra. "As for the other things, I would prefer not to discuss them. Leave her alone because I can't get her out of my mind. I want to convince her to come and live with me for a little while. I'll dress her in gold and silk. I'll give her whatever she wants."

"She won't accept," Chema advised him, rising from his seat. "I'm sorry, gentlemen, you will have to continue the discussion without me. I'm making preparations for my next trip."

"Where will it be this time?"

"To visit the barren isles in the seas of this kingdom. Goodbye to you both." He makes an apologetic gesture and leaves.

"Poor wretch. What a face! Those woman have made him into a monstrosity," exclaims Melgarejo after Chema left the room.

"Ah! at least he doesn't think so, and I'm glad he doesn't. Chema hasn't harmed anyone. I can't say the same about you. Pancha told Altagracia that you stole from her grandfather."

"Bah! If you're talking about that worthless trinket, you're exaggerating. I bought it from him. Anyway, I already told you. Did you forget?"

"It's pure gold and you gave him a few reales," answered De la Piedra, ignoring the question. "Don't be a fool, give it back to him."

"I thought it was copper. The old man wanted to throw it in the river," he responded calmly.

"He can do whatever he wants to with it, it's his."

"Instead of defending him, you should be preparing for your wedding with Catalina," he protested, irritated. "It's not that your business is important to me, but I need to buy the farm so I can expand the mill. It's urgent. If I have more capacity, maybe the Jesuits will bring some of the wheat from their crops to the mill. Father José has promised Gertrudis that he would intervene in our favor, and you know that if I get their business, it would be a great deal. I don't want to lose those clients."

De la Piedra got up. He adjusted the belt over his stomach and coldly replied: "Don't ever mention the wedding to me again. I'll marry Catalina when I decide to. No one's going to push me into doing it sooner. Not her or your mill. You're going to have to wait if you want to be rich. And in case you haven't already noticed, the day has already begun. Go grind your flour. Money doesn't fall from the sky for me either. Oh, and leave the herbs woman and her grandfather alone if you don't want problems with me."

Melgarejo, silent, thought "We'll see about that. Those niggers are not your goods, swindler."

Damn you, swore De la Piedra inwardly. The two men smiled at one another with hypocrisy.

De la Piedra left to go for a walk. The discussion depressed him. Conversing with Chema and Melgarejo, he once again felt his memory become lost in a labyrinth of recollections. He was losing the ability to distinguish between what he had lived and what he had heard in a tavern, at the town fair, at the turn in the road, where he sat beneath the fronds of a ceiba tree, waiting for the sun to set. Why couldn't he distinguish between other peoples' experiences and his own true life? he asked himself, conscious that the present was getting shorter each day, and the past was in constant doubt.

The sound of riding horsemen coupled with the clamor of trumpets and kettle drums, made him glance towards the Plaza Mayor. In Clerk's Street the officials from the Holy Office of the Inquisition were riding, preceded by a town crier. He hears: " . . . so that turning to Him, the faithful Catholics earn the indulgences that the Supreme Pontiff has granted . . .," and pays no more attention to them. He imagines the procession of the convicted, carrying green candles. The witches and the bigamists are always followed by the Judaizers. Those who will receive lashes march behind, carrying thick ropes around their necks.

In Lima, the capture of Jews began the same Friday that Antonio Cordero refused to sell someone match sticks for lighting candles. His store was open, but he said that it was dark and that he did not run the business from sundown to Saturday sunset. If it was not that person, it was the owner of the adjacent store who denounced him. They did so secretly. There were no witnesses. Regardless, the green coach of the Holy Office did not make him wait for the arrest and confiscation.

In the interrogation, Antonio Cordero denied what was said about him. He denied that the incision on his penis was a sign of his alliance to the Jewish faith.

"When I was a boy, a dog bit me. It was an accident," he shouts at the first turn of the rack.

At the third turn, his thighs and shin bones creak with the screeching of rusted hinges, but he still denies it. After more turns, his knees are about to burst out of the joints. They seem like ripe apples. The executioner perspires. He rests a moment. Once again he adjusts and strengthens the cord. The yells echo in the Holy Office dungeon.

Cordero's cries overflow and fall, wasted. In the Jewish home there is never a lack of crystal flasks to hold the fallen tears.

Those that are tortured believe in Adonai, and this is why they only eat food cooked with olive oil. They do not consume pork, nor fish without scales, nor hen that has not been drained, says the Talking River.

So that no one finds out, if they are invited to a meal, they eat even during the days of fasting. True, upon arriving home they stick their fingers down their throats and vomit the food fried with fat, the impure meats, the roll kneaded with grease. This is why Antonio Cordero gets cleaned up on Saturday. When his people die, he buries them with coins in their mouth. He empties the water from the jugs in the house, and during the seven days of mourning, he only nourishes himself with unsalted, hard-boiled eggs. This is what the water echoes.

⋙⋙⋙

De la Piedra imagines the condemned, on the day of the Auto-da-fé, dressed with cone-shaped headpieces and sanbenitos painted with flames and snakes. There would also be an ebony cross with bronze corner pieces. The nobility and the riffraff. It is a festive day. A terrible bonfire burns. Smoke swells up from the bundles of firewood. Someone stokes the flames, and the crowd roars as they hurl waste at the Judaizers. Two of the condemned embrace before the inquisitors can stop them. They give each other the Jewish kiss of peace.

> *With the arms of Adonai I go armed.*
> *With the cloak of Abraham I go protected.*
> *I carry Daniel in my heart.*
> *For wherever it may be that I go,*
> *good and bad I will find,*

The multitude jeers the last oration. They throw trash, stones, peelings. A rotten fruit flies through the air. Someone strains their eyes to watch it fall. An uncontainable shudder overcomes De la Piedra. Without being able to organize the shreds of his memory, he sees the fruit fall on the face of one who stares, accusingly, at him.

My silence comes at a price. Moist and black eyes are immediately revealed. The image of Catalina Ronceros is lost among the smoke from the bonfires, in so much shouting. He does not know if it was her. It could have been or not.

The street criers announce that soon twelve Jews will burn in the Lima blaze. Among these they name Juan Bautista Pérez, forty years old, and a native of Coimbra in the Kingdom of Portugal. De la Piedra calculates that Bautista will leave a fortune of three hundred thousand pesos, perhaps the biggest in all of Lima.

All at once, De la Piedra decides to walk to Martínez's silver shop. He enters. He makes sure that there are no clients and, lowering his voice, without even greeting him, he asks the silversmith: "Can you trust that Guararé?"

"As much as any slave. No more, no less. He won't talk, no matter what. I treat him well and he doesn't have the slightest idea who requests the work that I make him do." The silversmith is polishing a perfume spray, done in the ostentatious Lima style that is made in the shape of a turkey. Both look nervously towards the street each time someone passes in front of the shop.

"I'm relieved to know that. I hate informers." Then he is quiet. The silence is broken by the silversmith, who murmurs, "I'll be happy once you've taken the gold bars. I've already melted them down. I'll keep one, and please don't tell me how those candelabras came to be in your possession. I don't want to know."

"Agreed. I'll send Nazario to pick them up. Wrap them up as if they were packs of goods. If they see them, they won't be suspicious."

"I'll know what to do. It's not the first time. Don't worry about it. Let's talk about something else. Here come some customers." He raises his voice. "And tell me, how're things going with your tenant?"

"Chema's fine. He's recovered from the accident and now he wants to travel. He's going to get to know the San Lorenzo islands, the ones in Chincha, and I don't know how many more. It's the best thing for him. Do you have anything you want me to ask him? If so, I'll let him know before he leaves."

"No, I was just curious how his face turned out. That's all. Tell him I said hello."

"I'll do that."

※※※※※

In the back room, Guararé works a vein of metal to form a filigree. Close to the oven, crouched on a mat, he stretches it to a fine spiderweb. He is skilled with the pliers and the jeweler's pincers and gets lost in the shimmer of silver horizons. He finishes a pair of earring studs and then cheap ornaments with orange blossom motifs and butterfly wings. He creates piece after piece, without stopping, finding new shapes in the vein of metal, but no comfort, only emptiness, desperation. Chema Arosemena's broken promise hammers him, flattens him, with the same intensity that his hand strikes the metal.

But he now knows that Chema lives in De la Piedra's big house. He just heard it. He'll speak with him again. One of these nights he'll visit him.

Chapter VII

. . . That river, with the moon shining white like that and you only see half of it, is the most beautiful black girl that I've seen in my dreams. She is Ochún, the mistress of sweet water, which is Ogún's fault. Now she lives in the rivers, lagoons, and springs.

It turns out that one day Ogún was at a crossroads looking very self-satisfied because of the way the hunters offered him a red rooster. He saw Ochún gathering those little yellow flowers that they call "amancayes" and right then he was hooked on her. It didn't matter one cumin seed that Ochún was having a love affair with Changó, whom Ochún knew well, because sometimes Changó scared the animals with his lightening. But that's how the gods are. They too have their cravings. Hiding himself amongst the plants, Ogún pursued her without the hunters discovering that he was disrespecting them. When they went off to another hill, he planted himself in front of the woman and tried to take her by force. Ochún, upon seeing him wild, barely covered with a deerskin—or maybe even naked—I imagine that she got scared. One thing that's true is that she took off running with Ogún right behind her. Stubborn, hounding her, stepping on her heels, because this fellow knows the scrubland better than anyone.

Desperate, Ochún dove into the river, and the current carried her away. She didn't drown. Yemayá, the goddess of the sea, saved her and gave her the sweet water as a dwelling.

When fishermen are setting out their traps for shrimp or hauling in their nets and by chance see Ochún, they immediately drop everything and go. When she falls in love, there is no way to free your body from her. She helps fishermen. She weaves wicker baskets from large reeds and fills them with delicious fish. But pity the man that does not love her in return, that does not indulge her and give her coral jewels. The day least expected, she pulls them into the water, but not to drown them. She keeps them until she tires. She may have them a few hours or months. Here, on the Rímac, without going very far, I have seen a fisherman walk out of the water and not have a drop of water running off of his clothes or hair. He comes out good and dry, but very dazed, too, and you have to make a lot of offers to Ochún so that she takes pity and lifts the spell.

Ochún yeyeo apetebi nombale
Ochún yeyeo apetebi nombale
Ochún, moriyeyeo obiniri aro abebe
oun ni, kolala ke, Iya ni koyuo
son yeye kari, guanarí guanarí
ogale guase ana, ago
Ochún yeyeo apetebi nombale
Ochún yeyeo apetebi nombale

Tomasón dropped the piece of coal that he used to draw the mural and sang softly to the beautiful Ochún.

Sickly as he was, he began to feel compassion towards things that hadn't even been in his consciousness before. He took time to discover all that surrounded him. He would go to the door and contemplate for hours the wooden doorway of the slaughterhouse, the people strolling by on the streets, and each one of the leaves of the Malambo tree. He would let out an amazed little laugh for all that his eyes were able to see. However, as soon as he felt happy, he could also lose his good mood. Especially if he saw Pancha shaking out the dark dust of the shack. He had become accustomed to the fine dust that settled on the table and that accompanied his eating. The dust covered shelves. It adorned the blankets and the clothes, he thought. He was fascinated by its opaque brilliance laying on the back of his hands, highlighting his fat veins and the yellow of his thick, curved fingernails. In opening the window, the blinding light made it dance in speckles of velvet. He spent the entire morning trying to trap it, with the intention of saving it underneath his pillow. He lay down knowing that it would be difficult to sleep many hours at a time. He was nodding in and out of a light sleep when Juanillo the water vendor woke him and asked that he paint more saints from Guinea.

Later, Venancio entered. "But Tomasón, stop painting that wall and finish this San Benito de Palermo. Don't let it happen that your master gets mad and decides to come here."

Tomasón went back to outlining a blurry figure. "Don't bother me and let the master wait. I'll finish this and then I'll paint the Crucified Christ for Altagracia. Look, with all the black dust that's in here, you'll see that it's going to be miraculous. But let's leave that alone and tell me what's going on. You seem worried."

"I'm frustrated. The fish have all gone. Anyway, I brought you three catfish. It's all I could catch."

"Go ahead and clean them up. Pancha's not here. Don't worry, better times will come. How's Altagracia's arm?"

"Bad, it's real bad. I also came here about that. I want Pancha to cure her. Where's she gone off to?"

"She went who knows where in a hurry to find male and female *huayruro*—that little red bean with black specks that they use to quiet a cough." He shakes his head, accentuating his words, "But I'm telling you, I don't like it one bit that she has to go so far away to look for healing herbs."

"That's her job. Anyway, she does it well. We should give thanks to Francisco Parra that he decided to come here with her, because he could have escaped on his own and left Pancha where she was."

"That Francisco Parra!" Tomasón complained. "A good father he was for Pancha. Why in the devil did he have to leave for Lima the very night that they arrived? I rack my brains asking myself: what was he looking for there?"

He had began to paint a Christ, but he left it to watch how Venancio cleaned the fish. "They killed Francisco for a reason, yes sir!" He walked to the head of the bed. He was looking for an image on the wall. He stopped and called for him.

"Look, Venancio. What do you see here? Ahh? Look well, because it's disappearing."

Venancio approached with the knife in one hand and the fish in the other. Between many dust and soot stains Tomasón pointed to what seemed to be another stain the size of a fist. After looking at it long enough, and out of the wish to appease him, Venancio found a shape.

"Now I know," he said. He outlined the figure with the knife. He added victoriously, "It's a man carrying a sack."

"That's right, it is."

"He's coming back from the harvest. Or he could be a vendor," he ventured, more confident than he should have been.

"What do you mean, vendor or something? That's Francisco Parra with a duffle bag in his hands." Tomasón was riled.

"Ah, *caramba*! Then that's Pancha's father!" Venancio went back to cleaning the fish. "And how do you know?"

"It's that you can't see he's missing two fingers." Tomasón almost angry made him look. "Here it is clear as day." Tomasón showed him the precise spot.

"Yes, now that you tell me, I can see it," admitted the other, so as to not contradict him. "And you haven't dreamed any more about him?"

"Of course I have. All the time. He's over here and over there, high and low. Just wandering. But since he doesn't have a tongue, he can't speak, nor does he have eyes. He can't see. How's he going to call out for help? Poor Francisco Parra. I think that they have ruined him forever. I hope I'm wrong."

"Don't say those things. I know that Pancha has been checking around to find out who put him that way. Maybe she'll be able to get a clearer idea of what happened."

"And then what? The only thing that she'll accomplish is that someone out there will recognize her, claim her, and take her back to the hacienda that she escaped from."

"I didn't even think about that."

"And when are you going to start thinking about these types of things, Venancio?"

〜〜〜〜

Walking along the riverbed of a stream, Pancha figured that she was now close to Catalina Ronceros' farm. When she crossed Melgarejo's property, she took a detour so that she would not run into him. Pancha walked quickly. Her copper bracelets jingled with her bare steps. She had let her big, loose shirt out over her skirts, and in spite of her hurry she delighted in the pleasant tickling of the small rocks under her feet. It could only be her, Pancha thought, when she saw a woman fanning herself under a plantain tree. She approached her.

"Yes, it's me. What do you want?"

"By chance, I heard Antón Cocolí—the boy who sells eggs—say that you once found a dead man near the river. I wanted to know if it was true."

"In part. I didn't find him. It was many years ago that happened. Why do you want to know?"

"I think he was a relative of mine."

"Well, if it's like that, I'll tell you that, truthfully, I didn't see much. But if it helps you out. By chance, I was walking by the dungheap at that time the current was carrying a dead body that no one knew. It wasn't the first time that bodies floated in the river. That's all."

"Who else was there?"

"A few people. An old man, I don't know who he was, and the young man who sells fish. Everybody else looked and kept on walking."

"Do you remember what they were talking about?"

"Unimportant things. The things you always say in front of a cadaver."

"Please help me," she begged. "I want to know why they killed him and who did it. You don't remember anything else?"

The fan and its hissing stopped.

"You come from Malambo?"

Pancha nodded in agreement.

"Then go back, it's already late. You don't want night to fall while you're on the road. And don't waste your time asking around. It will serve you little or nothing at all if you find out who's responsible. The pain, no one can take it away from you. It must have been some mess over women, or over money. Men always are getting into those kinds of fights. At least that's what I think Nazario Briche said. Now that I think about it, I also saw him there. What's your name?"

"Pancha Parra. I'm an herbs woman. Thank you very much. Maybe you've helped me, I still don't know. And you're right, I'm leaving it's getting late. Send Antón for me when you need me." She waved goodbye.

On her return, she took the path that passes by the flamboyant tree, flowering in scarlet blazes. She asked permission to pluck the red-black seed from its pods. And then she turned towards Malambo, promising herself to visit Nazario Briche the following day.

〜〜〜〜

"I'm late but I found what I was looking for, Tomasón," she said quickly. She gave him a big kiss on the forehead, happy to see him with an appetite, eating fried fish.

"He hasn't been alone. I've been with him." Venancio made her note his presence.

"Yes, I imagined so. It's been a long time since we've seen you. Where have you been? We've missed you."

"On the other side of the river. In Lima, helping my sister. Her arm has gotten infected. I didn't want you to step foot in the house, Pancha, but Altagracia needs you."

"I'll go. I'm not afraid of her master. Anyway, I want to meet her husband, the coachman."

"Huuumm." Tomasón grunts. "And why? You're not going to try to find out things from him!"

"Yes. They say that he saw how the river's current carried my papa."

"Me, too, and that's not going to take the death out of your father. That Nazario, if he knows anything, he's not going to tell you. And it's not that I have anything against him, but who would think to keep a box of people's bones! Huh? That man walks around this world as if he were dragging something terrible, and to top it off, Altagracia and his master joke about him. This is not going to turn out well. Jaci says it and I say it too and we've been around. Our eyes have seen everything," Tomasón argues. "Remember: the devil knows more because he's old than because he's the devil."

Venancio added: "I hope it's not like that. But I'm really worried. That's why, as soon as possible, I want to get her out of that house. I'm even thinking about leaving for a while to fish on the beach to save up some pesos."

"The beach . . . ?" Tomasón talks with his mouth full. "The beach is big. Where?"

"Around the south part. Between El Callao and Paracas there's a bunch of nooks and coves to throw my hook and where you can fish out at sea with nets. Without going very far, in San Pedro de Chorrillos Bay, you can fish for dogfish, kingfish, and sea bass. Maybe I'll stay there."

"But is fishing in the river so bad that you have to go to the other side?"

"Yes. I barely get enough so I can eat. And I already told you I need more money. As soon as I can, I want to buy my sister's freedom."

"How much is Don Manuel asking for Altagracia?"

"I don't really know, but that's not the only reason why I need a few pesos more. I also want to save because I want to build me a shack. I'm tired of sleeping wherever," he stuttered.

Pancha stopped smiling. She wrinkled her forehead and frowned. With her eyebrows close together, she avoided looking at him, to keep his hands from absentmindedly stroking her back.

In spite of the fact that very same night while, combing her long ponytail, she regretted that Venancio had not done it and she yearned to have him close.

"If it's pesos to buy Altagracia, you could negotiate it with her master. Now that her arm is damaged, he wouldn't ask that much for her. If it's to build a place to live, you don't need much. There's more than enough cane here and the people will help you put them together to make walls. Even I can help," Tomasón tells him with a thread of his voice.

"Well, it's not just for that and nothing more. Jaci says that if I go far away for a while, I'm sure to come back with a woman, because now I'm too old to still be single."

"Don't believe anything from that Jaci Mina. He talks just to talk." Tomasón saw that the Pancha's face had darkened. She was sad and crestfallen. Hoping that she would go back to being the Pancha of before, he changed the subject.

"Have you seen Inka, Venancio? It's been a long time since he's come around here, and I have something to tell him."

"No. If I see him I'll let him know." Venancio turns to Pancha and asks her, shyly. "You want me to bring you some water from the well?"

~~~~~

After a long while, she finishes washing the dinner dishes and lights the small oil lamp. She sits in the corner and in silence takes up the garment that she is sewing for Tomasón. A light breeze begins to move the hide that covers the opening of the window.

Tomasón observes how the flickering light gives life to the bull painted on it. Wind and chiaroscuro beat down on the alabaster horns. They shake him. The beast tilts his head. He advances his agile mass of flesh; he plants his tense hooves in the ground. He draws back a little. His restless tail whips the air. A brief shiver, and then the bull strikes out to give the decisive gore. For an instant, the painted bull seems huge and now too close to Tomasón. He is filled with an immense distress. He turns his eyes away from the window and forces himself to forget the bull. He begins to draw the goddess Yemayá on the wall.

. . . The world was still pure fire and not even the great Creator wanted to set foot down here. But so much desolation pained him, and this is why he filled his cheeks with air and blew and blew and put out the world's flames. From then on, things improved, though not a lot. It was still a bare mountain around here; a little bit of ash there.

There were many hot rocks—very small ones and also very large ones (which are great to make a barbecue). But everything was covered by a dense smoke, so you couldn't open your eyes without feeling them burn. At least it was clearing. And then, from the heavens there fell a jellyfish that was the very Yemayá.

Ever since she fell to the earth, Yemayá never stopped giving birth to creatures. In her womb were created all the gods and the animals. From the smallest animal that I know, which is the big-bottomed ant, to the biggest, which is not the ox but the elephant. Just like that, the fish came out, like the one I like to eat so much, that one they call "bonito." And that one (caraaá I hate it so much) called "monkfish." Then the yucca plants grew, and the maize, and the mint (which is not a plant but a herb and you eat it with potatoes) and the groundnut plant (which you also can eat with potatoes). Afterwards, the people began to appear, and as I said before, the gods were born from Yemayá.

It was already past ten o'clock at night when the creaking cart stopped in front of the house.

Venancio opened the door and was surprised to see the constable and his assistant.

Tomasón was engrossed in a fuss of shadows raising up from

the black dust. He delighted in the contrasts they made. He wanted to touch them. He could not. The dream and Bernabé's drum attracted him.

"We have received an accusation that in this house you are violating the nigger ordinances," the constable said with the voice of authority. "You possess a bronze cot with a canopy and an awning."

"You well know that it is prohibited for blacks whether they are freed or slaves to sleep in a cot and wear jewels, silks, ribbons or embroidery or use gold," repeated the river pebbles on that clear night.

And it was because of this talk, and because of the voices of the skins, that Rosalía forgot to fry the fritters; that Mercedita forgot to enclose the chickens in the corral; that Ramón let his porridge get cold; and that Emitelia, to hear better, opened the door in spite of having just fumigated. She got a crick in her neck.

What did it matter to Melciades that the sweet potatoes baking in the horse dung turned into coal!

What did it matter if envy finally paid off and the constable took away the bronze cot and the bedspread with a banister from Flanders! They confiscated Pancha's leather-covered chest, with its inlaid cabinet. And her skirts, perfumed with lavender. Maybe they did not even leave her sandals with silver bells, or her big linen shirts, or the beautiful hemmed blanket. Maybe.

〰〰〰

On the other side of the Rímac, Altagracia was sweeping the kitchen, listening to the playing of the drum that had arrived from Malambo.

"It's not a good sign." She was bringing her wine eggnog to a boil. She finished washing the pots that she could. She dried her hands on her apron and went up to her master's room.

"This wine that Nazario buys in the Surco vineyards is not what it used to be." De la Piedra sipped the warm liquor. "The grapes have a bitterness that doesn't sit well with me."

Altagracia said that it was due to the clove and the cinnamon. With her healthy arm, she untied her corset.

"Where is that racket coming from?"

"From Malambo . . . from the hill . . . I don't know. They say that it's Bernabé's drums." She was tired. Without shedding her petticoat, she slid under the blue mosquito net.

〰〰〰

Before dawn, Altagracia was crossing through the kitchen to her room, when out of the corner of her eye she saw that someone had moved the fulling hammer stone.

It must have been the late Candelaria. I should light her a candle before I spill salt and she damages my arm more, she thought. She lit a wax candle and crouched down to put it on a plate with water beside the heavy stone. She got up with a pleasant fluttering in her stomach. Finally, she is growing fond of me. She must feel lonely. Poor Candelaria! Altagracia wants to sit down in the kitchen, if only for a moment, to give her company, but Nazario will not be long in returning from his escapades. She left to go to sleep.

The whole blessed day she had felt trembly. Even when pleasing herself entering onto the body of her master, she could not control the queasiness that flustered her. She tossed and turned on the straw mattress, unable to fall asleep. Wrapped up in the wool blanket, she was a ball of fatigue and sleeplessness when Nazario Briche entered and lay down by her side. Altagracia felt the always cold body of her husband.

"Where did you go?"

"Round about, to walk."

"Ah! Did you hear the drum?"

Nazario yawned. He covered himself with the blankets, and Altagracia's warmth awoke his desires.

"What drums are you talking about, woman?" He tugged softly on her cheeks and pinched her nose.

"You didn't hear any drums?"

He rubbed her hard, rough arm, which seemed more like a dry stick. He massaged her thighs and calves.

The morning light arrived. He filled his hands with her breasts and drank from her mouth.

"What drums, Altagracia Maravillas?" He smelled her to discover if she held the scent of another man hidden in some corner.

"I heard them playing the drums," she kept repeating.

Her armpits smelled as they always did. He breathed in the acrid aroma. He recognized the ooze from her womb. All of her smelled of cumin, garlic, and pepper. Girl, you smell good!

"Jasmine! Spices!" The cry of the jasmine seller who also sells *caramanducas* and flower decorations was getting lost in the streets.

Now it is five o'clock in the morning and the coachman does not tire of purposefully taking in the aroma of his woman—the seasonings and the smoked firewood. He encloses her in his arms. He gets comfortable and positions his weight on her. And suddenly he realizes that nothing will be the same as before.

"Altagracia Maravillas, you're pregnant."

Chapter VIII

After they confiscated Pancha's bed there was a bustle of people entering and leaving Tomasón's house. Pancha looked for work in the garden.

She did not want to see them. She furrowed, watered, and pulled herbs until the fresh basil and the *yerbaluisa* eased her anger. Adorned with a bouquet of camomile in her long ponytail, she remembered how Venancio blocked the constable's entry and laughed inwardly about all the commotion.

〰〰〰〰

"Get out of the way, Venancio. This doesn't have anything to do with you," the constable had said.

"Yes it does: I'm going to marry Pancha as soon as I build my house. Tomasón promised me the bed as a wedding gift. So, you, sir are taking away my property." He did not move from the doorway.

Shadows halfway hid Venancio from Pancha, but she could see that he was rabid. The locks of his reddish wavy hair were standing on end.

He's lying, she thought, and looked out of the corner of her eye at Tomasón.

The old man smiled mischievously, showing the gums of his half-open mouth. He moved his eyelids in what seemed like a conspiratorial wink. He breathed deeply.

"I slept like a rock, and I dreamed wonderfully. Why are you looking at me like that, Pancha? Did something happen?" he asked upon waking.

"Well, nothing is yours now, nigger," said the constable, mocking Venancio. "I'm glad you'll be giving me the bed right now and not after you get used to sleeping softly and up high. Go back to sleeping on the ground. Maybe you've hurt your back."

"You can jail me as long as you like. There's nothing stolen here."

"I'm sure that's true. No one's accusing you of stealing." He changed the tone of his voice from the type that is used towards a child to something more benevolent. "Negroes are forbidden to have them, Venancio. The law's the law and it has to be obeyed."

"What harm does it do if a nigger sleeps on a bed? Tell me. Anyway, since when is the law obeyed in Lima? Everybody says that God is in heaven, and that the king is in Spain, and that at home, the owner reigns."

"Enough already! Enough! Watch your mouth. You may use it too much and end up in jail, Venancio."

Venancio, fearing his own rage, stepped aside to let them pass. The constable and his helpers rummaged the shelves, turning over frames and canvasses. Finally, they loaded various articles of clothes and the bed onto a cart. They left. Venancio followed, unable to abandon the bronze and damask vision of the bed.

Tomasón, who awoke fully only after everything was finished, listened to the visitors who entered Pancha's empty room. They told him what happened. He accepted their mournful gestures and their embraces, their resigned pats on the back. At first, he was entertained by watching them attempt to put on the facial expression they used at a wake, without any dead to bury. Of course, this amusement only lasted a little while. After two hours, he had already grown tired of seeing, behind their sorrowful faces, the glow of a secret happiness. Some tried to hide it with their hands, as they rubbed their palms together in front of their faces. They claimed to be easing the cold, but the rubbing was too short and pleasurable to warm them.

Others allowed only one of their eyes to express their joy. With one eye attending to the conversation, the other turned away to study Pancha's room again. True enough, the bed was no longer there. Tomasón thought some of them might remain cross-eyed from their efforts.

Those that faked it worst were the ones who curled their mouths into a sad pout, even as the corners of their mouths betrayed them with a subtle smile.

"Ay Caraaá! When is Jaci going to get rid of these people for me?" Tomasón thought. He did not have to wait long.

"Whoever doesn't get out right now, through the door, I'm going to get out through the window!" Jaci Mina's promise motivated even the most dense among them.

"Since when could you read my thoughts, *cumpa*?"

"Ever since you started saying them out loud," said his dear friend.

"Look at that! I didn't know. What's happened to Venancio? I don't see him anywhere."

"No one's seen him since he followed the cart that they carried away the bed on. I think he must have gone off walking, to get rid of the bad taste that was left in his mouth after he couldn't help Pancha. He'll be back. He'll want to know who reported her. Who do you think it was?"

"What do I know! I don't have the slightest idea. But surely it was someone who wanted to do her harm."

〰〰〰

Altagracia wrapped three fritters in a napkin and invited Antón Cocolí, the boy who sells eggs, to have them. A black child about eight years old, he was sharp, vivacious, and always eager to carry a message in exchange for a treat.

"Take it. Run and go tell Pancha to come and see me as soon as she can. Now don't you forget about it. You know where she lives?"

"Yes, yes I know. Are the fritters for me?" He smelled them. They were recently made and still warm.

"For you, silly, who else would they be for?"

"For my mistress." He ate them quickly.

"I don't even know who your mistress is, and I'm going to be sending her gifts!"

"You don't know her, but Don Manuel does."

And Altagracia, who always bought eggs without caring where they came from, was suddenly interested.

"Aaha! And what's her name?"

"The widow Ronceros."

"Ah. Are the eggs from her farm?" She gave him time to chew.

"Yes, and my brother Ramón says that Doña Catalina is going to marry Don Manuel, but I don't want her to because I like to be with the hens and I don't want to come and live here."

"What are you talking about! Are you funnin' with me?"

The boy said no. He had left the basket with the eggs on the ground, and as he gobbled up another fritter, he pulled himself up on Altagracia Maravillas' shoulder to look at the interior of the house.

"Do they have a coop to raise chickens here?"

Altagracia rubbed her hurt arm, deep in thought.

"Yes. That story could be true, even though I've never heard master mention that widow's name."

"Well, just like that, things change! If there's a coop maybe it's good that Doña Catalina marries and sells Nazario."

"What . . . what?" Altagracia jumps with surprise. "Will they sell me too?"

"I suppose so. Why wouldn't they?" The child shrugged his shoulders, since he knew few details. Licking his fingers, he added, "Now I have to go to where Pancha lives because it's getting late, you know." He gave her the napkin, and, lifting the basket from the ground, turned around and left.

Altagracia, confused from what the child had said, entered the kitchen. She would embrace the comfortable routine of the big house, and not allow the child's news to bother her. When Nazario arrived, she stopped beating the eggs for lunch and repeated what Antón Cocolí's had told her.

"Is it true?"

"Hummm. There is something to it." Nazario spoke in a quiet voice. He took a jug full of water from the stone filter and drank from it.

Altagracia Maravillas would never grow accustomed to his strange ways. "Will he marry her?"

The coachman looked down and shaking his head, said, "No!"

"I wouldn't be so sure. How do you know?"

Nazario again drank the water that had been filtered, drop by drop, with the porous stone. He left the jug on the table, and spoke to Altagracia in his lazy way, stretching out his words without adjusting his lips.

"Altagracia, don't cook tortillas again because the scrambled eggs are going to spoil." He added under his breath, "That's what always happens with pregnant women," and left.

Nazario was right. After a little while the eggs were a yellow liquid that did not have any foam. They had no body. They could not be used to make the delicious potato tortillas.

Altagracia cried, and on that day there was no one else to prepare another lunch.

〰〰〰

Antón Cocolí arrived at the farm later than usual, and he gave the sack of money earned from the sale of the eggs to Catalina Ronceros. She counted the reales and returned them to the sack. She gave it back to him.

"Put them in their place. Today you didn't break any but you took all morning to sell them." She scolded him. "Your brother came back a while ago to help me. Melgarejo is coming to have lunch. Were you playing in the street?" She waved her fan, waiting for an answer.

To Antón, it seemed like the hissing fan made the same sound that a snake makes when it slides through the corncobs set out to dry on the roof of the henhouse.

"Is it true that snakes are the spirits of the dead?"

"No," she said curtly, "and don't be so long in the street, because I worry about you. Now go. Wash up good and dress respectable to help me serve the table. And when Melgarejo arrives I don't want to hear any talk about spirits or dead people. Be careful with anything you say around him. Better yet don't say anything. And wash yourself good. You understand me? Do you understand me, Antón Cocolí? Wash-your-self-good."

Antón nodded his head up and down, with his eyes opened

wide. Then, he left, running. Catalina smiled at seeing him disappear without saying a word.

Soon, he entered the dining room dressed in white socks, a large linen shirt and baggy, dark velvet pants. At first glance, he seemed impeccable. But he had not washed. And later, given what happened during the lunch, he was happy that he had not wasted his time lathering up his face, his hands, his ears, and maybe even his neck.

〰〰〰〰

He kept the porcelain soup dish far from his body. He feared it burning him. He approached Melgarejo, who took the lid off.

Melgarejo served himself a smoking broth, thick with vegetables. Without lifting his gaze from the plate, he tasted it. He knit his eyebrows. The broth was tasteless and the hen was tough. He blew on it, pondering how to convince Catalina to sell him the farm as soon as possible. Maybe it would be enough to reveal the love affair between De la Piedra and Altagracia. He knew he needed to concentrate, in order to find the right moment to do so. But it was difficult for him because his thoughts wandered back and forth through the outskirts of San Lázaro, in alleyways of Malambo. At last, thanks to a subtle work of intrigues, slander, and partially developed lies, he had persuaded the constable to raid Tomasón's hut. But the deed had been in vain. The constable found no more little gold statues like the bull, nor anything else of any real value that justified confiscation. To cover up the disaster, the constable had no choice but to invoke the ordinances and confiscate some trinkets, some clothes, and Pancha's bed.

"Would you like bread, Jerónimo?"

Melgarejo took a slice. He tore it, and while he was chewing, he once again felt the pressure of his urinary problem. He pushed back his chair and got up from the table.

"Would you excuse me a minute, Catalina?"

He left the house. He turned the corner and hid behind the pomegranate bushes. And the warm sensation running between his legs disappeared. Another false alarm, he thought, irritated and he returned to the dinning room. He apologized. Catalina had finished her lunch and was fanning herself. She smiled at him. Surely she too was aware of his sickness, he thought, and he blamed Manuel De la Piedra for his indiscretion.

"In regard to the sale of your farm, if it's not inconvenient for you, let's arrange the price between us. Manuel is more and more forgetful each day and he doesn't know about these land issues."

"He has the titles to the property. I gave them to him."

"Ask for them back. He'll do it. Between the two of us we can come to an agreement."

"No, I don't know anything about sales. Anyway, I'll stay here until the day I get married. If not, where will I live?"

"Now don't misunderstand me, Catalina. The thing is . . ." He coughed and cleared his throat. "Manuel will put off the wedding as long as he can. I would even go so far as to say that he'll wait until you get tired, give up, and get another suitor. I'm sorry that I'm the one telling you this, but he doesn't show any interest in rushing the marriage."

"He's going to marry me. He's obligated to look after me."

"I don't know why he would have to. Of course, you know better than me. I don't know what secrets there are between the two of you! Nor am I interested in knowing! The truth is, I need your farm right now. As soon as possible, and if you don't pressure Manuel, you'll keep being the widow Ronceros. You see, Manuel lives with a great deal of liberty in that big house . . . he is . . . he is too comfortable under the skirts of the niggers to abandon his ways and marry you." At last he told her.

"Does he have a favorite?" She spoke slowly, stretching out her words. She fanned herself faster.

"Yes. Altagracia Maravillas, a slave, and I don't want to mislead you—as far as I know, she is the only woman that knows him and that he tolerates." He abruptly abandoned discretion. "For a number of years now, they've lived together. Though he bought her for his driver, he made her his lover and . . .," he stammered and was suddenly quiet. A sigh deflated him: "I just peed on myself, Catalina. I'm sorry." He lowered his head and looked without understanding at his wet corduroy pants and the puddle of urine growing under his feet.

Antón Cocolí observed how new red blotches began to appear on the face and neck of his mistress. On her fan the golden yellow snakes, the color of dried corn, hissed more rapidly. They were about a foot long and fat like fingers.

"Antón, bring a rag and clean the floor."

At least he had only pretended to bathe himself! He cleaned the floor as he was told.

〰〰〰

Pancha walked through Malambo, carrying her basket. It was full of purple basil, cilantro, and rosemary. She was asking about Venancio. The washerwomen scrubbed with soapbark and lathered the white sheets even more, extending them like white flags.

"We haven't seen him." They waited for Pancha to leave so they could lean closer to the river, to better hear its murmur, as it ran through their legs and bright colored skirts.

"It's been three nights that Pancha has slept on the ground on a miserable straw mattress on a miserable straw mattress miserable straw mattress."

The river's whispers were muffled, and Nazario could not understand its words about Pancha. The aroma of the seasonings from Altagracia reached the backyard. A corner of it, covered with matting, had long served as a stable for the mule and the horse with light-colored fur. Actually it was a just colt, tied to a wooden post. The colt let its back be scrubbed, without bothering to look at who had arrived. The mule appeared to be sleeping.

Steel hooks, reins, leather whips, a pair of wooden stirrups, and a saddle hung from the adobe wall that separated the yard from the street. Pancha calculated the height of the wall, and imagined that the neighboring big houses featured similar barriers. The same ones Nazario climbed at night, her father, too, would have scaled. Climbing carefully among the cracks in the weathered adobe, and analyzing the shadows, he would have fallen silently on the other side, she thought.

Nazario gave her a glance with his yellow eyes. They were intensely empty and quiet. He continued to rub a rag on the backrest of the buggy. He gave the impression that his thoughts were elsewhere. He paused and asked Pancha to repeat what she had asked him.

"Something like four years ago, they found a dead man in one of the dumps along the river. I want to know more about it."

"The one that the painter and Venancio sank?"

"Yes."

"Ahhh! That wasn't the first time that I saw him. I met him a week earlier, but he was already badly injured. He was able to tell me that his name was Francisco Parra. He told me that he was a runaway slave, and then he died." He told the story with indifference.

Pancha felt that at last the certainty of his story let loose the great pain held deep inside her. A handful of tears and anguish lightened the heavy basket that she carried in her arms.

Malayerba, she thought, and waited for the pain to distance itself from her.

"Where did you see him?"

"Climbing a wall, I believe it was." Nazario got quiet. He slid the rag against the grain of the wood. He lathered it in a bucket with water and wrung it until his knuckles lost their color. "Are you his daughter?"

"Do you know who killed him?"

"What does it matter! He's still not alive."

"Who was it? Why did they do it? Who carried him to the river?"

He shrugged, made gestures of not knowing. Not even the insistent Pancha, as Venancio would say, could break Nazario's silence.

Defeated, she left him and went into the kitchen. There, Altagracia showed her her bad arm.

"What were you talking to my husband about?"

"I asked him about a person that I met."

"And . . . he was able to help you?"

"Yes, in a few things. But he's too quiet."

"He's always like that. He doesn't talk a lot, but he's aware of everything that happens."

"Maybe it's because he doesn't trust me. I'll wait until Venancio comes back. Maybe he can convince him to tell me how everything happened. But let's talk about something else. You sent for me about your arm, so let me see it."

"No. It was because of something else. I'm pregnant. And Nazario—I'm telling you this so that you know him better—he knew of my condition before I did."

"How strange! What are you thinking about doing? Have you already told Don Manuel?"

"Not yet." She became quiet and deep in thought.

Ever since she had learned of her master's plans from Antón Cocolí, she knew that nothing in the big house would ever be the same. Nevertheless, she wavered in asking Pancha for some tisane and rue to drink to terminate the pregnancy.

"Have you decided what you're going to do with the child?"

"No, and to top it off my arm gets worse every day. It doesn't itch or hurt, but it keeps getting harder, and it weighs on me like a condemned soul. How does it look to you?"

"Very bad. You should have called for me sooner. If it doesn't improve, they'll have to cut it off."

"I won't let them do that! This thing of dying piece by piece is a disgrace. I know of people whose leg still hurts, though they lost it when the machete blade slipped cutting cane. Others, without a hand, open and close the fingers they don't have, and still feel the crunch of the bones crushed by the sugar mill. Though you don't believe me, a foot permanently lodged in a cart's wheel always hurts. Anyway, I don't want to live without my arm, Pancha."

"You waited too long, but have faith. There're herbs that do miracles. Try to calm down."

"Keep talking to me like that because I'm very sad. I don't know what to do. Did you know that the master is going to marry?"

"It's natural. He needs heirs."

"Yes, but surely he'll sell me, and I don't want to leave here."

"Has he told you so?"

"Not yet, but I suspect he will. It's always like that. He's marrying a certain Catalina Ronceros. Do you know her?"

Pancha briskly rubbed the damaged arm with tobacco leaves that were very green. A few drops of juice splashed on Altagracia's skirt. She did not notice.

"Yes. Not long ago I spoke with her. She's nice, very quiet, seems like one of those people who wouldn't hurt a fly. At least she gave the impression of being nice and having a good nature. I imagine that she'll change when she finds out that you're pregnant by her boyfriend."

"Yes, Pancha, she'll change. Nothing is going to be like it was."

Chapter IX

It had been a number of weeks since Chema had said goodbye to De la Piedra. They had drunk thick cups of chocolate. Those oily bars made from cacao fruit had arrived from Cuzco. Boil them with milk and a slice of cinnamon, and it is a delicacy of the gods. Accompany it with a roll baked with wheat flour (which continued to replace maize), and you could, some enraptured voices said, glimpse the glory of eternal heaven. Others thought that drinking chocolate was an incurable vice.

"And do you think, Chema, that chocolate has harmful qualities?"

"No, although in excess it provokes insomnia, which would not be that bad for the trip. I'll be gone a good while. Months maybe. I want to know the islands well, even if they're presumed to be deserted, which I think doubtful. Islands are always populated, if only with legends." He said goodbye to De la Piedra with a warm handshake. They had stood directly in front of each other, forcing him to see Chema's face, without looking away.

De la Piedra did not bat an eye. He maintained his glance with the same detained concentration with which he read the log papers or deciphered the enigmas of a work of art brought from the Orient. He did not tell him because he was not sure how Chema would react to his opinion. But he judged that now, at least, the beardless face of the young man had its own character. He should give thanks to those women from Malambo. It turned out in his favor. Besides, the story would make him famous, he thought.

"I fear that it's not true. In those islands you'll only find birds. Believe me, you'll be disappointed. Go to the kitchen and have Altagracia give you a jug of wine so that the trip doesn't seem so long. The effect that wine produces is superior to that of the best chocolate." He laughed. "And this time, take good care of yourself. Will you?"

"I will, I will. Sometimes you act like you're my father, Manuel."

"I wish you were my son. I wouldn't let you get away from my side for an instant. Have a good trip." He saw him off.

〰〰〰

Through the window grating De la Piedra observed how Altagracia Maravillas accompanied the traveler to the entrance hall. Chema, always courteous, received the heavy jug. She was holding her sick arm against her body. Then she gave three turns to the lock to open the heavy cedar door, just as she had done the day of the slave auction, when Chema reappeared after having wandered through the alleys of Malambo.

Altagracia had gone up to the bedroom to accompany De la Piedra in his siesta when she heard the sound of the door knocker. She paid no attention to the noise. She had no intention of opening the door. Besides, her sick arm weighed too much to be coming and going for anything but pleasure. Finally, irritated by the knocking, she gave in, and hurried to open the door.

She did not scream upon seeing him, but she choked down bile eating at her throat. She had to jump twice and hit her chest to suppress the bitterness, and between tears she took pity on the state in which she found the tenant.

He was drunk, on the border of unconsciousness. His face was bloody and covered with wounds. She laid him down in his room.

Later, no one remembered who had advised him to apply a poultice of grease, raw mercuric chloride, whiskey, salt, and ashes, to heal the wounds on his face—and just in case, to drink the hot blood of a black chicken, to take away the shock he had suffered.

"Truthfully, I didn't drink the blood. But the other things helped me recover. My face burned like a thousand devils, but I didn't have a fever or anything," recalled Chema during the period of his convalescence. "Now, that must have been the ashes or the whiskey, but what do I know? The truth is that where I don't have marks, I have blotches," he said, pointing out his face and neck.

And he would have remained streaked for the rest of his days if it were not for Pancha, who had prepared for him a parsley ointment with other herbs known only to her.

He had had enough of those two women from Malambo who gave him the *chicha* to put him asleep. He distrusted even Altagracia and Pancha and their cures. But the sight of himself in the mirror was more powerful than his distrust of them. He began by smearing the refreshing paste from the roots of his hair to his neck. The blotches faded. The scars, however, were indelible, and settled on his skin in fine grooves.

Up close, his face looked like a delicate tablecloth embellished with a perfect finish. The two women from Malambo had tattooed him with a fine embroidery needle, Chinese ink. From his forehead to his neck Chema bore an intertwined *C* and *B*. They were very wide, of course. Precious! Openwork in French lace point. On each temple, there pulsated an *L* in feather point. The nose was an *S* with fringe stitch, with chain stitch from the septum to the wings. His cheeks had two *T*s in hidden stitch. Above the horizontal line they had embroidered three crowns and a star in cross point. They were the initials used on the brands of some of the Lima families. The same ones, though much coarser, still marked the bodies of their slaves.

~~~~~~

Meanwhile, Venancio, far from Malambo and Pancha, began to strike up a friendship with the sea. He was convinced that he needed to try his luck fishing on the beach. The keels of the boats barely grazed the fine, dark sand, as the emerald water approached and pushed them out to sea. The launches rested safely far from the gale and ferocity of the waves. He offered to take the fish out of the loaded nets, and to wash down the craft with the same salt water that bronzed his skin. He pretended not to be a native of the port. He walked with a slow, swinging gait that imitated the old sailors who, even on land, maintained their equilibrium like someone navigating the high seas. Sometimes he almost walked like them, but only recently did he experience the jolts that true waves give — the waves on those mornings when, looking at the agitated sea on the horizon, most fishermen decide to stay home.

During the night, the strange light had shone again on one of the big stone islands. The wind did not cease to strike with a shrill whistle, like the spent laughter of a woman.

Venancio set sail in a barge whose captain neither feared the foaming sea nor believed in bad omens. In a matter of a few hours, the boat sank. After trying repeatedly to fight the tall, salty waves, he realized that he was not strong enough to swim back to the shore. He let himself be carried instead toward an island with rock faces that stretched up into the clouds.

It was an island of living rock, populated with flocks of pelicans, *potoyancos*, and cormorants that bellowed like pigs. Armless birds, almost without feathers and without wings; small sea ducks with iridescent necks and eyes red-ringed.

What a desolate place! Still dazed, he took in the hills of lava formed by the birds' excrement and feathers, incapable of distinguishing, at first, a tangle of hair and beard growth that approached him.

He was an elderly man, though he seemed more like an animal. He wore a hood made of sealskin. He was trying to protect himself from the constant bird droppings. He was followed by a band of simple-minded birds that walked erect like children, with black liveries and big shirts made of white feathers.

Venancio did not see him until he was close. The fisherman moved back trying to escape but the man jumped at him. With a shove he made Venancio fall to the ground.

"You must be one of those slaves from the galleys who jumped overboard. I'll give you what you deserve." He had a hoarse tone and his out-of-tune voice resembled the cackle of the birds that fish by nose-diving into sea.

"No, no." Venancio feared his violence.

"Who are you then?" He spoke in bad Castilian, in a foreign accent with few clear vowels, fewer *rr*s.

"I'm a fisherman. Venancio is my name. My barge sank. I was fishing. Tell me, please, how can I get back to the beach?"

"It's simple. You wait until another ship passes by and picks you up." His tone was sarcastic. "Meanwhile, you can keep me company. It's been fourteen months and nine days that I've only talked with the birds."

"But in all that time, there hasn't been a single boat to pass close to the island? That can't be!"

"Of course, Spanish boats sail by, ships from the English fleet, and Dutch ships. What I don't have are plans to leave the island. My name is Lionel Sterling. But call me Sir. Sir is a gentleman's title. Understand?"

"Yes, I understand, Sir."

"No, you don't understand anything," he uttered infuriated.

"No, I don't understand, Sir." Venancio gave in to him.

"You're wondering, what's an Englishman doing on this island?"

"Yes, Sir."

"I'll tell you."

He sat down on the sand without concerning himself that he and Venancio would be soaked by the waves. Surrounded by birds in livery, he pulled on the hairs of his beard as if he were trying to remember something. He began to speak. Venancio shivered with cold.

"Like many sailors of my land, sooner or later, I, too, was taken in by the greed for gold. So I set sail from England in one of three boats of the Hawkins expedition, promising to return with silk riggings and damask sails. Have you ever heard talk of Richard Hawkins? Of Ricardo Aquines?"

Venancio nodded. On some occasion he had heard a song praising the pirate.

"I thought I would make myself rich with just one trip and return to Europe to enjoy the loot. We touched land in Brazil and sacked various ports that were so insignificant that we didn't see the need to burn them. They had told me that after crossing the Strait of Magellan, the good part would come. In Valparaiso, Coquimbo, and Arica, we won great spoils of gold and silver. We supplied ourselves with water, provisions, and barrels of good wine, and lifted anchor without problem," he continued enthusiastically sharing his memories. Soon he got up and walked from side to side, excited and gesturing, followed by his entourage of birds in livery. "But we didn't get very far. By the coast of Ecuador, the Spaniards surprised us. They defeated us and imprisoned Hawkins."

Venancio ignored Sir and paid attention to the sound of the waves. He studied the island, looking for someone else who might be shipwrecked, or maybe a boat. He had recovered from the accident and wanted to return as soon as possible to the port. Or maybe he should go back to Malambo and fish in the river that speaks, even if he had a bad season.

"I need a boat," he interrupted him.

"What are you talking about?"

"That I need a boat or a raft that you could lend me."

"No. And there's no way for me to make you one. Trees don't grow here." And then he returned to his story, reliving his voyage, basking in the details. With his filthy hands, he imitates using a musket or a dagger, attacking, and defending. The galleons of his story become bigger with each telling. The booty more fabulous. "I joined with a band of pirates and while I filled my bag with gold, the years slipped away from me. Until at last I was rich and I came to El Callao to embark for the return to my land. But I got into a quarrel and lost my fortune and the vengeance of one of the locals ended my plans. You're wondering how I ended up on this island?"

Venancio nodded again. He had no choice but to wait for the story to be finished.

"I fell back into my greedy ways," said Sir, with his guttural accent. "An Indian confided to me that this island held a treasure. I believed him. Contrary to what you think, it turns out to be true and all of it is mine. But I don't know how to carry it away." He opened his arms, exulting in the walls of rock, whitened with excrement. "All this fortune is mine!"

"What? I don't see it."

"Once again you don't understand. As far as your eyes can see, all this is pure gold."

Venancio would rather not waste his time arguing with a foreigner.

"Uh huh . . . Aside from your grand fortune, do you have a boat, Sir? Lend it to me. El Callao isn't very far. I want to leave. There, they'll think that I have drowned. I'll bring it back."

Sir considered this for a moment. Then he ordered, "Follow me."

Venancio climbed the steep and slippery peaks, crawling on all fours. He buried his hands in the fresh excrement. It was white, greenish. The strong odor burned, penetrated his throat and burned him. His eyes watered. Lightheaded with contentment, Sir stumbled over the slow-witted birds in livery and proceeded to the entrance of a dark cave.

"Here it is." He showed him a raft rotted by the salt, unusable, with timber barely held by the rusted nails.

"It'll sink before it gets to the port, Sir." Venancio was deflated.

"I hope so," said Sir with an air of triumph.

Venancio hated him as much as he hated the constable who took Pancha's bed. He had seen the Englishman's sort before, one of those adventurers who arrive from far away and end up failures, tired of doing the Americas without acquiring riches. Just like the vagabonds and desperados gathered in the evenings to play cards at the sides of the cathedral or in the Plaza Mayor. In order to win money for a return trip to their native land, they gamble with the few coins in their bags. They lose. They wager their capes. Their doublets. Their boots. They gamble without regard. By the time they add up all their losses, their prized swords change hands, and they begin to wager the only thing that they have left: their lives. They provoke a quarrel, a knife fight. And then, strange thing, luck smiles on them, and since their lives continue, so does the gambling. The only thing Sir possesses is a miserable existence. Venancio knows that if he does not flee from him, soon, he will either die or have to kill Sir.

"I won't hurt you." The Englishman seemed to read his thoughts. "I need you and you need me. There's only one fresh water spring and without my help you're not going to find it."

"You're crazy. You're out of your mind."

Venancio left the cave. He heard the chattering of his teeth. He felt his body coil, preparing itself to spring like a beast to finish off the Englishman. He ran down to the beach. He preferred escape to the violence that was now filling him like a breath of bad air.

"You can't escape me. You can't escape me. You can't escape me. You'll stay with me until a boat passes." Venancio heard him shouting, and then the shadow returned and grew before his eyes.

He heard the tam-tam beating in his temples. The fierce sea somersaulted into the clear sky. He fell, wondering how the sound of Bernabé's drum could reach this distant isle. But the tam-tam now grew distant, was reduced to a tiny sound that would fit inside of a sea shell, a nothing in a sea of foams. He was hurt. Blood from a deep wound that is only cured with a phenol bath. The memory of a woman with a long ponytail came to him with each wave. And there were two old men, waiting for him.

〰〰〰〰

When the herd rustles through the streets of Malambo to be sacrificed in the slaughterhouse, a jovial atmosphere is created. The herd, fattened on the small alfalfa farms near by, advance in front of Tomasón's house once a month. The parade of beasts lasts an entire day and converts into a fiesta. Two muleteers guide the animals in groups of five. The mooing is accompanied by shouts of joy from the people, the racket of whistles, cornets, and rattles.

Tomasón, fearful, does not step foot outside of his hut on this day. Every once in a while he stands in the doorway and extends himself, only a little, to see better. He cranes his neck, waiting to discern the silhouette of Pancha from one moment to the next. Her delay has him on live coals, but today he does not dare go out to find her. The beasts' mooing bears down on his heart with the anguished conviction that a tragedy will happen. He does not stray from his four painted walls. The shouts of joy from the people depress his spirits. Each month the same spectacle takes place.

Ay caraaá! One of these days something ugly is going to happen, he says to himself. He watches as some mischievous boys cut the rope that ties one of the bulls when the muleteer is distracted. They free it and the general raucousness is amplified.

Toro! Toro! Torito! Torito! They rouse him and tease the animal, waving a cloth. The bull hesitates. He steps back. He seems to judge the men's position, as they make signals at him. He goes to find them. They have already drunk throatfuls of *aguardiente* and whiskey: they are drunk with courage. Delighted, they dodge the animal's gorings and charges. Toro! Toro! Toro! They celebrate and there is no lack of people trying to grab him by the horns and mount him.

Only after they enclose the last animal does Tomasón decide to go out. He rubs his numb bones, fighting the lethargy that makes him yawn continuously.

"At least now the racket and the bulls are done with. But what a commotion, caraaá! Now the only thing left is for it to drizzle."

In spite of his years, he had only seen it truly rain once. He was a snotnosed kid at the time and lived in master Valle Umbroso's house. A downpour toppled the roofs and snaked through the streets of Lima. The road was converted into a tremendous mudbath good only for drowning people and getting wheels stuck. The Talking River fattened and entered the big houses. It spoke loud. To tell the truth, it was shouting. It pushed open the doors and soaked the silk rugs and the cushioned chairs. And then it left through the windows, as if it were nothing at all.

Soon the roar of the hills that surround city was heard. Because of the rain and the flooding of the river, the hills began to walk on their own. They slid from their summits, in alluvium, in *huaico*, dragging along with them planted fields and stored crops, Carmona's three cows, and Juancho's horse. Nevertheless, a drum remained intact, as well as, two simple flutes, five shovels, several pickaxes, a skinny little goat, and guinea pigs (which no one claimed). The people survived because they preferred to abandon the fields and let the earth drink all it wanted.

In Malambo mud walls had already been weakened, soaked by the rain, when the sky opened up with a burst of thunder and lightening. To this day there is not a *taita* who denies what happened, even if he was away and did not see it with his own eyes. They are certain it was like this, and they assure you that they are telling the truth. They swear and double swear by the Virgin Mother that Changó himself appeared. They sing:

Barikoso, barikosoooo
Alardemi, eaaa
alardo cabo
alardemi eaaa
Obakoso kisi eko akama sia okuni

buburu buburuku ki lo aguo oba
chokoto kaguo kabo sile. Ago.

Tomasón would like to have been in Malambo then, to paint the scene. Those who had already learned the song in Guinea took a thread of rain in their hands. Singing, they held the water reed tightly. Fist over fist, singing, splashing about, they rose to the sky of the *taitas* and they left with Changó. They never returned.

"Yes, it must be true," said Jaci Mina.

"What must be true?"

"That Venancio was around El Callao, but he's not there now. He left. No one knows what happened to him. They think he drowned."

"Noooo. He's more alive than I am. This I'm sure of. I didn't dream it. He must have gone to the other side."

"Yes, but like that, without letting anyone know?"

"Hummm. He probably has his reasons."

"And what's yours to be standing in the middle of the street when it's so cold? Are you trying to get sick? Come inside." Jaci thought that Tomasón might have a bit of a fever.

"I'm waiting for my granddaughter, for Pancha. And you, where are you going in such a hurry? You don't want to eat a piece of jerky?"

"I'd love to, if I were hungry. Anyway, I'll stay with you for a while. You're right. It's no good spending the entire day like a grasshopper jumping from here to there. I was going to look for a little firewood."

"To look for a little fire wood." Tomasón scolded. He forgot his aches and pains. "Don't you want to rest? You're not a slave anymore. Why do you have to work almost seven days a week?"

"It's because I'm used to it. I've never been one for just standing around with my arms crossed. If I'm busy doing something,

I can't stop to think about all the things I did wrong in my life, and all the things I'd change if I could go back in time. Also, for a while now, I've had a debt with Don Sinforoso."

"The man that used to be your master?"

Jaci nodded.

"I thought that he had returned to live in his land."

"He came back. You know that he didn't treat me that bad, so to speak. And when his wife got real sick, she asked that I should be freed if she died. He kept his promise."

"Of course. She wanted to earn the indulgences needed to avoid purgatory. She wanted to go directly to heaven, and he was scared that the dead would settle the score if he didn't keep his word."

"Be that as it may, the same day that the mistress died, Don Sinforoso told me, 'You can go, you're free.'"

"You've told me that story at least a hundred times, Jaci."

"Let me finish. Life is full of highs and lows. It turns out that not long ago I found out that Don Sinforoso came back poorer than a rat. Now it's my turn, I thought. I looked for him. I gave him my savings, and from that day on I started to give him part of my salary." He watched as Tomasón absorbed what he had said. Jaci took out his clay pipe. "Do you have any of that tobacco that Inka sent you?"

Tomasón nodded. He made a long moan before he spoke.

"Ohh Jaci! There's no cure for your sickness. You'll never learn to be a free man. Doesn't it make you feel bad to give away your salary?"

"No, I'm not ungrateful. If it weren't for the masters, many blacks would have had a hard time. I don't know why you wanted to escape so badly from where you were." He sucked on his pipe.

Tomasón twisted his face with displeasure and coughed as he blew out smoke.

"Look Jaci, I was tired of the abuse. I'm not like you, who can't figure out how to keep his bones busy, and you go from here to there, from when God wakes up to when God goes to sleep. Even when I'm asleep I work: I dream." He was irritated. "Look *cumpa*, last night I finished painting the Christ that Altagracia ordered from me, and that cursed Venancio still hasn't shown up to pick it up and take it to the *cofradía*. Do you want to see how it turned out?" He uncovered a piece of wood.

Jaci Mina ignored him. He did not turn to look at and praise the painting. He was offended. It was true: he was not a slave anymore. Tomasón was right.

"But only by working can I forget about my dear pueblo." And then softly: "Dondo." He inhaled the tobacco's aroma. A long drag consoled him and gave him the idea that the world remained intact, just as he had left it.

〰〰〰

In his memory, in his distant village of Angola, even that thread of water, the river Cuanza, remained the same. The dwellings were constructed in a circle, with open space in the center. It was used as a gathering place. There, the elders sat and listened to the stories of the warrior king, Ngola Kiluanji, while they crumbled and squeezed the fresh tobacco leaves. Afterwards, they rubbed the shreds between the palms of their hands and made balls that fit the mouths of the sculpted, ebony pipes. They let the tobacco soak in a container before smoking the pipes.

"Why do they keep talking about the king? You can reach Kalunga, mother of the rivers, with or without the king, by following the thread of water." Lucala knew that his friend Nganda spoke the truth. They had been born on the same day. They had grown up together, and after twelve harvests they went to the feared circumcision ceremony. They vowed not to complain about the pain, and they did not. As adults, they became hunters in the forests, but since the last rain, their paths had separated. While Lucala spent his days trying to spear an antelope with his lance and gathering many skins so that he could marry before the passing of four new moons, his friend Nganda had joined with some of those young warriors who attacked neighboring villages.

These attacks were not about territory or power, where a person had the opportunity to demonstrate his honor and courage. These were quick raids, in which they abducted people to sell to the white men who governed northern Congo, and who had begun to take over the kingdom of Angola.

They had to deliver at least a hundred young men and women in good condition, and by the specified date. In exchange, they would receive firearms, gunpowder, bright materials from India, mirrors, glass beads, and, above all, *aguardiente*, the color of honey and tastier than palm wine.

"It's easier to do each time," Nganda boasted. "We don't have to trap them and worry about hurting them anymore, as the Portuguese ask. Now the village leaders are the ones waiting for us, with captives tied and ready for the trip, as long as we share the profit with them. Not only do they deliver their servants and slaves, they even sell their own families."

"I would never do anything like that."

"Me neither, but I'd sell people I didn't know or that caused me problems. Look at what we've earned for twenty slaves." He showed him his clothes. No longer did he dress in the comfortable loincloth in the hot season, or cover himself from the cold with the soft, crushed fiber of the rubber tree that made the water run off. He wore two uncomfortable garments sown from cotton. The first he put on by pushing his legs through two openings, one for each leg. The other, he pulled over his head. It had three openings and looked uncomfortable—it covered his arms and separated them from his body.

"Now my name is Santos and I can make myself understood in their language. Don't you want to learn about a large village? You stay and live there all your life." He told him about how the dwellings had four high walls that formed a square. "Their windows have colored glass, the entrances three steps, and the roofs are hooded and they even decorate them with metal bells. Come with me. You don't have to hunt people. They also need interpreters who speak our language to ensure that the slaves don't throw themselves in the water when they board the boats."

"Will I have to kill anyone?"

"Only if it's necessary. I'll say that your name is Jaci Mina and that you're already a Christian. I'll teach you to talk their language."

Jaci Mina smoked, repeating the strange name his friend gave him until it was fixed in his memory. In his mind, though, he still called himself Lucala.

"You'll say that I'm Christian? What does that mean?"

"I'm not really sure. The only thing I've been able to understand is that they rub your forehead with water. They call it baptizing you."

"Ohh! And the name Jaci Mina, what does it mean?"

"Mina is the name of a town and Jaci or Jacinto is the name of a guardian angel. I'll say that you're named the same as he is so that you get into their good graces. Understand?"

"I prefer to keep the name Lucala."

The things that his friend Nganda or Santos said disturbed and confused him. He was so curious, and this weighed on him day and night.

"Forget about Lucala. Forget about Dondo. Forget about the balls of tobacco. Forget about all that."

It was in order to know the city of stone and clay walls that he forced himself to do it. Following the thread of water from Cuanza, they arrived at San Paulo de Luanda.

Jaci sucked on the cola nut and Santos drank a golden liqueur. They studied the large canoes with swollen sails that moved calmly on the mother of rivers.

"We're going to see the fort. It's the prison where they keep the slaves until they board." Santos was now his guide and the one in charge of the situation. He knew this world like the back of his hand.

Until this moment, Jaci had not asked Santos how big this Portuguese kingdom was that it needed so many slaves. Where was it? On the road to Luanda they had seen the empty villages. The harvest season had passed without anyone to gather the grains, cut the cane, or feed the goats. The trees bent to the ground, loaded with fruit. The abundant palm leaves dried without anyone to cut them. No one folded them one over the other, to repair the cabins, to weave baskets, to make the masks worn proudly for the festivals.

"Their kingdom is on the other side of the water. In fifty or sixty days you're there."

"Is it so big that they need that many servants, warriors, and slaves?"

"It must be." Santos wasn't interested in such questions.

"You don't want to go visit it?" They walked and observed that the arrangement of the houses was very different from that of the village. The houses were out of order. They looked uncomfortable and the walls ugly. The doors closed from the inside. Nganda did not like how he felt when he walked here with Luanda. He felt watched.

"Go visit the kingdom?" Nganda paused, seeming to think it over. "No. No one returns from there," he responded somberly.

They were now close to Igreja. He showed him the house with the cross on the roof and afterwards they saw the fort in the distance.

They were sorry they could not see the interior of the prison.

They would not have believed it if someone had told them that within thirty days and nights, they would know the inside intimately—every corner of that imposing stone mansion, with its watchtowers and armed guards. And they would know that its name was "Fort Luanda."

Years later in Malambo, Jaci remembered how he and Santos had been talking.

"Not even in front of a leopard have I felt as much fear as now. Yesterday they brought in people from Banguela and I was able to talk with some of them. No one knows what's happening."

Santos paid him little attention. Underneath his shirt, his muscular and agile body was still that of the hunter, though the game was different. He moved so beautifully, in complete control. At the same time, his gestures had the precision and inflection of the village chiefs and the priests, who decided about life or death.

"It's simple. Times change, Jaci. They pay you well for working as an interpreter and they pay me to hunt for slaves. If we don't do this job, others will. Now if you still want to return to Dondo, do it. Wait a few days and I'll go with you to the river, and from there you can continue alone. Is that all right with you?"

Jaci was grateful to him.

They walked slowly, certain that their lives would separate forever. Their paths would never cross again, ever. Their true names or the new ones they used would be mere memories in each of them. They proceeded in silence. They moved slowly, but still without seeing the many traps in the fallen leaves. They stepped on them.

The hunters were three men whom Santos recognized immediately. A Portuguese and two from Congo—they did not listen to their pleas. They shaved their heads. They fastened a chain to their necks, shackles to their ankles. The two joined a caravan of slaves, and, with them, got to know the cells, the dismal passageways, the humid and dark caves of Fort Luanda.

On the prison floor, in his cell in the basement labyrinth, Jaci could hear his friend talk with the servants who brought the sole daily meal. Santos begged them to help him escape.

"Lucaaaala, Lucaaaala" Santos called for him, ceaselessly, by his true name.

He did not respond. It made sense not to do so. He was gathering his strength to survive the trip of fifty to sixty days and nights to the Portuguese kingdom.

They did not travel in the same flat-bottomed cargo boat, but they found each other again in the living quarters in Cartagena de Indias. Santos was ash-colored. The hair that he had once rubbed proudly with castor oil had turned thin, and even had some white threads.

"You are Nganda, from Dondo." He embraced him, happy to see him.

"Yes, Lucala, it's me. I'm glad to know that you're alive."

"Finally I've found you! Where are we? Is this the kingdom of the Portuguese?"

"I don't know. They speak a similar language, but it's not the same. I almost don't understand it." He lowered his head. His voice became quiet and thin. "Do you still miss the village, Lucala?"

"Yes, but I think I'll never see it again. What will become of my father and my mother, Nganda? They will be looking for me."

"Don't grieve. You'll forget about the village. Now we are each other's family." He passed him some tobacco leaves without letting others see. "They're not like the ones from Dondo, but certainly they're smokeable." He left, but not before promising, "I'll see you again another day."

They never saw each other again. The following day Jaci was sold with a group of slaves destined for Peru.

A while had passed since Jaci's tobacco had burned out. Finally, he decided to criticize Tomasón's painting. He was still offended by what he had said. But as upset as he was with the painter, when he turned to look at the Christ of Tomasón's painting, he could find nothing to disapprove of. It was his friend's best work. The Christ moved him. In the Christ there reverberated a splendor of light that was like the light of the hut, but the Christ also expressed something of darkness, a broken reflection of the dark dust.

"Sometimes I understand why you live in Malambo." Jaci stepped back from the image to better appreciate it.

"It's about time, caraaá! Yes, it seems like a miracle," exclaimed Tomasón satisfied.

Tomasón found a jacket lost among the junk and put it on. He was still losing weight. He was drying up like a raisin and his skin was turning thin as silk. In the mornings, his fingers cramped from holding the paintbrush, and he had to rub them vigorously to relax the muscles. But he did not complain anymore about his bad health. Always busy dreaming and painting, he had no time left to feel sorry for himself. Sometimes, he did imagine that his chest was filling with earth. He was the very ground, a crust of trampled earth. Any day he would wake up with his arms converted into willow branches. He said to himself that when his entire body was paralyzed, it would not be because he had died. Instead, he would have begun another life, with another form, in another place, with another destiny. Maybe like the dark dust does, right now, in this very place.

"What was that?" He was startled by the ruckus and shouts in the street that had recommenced. "It looks like they've started a fuss at the slaughterhouse. A bull has escaped."

Jaci opened the door cautiously.

Tomasón watched as Jaci's jaw unhooked with surprise. He ended up with his mouth wide open.

"Tell me what's happening. But tell me carefully because today my chest can't tolerate much of a shock. And if it has to do with Pancha, better be quiet first and think about it well, *cumpa* Jaci."

"Don't worry. It's going to be hard for me to tell you because I don't believe it myself."

"Then it's better not to know anything. Let me paint a barge. For a while now I've had it on my mind and there must be a reason for it. Someone will be asking me for it." Just then, there was the squeal of a cart's wheels as it stopped at the door.

"Look! It's back," exclaimed Jaci.

"Who, Venancio?"

"Noooo, Pancha's bed."

〰〰〰

The neighborhood of Malambo celebrated with the same ruckus that they reveled in the bulls. They helped to lower the bed carefully from the cart, but Tomasón stopped them from bringing it inside.

"No, that bed does not come in here unless Pancha decides so." He closed the door again. "What does that constable want? Do you understand him, Jaci?"

"Maybe he regretted it. The bad thing is that with all this, I don't even want to go look for firewood. I'll stay with you, and since Venancio and Pancha are not here, I could cook for you."

"Yes, make yourself useful! Don't just sit there; I'm the one that's sick and about to die." The bed had renewed Tomasón's spirit.

Jaci pealed potatoes, cut onions. With his fingernails, he separated the llama jerky into strips that accumulated on the table. "If Pancha had married Venancio, none of this would have happened." He got upset.

Nevertheless, the bad mood of his friend did not bother Tomasón. And then without his realizing it, the dreams came over him. He slept.

The cart with the bed returns on the narrow road that borders the gunpowder mill. It is leaving in the direction that it came. It proceeds jolting along between the rocks. A pothole stops it. They have to push it to avoid breaking the wheels. It turns halfway.

The mule trots and stops once again in front of the door. Pancha opens it. She does not accept the bed. The cart goes back to circling the hill.

"Now the bronze is turning opaque," says the river.

The neighbors make it shine, patiently polishing it with a cloth.

"And the mattress is hard."

There is no lack of volunteers to turn it over. They fluff the feathers. They return. Once again they knock on the door. Pancha does not accept it.

The washerwomen stop the cart. They shake the dust out of the pillows, air out the bedspreads, hanging them inside out so the sun does not damage the damask and the handrail from Flanders. Each Saturday they wash the sheets faded from sleepless nights and daybreak awakenings. Comings and goings. Turning over and over.

Tomasón woke up with an empty feeling and asked for Pancha.

"She still hasn't arrived," answered Jaci.

Chapter X

Pancha treated Altagracia's arm while telling her how once Candelaria, the previous cook, had confided to her that the young woman would never abandon Nazario.

"Her brother was born on the river and will always be unsettled like its waters. On the other hand, Altagracia must have been born underneath a tree because her feet have roots and people like that are difficult to uproot."

Pancha looked at Altagracia's feet. Sure enough. Her massive, wide feet broke down her crude clogs regularly, when it was least expected. They did not last her more than three months. That was why she preferred to use wooden sandals the few times that she went out to go shopping.

"Candelaria was right. It's true. I don't want to leave the big house! I don't want them to sell me again!"

It was difficult for her to get accustomed to strangers. She never enjoyed going out to the street. She felt comfortable in the seclusion of the monastery, serving the maidens. After marrying, when Nazario still let loose every now and then with one of his guffaws that brightened his yellow eyes, she thought that it might be possible to forget about the tranquility of the cloister. Perhaps her feet could be less heavy, and she less sluggish. But later, a few weeks after she slept the siesta with the master, Nazario abandoned his will to laugh. She considered retracing her steps back to the convent. Now it was impossible for her to leave.

But De la Piedra listens to the two women talk from the sitting room. He can barely hear the melody of their words and understands little of what they say. It bothers him to have Pancha so close and nevertheless so far away. The memory of her skirts stirs him. He drinks another sip of wine as he looks at the weak rays of the sun on the silk rug. Nostalgic for tropical colors, he dreams of that bright, orange, summer sun that inflames forests, dries lakes, drives away shadows from midday until past five in the evening.

While having lunch on the balcony, he realized that the midsummer heat would last a long time. From a branch, a parakeet fell on his plate. He tossed it aside and continued eating. That evening he watched a green rain of birds. The following day it became reddish-yellow. Parrots, macaws, and the toucans fell from the trees. Exhausted, they smashed against the ground and died. The hens too drove their beaks into the ground as they toppled one by one. Even the dog, long accustomed to the rigors of scabies, howled the entire night and died.

Months passed, or at least that is what it seemed, until finally there began to fall one and then another lazy rain drops. It did not become a full-grown shower until little by little, across indecisive days, it matured and at last fell. It pleased him that his woman, who had recently given birth, could get up. He helped her escape the hammock, sticky with sweat, so that she could get soaked in the downpour of fresh water.

Later, on the balcony, she lulled the baby boy to sleep with a song. She stopped sometimes to talk to him. Her words were like those of Pancha talking in the kitchen with Altagracia. She didn't worry about making sense. She was not pressed to do so. She did not care about what she said but rather the melody of her speech.

The heavy shower slid down like a rough blanket. She listened to the singsong of the rain as it fell. She interpreted its music as an expression of the gift that was her child. She received it. She watched the sky through the branches of the camphor tree. The fat clouds began to scatter, as the rain died down, the smell and sounds of the fields returned to her. A distant bark. The birds that had not fallen greeted her. She fell asleep with the child in her arms, without realizing that a curve of suspended crystals had taken shape in the trees. The light arranged them in strips. That day the brightness of the sky grew until it formed the most precious rainbow that human eyes had ever seen. They told her when it was already too late to catch it for her memory.

They thought about it as it quickly faded. He rowed the canoe without feeling the fatigue in his arms. The current favored him. He was pursuing that magnificent band of colors, in the very center of the river, until with the tip of his paddle, he was able to touch it and then loose it forever.

In the kitchen, Pancha was peeling the aloe when the knife slipped from her hands. The metal bounced and fell in a corner.

"When you talk about Candelaria, strange things happen in the big house." She sounded as if she were joking.

"Maybe she wants to talk with us. Go ahead and get it. It's under the fulling mill, I saw it fall. Pick it up," she indicated pointing.

From the office, De la Piedra recognizes the dragging sound.

"Careful! Leave that where it is! It's very heavy." He enters the kitchen. "I don't want any more accidents." In spite of his girth, he bends down nimbly and finds the knife before the women discover what is hidden beneath the heavy stone. He hesitates in returning the knife to Pancha.

"Have you come to stay? His is a supplicating look, a look that begs. "Don't be foolish. I'll give you what you want, stay here."

"What's he saying to you, Pancha?"

"I'm only asking that she come and help you." De la Piedra raises his voice in feigned anger. "With that useless arm, you're not good for anything. You've gotten slow and stiff."

"It's not my arm, it's my belly that has me like that, sir. I'm pregnant." She caresses her stomach.

De la Piedra falls abruptly in a chair.

"A child!"

He passes his hand through his hair and serves himself a glass of wine. He drinks it with one gulp and his glance remains fixed on her arm held inert over the table. Completely uncovered, violet, scaly. He finds it difficult to believe that it is still part of Altagracia. Only habit keeps it hanging from one shoulder, falling along her body, almost sticking to her side. It is no longer an arm! It's one of those fallen logs that gets in your way. Dried and rotten with woodworms, only out of necessity do you cut them with a blow of the machete for firewood. It cannot be said that they get you out of a jam. They do it, but badly. As much as they crackle and send off sparks and brilliant flames that blind you, they do not maintain a fire. Upon going out, not even embers remain as consolation. He lowers his gaze, and looks for a new curve to her belly. He cannot see that anything has changed in her. Everything is still the same. Altagracia has the same warm roundness inside as she has outside. The same dark softness as always.

"Are you sure? How many months have you been pregnant?"

"I have seven left, sir."

"I hope it's a boy." He gets happy.

"Nazario prefers that it's a girl."

"What's Nazario got to do with it?"

"He's my husband, sir."

"But the child is mine."

"Noooo. It's Nazario's."

"You're lying. You yourself told me that he doesn't sleep at your side anymore."

"Altagracia should know better than you." Pancha steps in, stubborn.

He shifts his gaze between the two women. He laughs quietly. The two of them are making fun of him. He swallows, clearing the displeasing taste of wine left on his tongue. Nazario must be buying it from a different general store, he imagines.

"Are you sure that the child you're going to have isn't mine?"

Altagracia had decided that the baby would only be hers. It would not be Nazario's, or the master's, because it was thanks to her that ordinary and empty form took life. She knew how to capture and absorb it into her body. She had taught him to give her the long shudders and the panting trembles. To pierce and create the warmth that she already knew how to find by herself, keeping the enchantment, not wasting the feeling in sentimentality and sad crying. She held it. She prevented the current from carrying it away; she guided it to that open flower. If it grows, it will be only hers.

In which siesta had it been conceived? Maybe it was the time that the chatterbox neighbor began to shout, "They're stealing the hens! They're stealing the hens!" She thought it was so funny that for a long time she imitated a rooster. She made the master enter her deeper and sang long cockle-doodle-doos, until the first tremor in her womb made her imitate the meow of a cat in heat. Meeeeeoooooooooow. Or was it the evening that she heard Nazario returning before the four o'clock bell? That time, he opened the gate, pulling the mule. Maybe he was already in the stable, unloading bunches of alfalfa, but she continued on top of the master: the fear heightened her pleasure. She counted three short spasms, which left her limp. When she entered the kitchen, Nazario was also entering, and he stopped, surprised at seeing her flush. He touched her forehead.

"You have a little fever. You feel all right, Altagracia Maravillas?"

She did not lie to him.

"I'm fine, just a little tired, that's all, and I'm sleepy."

Calm, without moving from where she stood, without taking a step that would betray the pleasure melting drop by drop from between her legs.

Maybe it was the night that she climbed to the bedroom and saw that shadow at the head of the bed. The next moment a gust of wind put out the four candles of the candelabra. Altagracia felt the presence of the late Candelaria in the "swiiiiish-swiiiish" that the sheets made when they rubbed against her. She was not sure whose hands had positioned her, as if on an axle, so that her body was used like a stone on the fulling mill.

"No. The child that I'm going to have is not yours. I'm sure."

"It's a pity." He deplores feeling the effects of the wine. "The idea was already growing on me of watching him grow. But it's probably better this way." It seemed to not interest him any more. He addresses Pancha:

"How's her arm coming along?"

"It's still not getting better."

"Then don't keep wasting time with prayers and herbs. The illness is very advanced. It will poison her whole body and I'll loose the 'piece.' I can't afford that luxury, especially now that Altagracia has begun to give me offspring. It's better to have a damaged slave than a dead slave! I'll notify a surgeon to come amputate her arm."

"Yes, and the sooner the better," reaffirmed a voice entering into the kitchen.

〰〰〰

In December the sun rises early in Lima, but Catalina Ronceros was awake long before it warmed. She pulled the curtains open and thought about the river that spoke. Its waters brought gossip, but she preferred not to listen. The blades of the nearby mills were motionless, with the exception of Melgarejo's; he would stay awake all night in order to be punctual for his few clients. Soon he would be owner of the farm and his luck would change. She moved away from the window. She took off her nightshirt and bathed, using the washbasin. She looked at the image of her naked body reflected in the mirror. The years had gone by as she fanned herself comfortably in the rocking chair, she mused while washing her hair.

She had been widowed by the time she turned forty-three, after only a year of matrimony. Eleven months to be exact. Now, ten years later, she did not remember what it was like to be married. The marriage had passed through her without leaving a trace. A certain Ronceros, by the name of Fernán or Fernando (at times he signed his name with the shortened form), was looking for a wife. He wanted her to be from Spain, from Seville, to be specific. If she was old or ugly it did not matter. He did not have a lot to offer, only a miserable farm. Her parents found out about the request. They sent her on the first ship that left for Lima like someone sending a gift to distant relatives in the Indies. As soon as Catalina climbed aboard, she felt her face turn bright red. Blotches appeared on her. She hadn't the courage to talk to anyone during the trip.

"Here they don't need old maids that are ugly and don't have dowries," her parents had told her. "After the marriage, arrange it so your husband sends us money so that your mother and I can also travel to that kingdom. And make sure that he doesn't delay, because we're not that young either." These were their parting words.

They never received the money. Fernán or Fernando Ronceros had completed seventy years of life and died before accumulating enough for his in-laws' trip. In truth, he never saved even a peso for that purpose. He was only looking for a wife to ensure that he had a tranquil death. The wedding distracted the attention of those who openly criticized his way of running the farm. He raised birds with dark feathers. He did not wring their necks to kill them. Rather, he preferred to slit their throats with a special knife, and then bleed them by hanging them by their feet.

"Ronceros did not profess the true religion," said certain rumors.

"Or is it that you're a converted Jew?" she asked him.

The farmer covered his lips with a finger.

Silent, he pointed to the river. He waited until what he later explained to be the Day of the Great Forgiving, celebrated on the eleventh day of the September moon, to go out with her. That was the first and the last time that they walked together through the city. He with a black suit, buttoned up; she with a silk dress. Fernán or Fernando took advantage of the walk to make short visits to relatives, friends, and clients. He introduced her. They did not seem to be very satisfied with his choice. Nevertheless, they accepted her amicably. Returning to the farm, her husband wanted to know her opinion.

Catalina realized that she would remember the few women whom she met, but there had been so many men and she had visited them for such a short amount of time. She was not sure that she would even recognize them.

"The people that you met will always look after you, Catalina. They've promised me. They will continue buying chickens and eggs from you even after I die. Remember, when you need help always turn to them." Two or three months later he died, and she preferred not to return to that chapter of her life. At least until Manuel De la Piedra began to court her.

She dried her hair and grabbed a hand mirror. Its handle was broken and the crystal opaque. She wiped a damp cloth over it and looked for the space that still reflected clearly. She made a smile. She could not hide the fact that she was missing three lower teeth and soon would have to extract an upper one, on the side, or maybe all of them. Her whole mouth hurt. She looked at herself at length. She should accept it without blushing: she was ugly. Although not as ugly as her parents thought. She decided that from that day forward she would never again get up early for the sole purpose of sprucing herself up. No more early-morning rice powders, rubbing carmine on her lips, or arranging her hair in that bun of complicated curls that took her two hours in front of the mirror. She felt liberated. Later, after lathering her hair with an infusion of bay leaves that made it glisten, dark and shiny, she marked a line with a barrette from the point of her nose to her nape, and parted her hair in two, letting it hang loose over her ears. She pulled two new gray hairs from her temples. She looked at herself satisfied. Her pale face did not have a trace of the red patches. In fact it was beaming. She got dressed slowly. She counted the coins that she still had and looked through the window at the empty bird corrals.

She put her fan in her purse and walked without hurrying, as if each movement had been calculated long before. She counted the eight steps from her bedroom to the living room, and from the living room, five more to the door. She closed it behind her without locking and went out to the courtyard. She wore her best dress, the one made of violet silk, with ruffles, a closed collar, and a fine line of pearl buttons. It had lace, white cuffs. Antón Cocolí wore his cabin boy livery of dark velvet.

This time he has listened to me and washed himself thoroughly, she noted smelling the soap from Castile that emanated from the boy. Both of them carried a heavy cage in each arm, packed tight with hens. They left. They knew that the walk would be a long one.

Lacking a mule, it was Ramón, the other slave, who followed them. He pulled a large, high-wheeled cart. On it were the wicker rocking chair and an oak trunk with a three-numbered lock. On top were an earthenware saucepan and three roosters with their feet tied.

A fluttering of feathers and crowing of the birds announced their arrival. Anton's footprints registered his impatience with her slow pace. He walked ahead, along the path. Catalina avoided stepping in the footprints. She stopped from time to time to fan herself and to clear the hair from her face. She smoothed down her skirts. She lowered her gaze before strange men who ventured to greet her.

Three vagabonds forgot their game of cards and dealt flirtatious and inelegant remarks. She continued on her way.

At eleven o'clock, they stopped to eat a lunch of hard-boiled eggs and rye bread.

"We're close now," said Antón Cocolí.

Then they passed in front of the tavern where drunken young men were singing a vulgar song. They advanced deep into the unsafe traffic and the dust clouds of the streets of Lima. They heard the street vendors praising the trinkets that they were selling at the top of their lungs. She heard the cry of the refreshment sellers. The general stores were stuffed with candles, with oil, with vegetables. The merchants, with materials. There, on the balconies, behind the filigree lattices, were the spying onlookers. Catalina felt herself blush once again. She felt the waves of heat in her face, but she did not stop to fan herself. She was a widow and ugly, but she was not inclined to spend her last days on a miserable farm, much less in a convent, when she had a man courting her.

After midday, Antón Cocolí pushed the leaves of the gate. He opened the door wide, and Catalina Ronceros entered Manuel De la Piedra's house to stay and live there forever.

〰〰〰

"If there's no cure, then they should cut off that arm. What good is it?" Catalina stares at Altagracia Maravillas challengingly.

"We'll talk about that later, Catalina." De la Piedra gestures for Altagracia to go to the kitchen. "Today . . . you're different. I didn't . . . expect your . . . visit," he stutters seeing her. He takes her to the sitting room. He is surprised that her hair is let down.

There are roosters picking incessantly at the carpet. They appear surprised. Those specks that resembled grains or worms are designs or decorations. They give up and forget about them.

De la Piedra is about to praise her silk dress. He sees a hen pecking at his rug. He is startled at seeing the chickens. He forgets to flatter her. Two black hens are sleeping on his leather easy chair. The red ones are nesting on his desk and looking for grains in the drawers. He recovers partially, thinking to offer her a glass of wine.

"No, thanks. I don't drink." She fans herself. Altagracia cries in silence so that the waters of the river do not announce her pains from shore to shore. The tears spring forward and her eyes overflow and carry the sad reflection of Pancha.

"They'll cut off my arm. That woman will make master kill me piece by piece. Look for my brother. Venancio has a few pesos saved, and he'll buy me."

Pancha crushes the aloe leaves.

"I can't leave you. Your arm is very swollen and you still have a fever. Run away! Hide in Malambo until the herbs take effect. It won't be long before Venancio returns. Tomasón and Jaci will help you."

"No. Nazario would bring me back here. That would be worse. Go, look for my brother. Look for Venancio."

"But, where? I don't know where to begin."

"Go to the beach. He should be fishing. Bring him here. Go on. Go for him before they cut off this arm. He can't be very far," she whispers.

~~~~~

Venancio endured a sharp tam-tam in his head since being struck by the stone. He felt far from the world that he knew.

"The only thing here is bird shit." He continues sharpening the knife to scrape the dried excrement from the rocks. He gathers it together in mounds, in exchange for a few sips of fresh water. The days are spent dodging stones, fishing, and lighting the bonfire on the summit. Because that is what the Englishman wants. Until he one day discovers in a fissure in the rocks the actual barge that Sir has prepared to set to sea. With hatred, Venancio waits for him to go swimming, which he does each morning, waits for him to float in the freezing cold sea, watching the birds circling above his island, his treasure.

Sir lets himself rock like a ship adrift, but returns to the shore exhausted. He wraps himself in sealskin and lies down. Venancio approaches him without making a sound. He loathes the greasy, matted hair of his beard. He pauses to quiet the crazy tam-tam beating in his head, but his hatred gives him patience. He does not know or remember how long he waits, but then he raises his hand and, with the sharpened knife, slices off one of the Englishman's ears. His shouts of pain are swallowed up in the happy cackles of the bird in livery that swallows it with one mouthful.

The barge is made of fragile wood. The sail will not hold the wind.

Venancio wonders if it will withstand a trip to port. He pushes it to the sea and ties himself carefully to it. Behind him is Sir and his treasure of excrement. Let him talk to his stupid birds. At last Venancio is leaving. He feels content. He will again see the arrogant Pancha, the sour-faced Pancha. Pancha, with the enchanted ponytail, who makes things grow in the garden. He melts at the thought of seeing her, smelling her herbs, and drinking a fresh, clear stream of water from her.

A thread of liquid blesses him, and grows and multiplies. It no longer has a bottom and tickles his ankles. It rises. In an instant, it kisses his ankles and embraces him. It caresses his face. It is not the gentle water from Pancha's well.

The barge is sinking.

〰〰〰

Deep into the night, Tomasón and Jaci listen to Pancha. Sometimes they interrupt her story with questions. She finishes. "That's why I have to find Venancio."

"To help Altagracia, you want to go look for Venancio?" Tomasón is skeptical. "Am I hearing you right, or is there something more? I think that you want him to come back to Malambo, for you, too."

"Leave the girl alone! After what Nazario Briche told her, now Pancha doesn't have a doubt that her father is dead. Maybe she also wants Venancio to know," Jaci Mina comments.

"Yes, and I told her that before that coach driver did. What happens is that Pancha is stubborn."

Angry, Tomasón turns again towards Pancha.

"I don't want you to leave my side, girl."

"Let her go. When your feet want to travel, you have to obey. Don't I know it, so far from Dondo!"

"I have to look for him. I promised Altagracia. Anyway, it's my fault he left."

"You're going to look for him so you can marry him." Tomasón is convinced.

"Then go then. Rest now, because the two of us have to think about where you're going to start looking for Venancio tomorrow," suggests Jaci.

"Yes, listen to him, Pancha. Go on, get some sleep."

~~~~~~

Now that they are alone, Tomasón feels a cold wind run through him. He hears the last street criers and the rattle of a tired cart.

"Could it be that the bed is still going around the streets, without anyone accepting it?"

"Pancha is old enough to take her first trip, Tomasón."

"Exactly. Do you think that she'll come back once she knows what there is outside of Malambo?"

"That's why we're here. To guide her."

"Will you help me, *cumpa*?"

"Tell me, when have I ever let you down?"

"You're asking me? I'm still waiting for you to make the window smaller."

"I already told you that I was going to do it one of these days."

"And why is it that time passes and that blessed day never comes, Jaci?"

"That's just the way Malambo is. You know it."

"It's true, it's true. Now make yourself useful and pass me the tobacco."

"Yes, I'm going to smoke too. We have a long night ahead of us."

Chapter XI

The 23rd of January, Saint Idelfonso in the calendar, and Tomasón spent the morning accompanied by a buzzing horsefly that announced something bad. He thought that it had entered through a crack in the hut. He let it dance in the dark dust without scaring it away. He did not even shake a cloth to remove the bad omen. He fell asleep with the paintbrush still in his hands. He had hoped that the insect would fly to the fragile mesh of his dreams and, stretching out its blue wings, become a good messenger, and take him to visit Babalú Ayé.

... Oh, Babalú Ayé! That troublemaker lucumí that couldn't be faithful to any woman so God Supreme, tired of warning him, punished him by completely filling him with those ulcers that eat away at the body like leprosy and that ooze a fine foul-smelling water. The ulcers never

ever scab and if the water lands on someone else, they get the disease.

Ochún and all the women who had been his mistresses didn't let Babalú Ayé lay a hand on them anymore. Aside from two dogs and the blowfly that announced his death, and that terrible sickness, no one wanted to be near him. When they ran him out of the village, only those two filthy dogs, which followed him to lick his wounds, were his company.

Babalú Ayé wandered through the streets, begging for a piece of bread and some soup, until he died. And good and dead he would have stayed if Ochún had not pleaded to God Supreme to forgive him and give him life once again.

Tomasón drew him with a tunic made of rags. His lacerated body was supported by two walking sticks.

"Someone is about to die," he said to Jaci, who had just entered. "He won't make it through the night. Who could it be?"

"Well, It's probably the heretics. Today the Holy Office is going to burn the Jews accused of high crimes. When I left, they had them tied to the stake. They're waiting for the winds to calm to set the torch to them. You should have seen the Autos-dafé that they did. With two platforms and all the dressings. With the viceroy there, all the authority of the city. But this thing about watching people burn is not my idea of fun, so I left. But there's also a relative of the *cofradía* from Angola who's about ready to leave this world. He has no one to cry for him, so we allowed him to join with us at the last minute. Not because he's from Angola. He's creole. We're taking up a collection of half a reale for the funeral, so we can bury him in a box. Do you want to contribute?"

"Aren't you all rushing things in preparing the burial of this poor soul?"

"No, he's in real bad shape. He's not moving. He's on his last breath. In fact, I should go there. I want him to give some messages to the dead." He is about to leave the hut when Tomasón stops him.

"Here, here." He takes a coin out of a big sack and gives it to him. "If it's not too much of a bother, tell him to ask Francisco Parra who wronged him like that."

"Francisco was Pancha's father, if I'm not mistaken, right? Then you don't believe the story that Nazario told Pancha either? I'll tell him. Anything else?"

"No. I don't like to give work to people who are in that trance, and even less to bother the deceased with problems. What are you going to ask of him?"

"I want three things. That he asks Salomé Valle to reveal the place where he buried the jug with the gold nuggets that his widow can't find. That he says hello to Miss Elisa on behalf of the washerwomen. And that he tells Meritón to remind his children to return my machete, because it was borrowed, and not given away. That's all. I'm not going to ask about Venancio, because he's still alive and he's not around there. Venancio is very alive and kicking."

"I think the same thing, I'm happy for Pancha."

"Well, I'm leaving."

Tomasón stops him once again.

"Before you go, Jaci, what is the name of the man who's about to die? Do I know him?"

"No. He's one of the blacks who arrived not long ago. He was sold in the last auction."

"Strong and young he was, caraaá. It's true what they say, that when death blows, like a leaf even the strongest goes."

Alone again, Tomasón pensively watches the horsefly race about. He decides to paint its iridescent wings. A gust of wind displaces the hide in the large window. He mutters as he gets up to adjust it and return it to its place. "All the master builders from Lima are a bunch of failures. A bunch of *hambones*! They don't know how to work the way God commands!"

He moved his bench closer, stuck his head out the window to yell this to Jaci so that everyone in Lima could hear his complaint when the Talking River repeated it in the echoes of its rounded songs. But Jaci had already left. There were the waters. And there a shadow traveled the path. A deep pain pierced him as he recognized Yáwar Inka. He was saying goodbye. Alone. Walking slowly, almost without touching the ground, almost without moving, almost transparent.

〰〰〰

De la Piedra felt as exhausted as he had the first days after arriving in Lima. He wondered if giving the chickens a portion of his fortune—maybe some of the bars of gold that he has hidden—would persuade them to leave his house. Not even the closed doors of the great room and the bedroom blocked their ruckus, and their clucking. The big house was becoming a farm, covered with feathers, eggs, and miasma.

On the other side, after extensive experimentation, Catalina positioned her wicker rocking chair in the long kitchen. It was in the way. When she did not have a book in her hand, she fanned herself. But she could not escape the chicken coop pestilence that inundated the house.

〰〰〰

"Just seeing them wears me out."

" . . . I didn't see you in the Plaza," continues Melgarejo. "Gertrudis and I got a good spot to watch the procession of Jewish heretics going to the fire pit. It was an impressive show they provided, don't you think?"

"I don't know. I left the city. I detest those spectacles."

"I don't," he said halfheartedly. "I always stay until I've seen them turned to ashes and then I watch the procession of the ones being whipped. It's fair that they pay for their sins, even though this time I couldn't see either of the groups very well. Gertrudis wanted to stay in the Plaza chatting with Father José, and I had to keep her company. The two of them have become good friends, if there's such a thing as friendship with a Jesuit. He told her that they jailed somebody who a couple of years ago stole heaven knows how much gold and silver objects from the churches. You remember? They even offered me a reward."

The trader nodded in silence.

"It was Yáwar, that Indian that they call Inka."

De la Piedra raises his eyebrows feigning surprise.

"Yes my friend, it was him and it's a difficult case to figure out. The Inka admits what he did but claims that it wasn't stealing. He doesn't want to reveal his accomplice or accomplices. Besides that, they didn't find a single piece of gold or silver in his possession. Whoever knows the truth reported him. But he's hiding and quiet."

"Do they know who was the informer?"

"Not even the slightest clue."

"It's a shame because this way he can't claim the reward."

"That's true. But it's possible that the fellow's also involved in the whole thing. Regardless, it's better for the Church not to talk anymore about the subject. The priests prefer not to cause a lot of commotion for fear that the Indians from El Cercado might rebel. At least with reliable proof, or even without it, they have enough reason to send Yáwar off in exile. By now, they are boarding him for Spain. Maybe by the time of his send-off, he'll give in and confess to Father José where he hid the candelabras, because he's never returning from exile."

"Is it true they don't have the slightest suspicion who reported him?" De la Piedra asks again, waiting to find out more details of the event.

"No, as far as I know, no. But talk with Father José if it interests you so much. The only thing that's important to me was to earn a few pesos, and now that's up in smoke. Bad luck. But it's not going any better for you than it's going for me. Tell me, how's Catalina?"

"It's easier for me to share the yard with the hens than to share the bed with her. Here, sign the sales contract." He throws the bundle of papers at him.

"Now the only thing that needs to be done is that a notary certifies it and the farm will be mine." Jerónimo rubs his hands with contentment.

"No, it's not that easy. The farm will be mortgaged under my name until you make the last payment. Naturally, you can begin to enlarge the mill and plant wheat and do whatever you want to with it."

"I'll only plant wheat, Manuel." He does not mask his anger. "Now you don't seem to trust me much."

"Business is business. Don't feel bad. Things turned out the way you wanted. You accomplished what you set out to do and that's enough. If it weren't for your meddling with Catalina, she wouldn't have known about my ties with Altagracia and you'd still be waiting for the sale of the farm."

"Don't take it that way. Sooner or later she would have found out. You know how gossip is . . . the way people talk . . . the river. And," he pats De la Piedra's back amicably, "that woman's worth little with a dead arm. Be happy that Catalina lives with you! Marry her as soon as you can! And look for another nigger girl . . . right? How are you doing with Pancha? Have you already convinced her?" He jokes calmly while he rolls up the sales contract.

"I don't know what's become of her. She doesn't come around

anymore. I've even sent for her. She's not at home. She disappeared or her grandfather's hiding her. As for Catalina, there won't be a wedding, at least not now. I've got my head filled with more important things. Did you know that a few nights ago a runaway slave got into my room? Did you hear about it?"

"Yes, and I congratulate you for giving him what he deserved. It'll serve as a lesson for the others."

"I hope so, although not everybody thinks like you do. The silversmith is suing me: he's asking for three thousand pesos cold hard cash for the slave. The *cofradía* of Angola has complained to the Town Council and accused me of excessive violence, mistreatment, and I don't know how many other things. I'm going to have to pay a huge fine to get out of all this. I was thinking about calling a doctor to come and amputate Altagracia's arm before the poison takes over the rest of her body and kills her, but she refuses, and I don't think that now's a good time to force her. I prefer to safeguard my reputation. With a little luck I can get out of this mess if her brother buys her before she dies on me."

"That Altagracia, she is also from that *cofradía* that is preparing a procession. You can't deny that the niggers are bigger believers than the Indians."

"No. They know how to put up a better front. They pretend they're praying to a Catholic saint, but underneath the image of Saint Bartholomew, the rainbow of liberty is what they see. Christ is the god Obatalá. The Virgin Mary, a water goddess from Guinea, and so forth. Don't I know it, since I earn my living selling niggers!"

"You might be right. I never thought about looking at it that way, but now it all makes sense. The painted walls in Tomasón's hut are not very Christian, so to speak." De la Piedra tells the truth. Melgarejo decides he'll mention it to Father José. "And why don't you free her the day of that procession. It would look good to the authorities, to the silversmith, to the other niggers, and even to Catalina."

"No! Catalina wouldn't accept it. You should see the two of them in the kitchen hating each other like cats and dogs. Now that Altagracia is sure that she won't lose her arm, she's done nothing but wait for an opportunity to slice the throat of one of the hens. And the one to blame for this mess is you, Jerónimo! I hope that your pissing problem lasts forever!"

"Too late to curse me," he mocks, "I'm getting better and that's because I don't want to live with regrets. Look how the herbs woman accepted my apologies, and how I paid her grandfather a fair price for that golden bull, that charm that I bought from him below price. I realize that now."

"Ahh! Better yet give it back to him. What good is it to you?"

"There's no good in it. But I'm used to feeling its weight in my pocket. I always carry it with me. Superstition, probably! I don't know. At least my bladder's under control, the farm is mine, and my business will eventually be successful."

〰〰〰

Pancha passed the village of La Magdalena a few hours after beginning her trip. She rolled up her flapping skirts with a knot and took off her clogs. She preferred to carry them in her hands. She felt freer that way. She was anxious to find Venancio as soon as possible.

Malambo was behind her, she thought to herself with joy, but it was mixed with some fear. She felt as if she were dreaming. She walked with skipping steps, determined not to grow tired in the two leagues she had to cover to reach the salty waves.

"Who knows if we saw him? There're many people that come to fish and to watch the beached whale." They pointed towards a group of large reed huts. The Indians in La Magdalena had copper-colored skin. They were short in height, solid, and strong. Apparently they knew Castilian, because they responded in a way that could be understood, although it took Pancha a while to make out what they were talking about. They had approached her to meddle and find out what she was looking for. When they found out, they answered:

"It's possible that Venancio's over that way."

"Don't you want to see how big this animal is?"

Pancha declined. She continued walking towards the cove where people fished in order to make beautiful creeper plants grow, to fill the arid hills with flowers.

The fishermen pulled clumps of *jallpakwa manan wañuq*: the earth that never dies. That is what they call it in their language. In furrows, they plant a seed and a fish. In each hole a seed, a fish, a little water, and hope.

Pancha inhaled by the mouthful the fragrance that inundated the cove. It already clung to her skirts. The delicate balsam unknown in Malambo was in her hair. She looked in the direction of the sea, and only a brief moment passed before a fisherman, coming out of the water, was drawn to her almond-shaped eyes.

"Where are you going?"

"I'm Pancha and I'm looking for Venancio. A moment ago I couldn't see you." She was surprised that something like this could happen. "It's probably the sun's reflection off the sea."

"No, it's because of the lovely smell of this place." The fisherman did not take his eyes off her. "I'm Paco the fortune-teller, 'the one who reveals secrets.' What's brought you here?" inquired the Indian.

Pancha studied the Indian, and saw in him a resemblance to Yáwar Inka.

"I'm looking for my friend Venancio. Maybe you've seen him around here? He's more or less my color and he has red hair."

"I haven't seen anybody your color, but the whale has a man

in its stomach. I'm not sure if you can see him. Maybe Venancio is stuck in there. If you tell me something, I'll take you to see the whale."

Pancha started to get upset and almost lost her temper.

"What nonsense! A man in the stomach of a whale! A man in the stomach of a whale!" she repeated and repented having left to discover the trails far from Malambo. She wanted to start running. To go back to being enclosed in the safe walls of the hut and to breathe the enchanted dust. She changed her mind again after consciously breathing deeply that completely new aroma. It was infectious and exciting, a strong perfume of amber. She let the aroma dominate her consciousness—it invaded her; grew within her, and calmed her steps.

"No. Venancio surely isn't inside an animal. What would he be doing there? Anyway, I don't have anything to give to you in exchange for seeing him."

"Give me one of your skirts." He rubbed the material with his fingers and laughed silently, like a mischievous boy.

"I have herbs." She freed her skirt. "I have mallow, *paico*, *pinco-pinco,* rue, juniper, royal sap, mint, *yerbaluisa*, *yerbasanta*, lime flower, broom, *llaque-llaque*, *jinchu-junchu*, thistledown, sweet grass, boldo, watercress, parsnip."

"Give me the herb that makes it rain or give me your skirt."

"I have the herb that makes you fly."

The Indian stopped laughing. He gestured to her so that she would follow him. They climbed up an inlet, until they reached a woven reed hut that sat beside a lima bean field.

"Now give me that herb that makes you fly."

Pancha untied a red scarf and loosened her long ponytail. She chose three splinters of bright wood. "They are wood from Guinea." She gave them to him.

He cupped his palms to receive them.

"I want to fly so I can see the source of the flame. Look at it, it's growing again." He pointed to a thread of smoke that rose from a small island not far from the beach. "Afterwards, I want to fly very high and learn the endless roads that the ancestors traced in the pampa of Nazca. The monkey with the long tail is my pueblo. Do you want to come with me?"

"No. Take me to see the whale."

"First tell me what I need to do to fly."

"In the early morning, put the splinters underneath your fingernails and repeat this three times:

Oyá is going to fly.
Oyá is going to fly.
He touches the wood and he's going to fly.

"Don't forget to give thanks to Guinea wood, before and after," she recommends.

"No. No, I won't forget. I'm giving you herbs with *yitiri*, with a lot of power inside, so that they help you. Ask them a question every morning and if they taste sweet in your mouth, keep looking. But go back a few steps if they turn bitter." He began to sing.

Pancha listened to his rustic ways as he let the coca leaves fall into her hands.

Jesus María coca from Yungas, against marriage with Pedro.
Llicta neighbor of Estarca, if anyone is in a jam,
they can ease them with a plan.
With my teeth I crush you, with my tongue I mush you.
With aguardiente *I impress you, with wine I bless you,*
with chicha *I refresh you, with* aloja *I caress you.*
I don't chew coca because of vice or wit
but because its benefits.

Behind the dunes she found a beached sperm whale. The fishermen, accustomed to its presence, had organized groups in charge of keeping the whale wet, while others fished and planted, maintaining their routine.

The animal was as big as the Government Plaza; its head alone, the size of the cathedral. Its snout was as wide as the altar. She was afraid to approach it. She sat down in the sand. It was growing dark. The whale let out an amber belch that echoed in caverns and wells.

The fishermen abandoned their nets and climbed up to the gardens in the hills.

"Now the time of God the Father is going to end. The time of God the Son is going to begin." A chorus had formed around the sperm whale.

Their voices put her to sleep. Very early in the morning, the cackling of birds woke her up. They passed by overhead, and flew in bands towards sea, around the islands, and far away. Pancha wondered if the fisherman who resembled Yáwar Inka was one of them, if at last he could fly.

. . . I don't know, Pancha, I don't know. I said it so many times, Oyá is going to fly. Oyá is going to fly. He touches the wood and he's going to fly. My voice grew tired and I ended up mute. I don't know if it was begging the sea so much to take back the beached whale, that the blueness of the water got into my eyes. Or that maybe I was seeing the purity of the sky. I don't know.

There I was, still, not even blinking, when they arrived at my side. I can't say that I saw them, but I knew they were with me, because of the beautiful sound of their wings. It was with me and nearly made me happy, though I still felt lonely.

When you gave me the Guinea splinters and showed me how to fly, I thought that finally I could do as so many Mandingos taitas. They go up in the air like dry straw and they glide towards the heavens.

You have to realize that what those Negroes lacked in wings and feathers, they made up for in abilities. They were slaves without ceasing to be free birds or wild trees.

Now I touched that soft, pink nothingness and basked in the place where the unborn live. I felt the pulse of a stranger's blood nourishing my body. I don't know if I could fly. My days are numbered. Even if I wanted to, I can't rise from the ground; I am called upon by my hut, my planted fields, my coffee beans, my yucca, my fish, my broken matting where I find myself now. Not sure if I ever had wings, if I saw the sky open up, if I planted my hands in the water, that fish would grow from my fingers.

〰〰〰

The sky was blackblack when Jaci Mina gave the messages to Guararé. He made the sign of the cross and wiped the sweat from his brow. Then he surrendered him to the night, so that it carried him forever.

〰〰〰

Guararé waited until the night watchman cried eleven o'-clock; then he escaped from the silversmith. He hid his fear amongst the shadows. He slipped away, staying close to the walls (avoiding two horsemen), until he arrived at the high wall of the big house. He climbed it and then looked in through the doors and windows for what seemed to be hours. But he knew he must hurry.

Looking for Chema's room, he entered the quarters of Altagracia and the coachman. The two of them were sleeping. In the stable, the mule smelled him, but continued to eat alfalfa. The horse did not move. He stood up straight.

In the darkness, he was barely able to make out Don Manuel, with his woolen cap and linen nightshirt. The bed was spacious but Catalina Ronceros was curled up almost on the edge of it. She hid her head, out of habit, from the hens.

But not everyone in the big house was sleeping. In the pale light of a wax candle, the late Candelaria was counting her reales over and over again. She saw him. She moved the stone from the fulling mill and extracted a brightness. She opened her hands and offered him the splendor of glow-worms. Guararé could not contain his fear. He tripped. He fell, bewildered, among crashing kitchen utensils and a meowing cat.

"Thief! Thief!" someone shouted, and approached with a candlestick in one hand and a whip in the other. De la Piedra ordered Nazario Briche to restrain the thief.

The coachman moving like a sleepwalker, still tied the knots well. He knew that Guararé was no match for his knots; nevertheless, he was thorough. He forcefully tied him up, securing his arms underneath his legs. He stuffed a scouring pad in his mouth for a muzzle. He shaped him into a bundle arranged for punishment.

Guararé tensed his muscles preparing for the blows of the whip. It was heavy, very thick, made from ox hide. He received the first blow from De la Piedra and relaxed. He tensed his body again. He waited.

Nazario counted five lashes before the young man stopped tensing his muscles. On the sixth, his body was already weakened, nearly bland. The coachman calculated drowsily that this way it would be easier for De la Piedra to whip him. If the boy did not put forth any resistance by the tenth blow, master would completely crush him. Nazario looked at the two of them and yawned.

Guararé felt the precise moment that the burning sensation produced by the whip became a nest of scorpions that ran blind and stung him without mercy. He could not scream or flee from the venom that tortured him, that tore away strips of skin. He shivered. A chill froze his bones. Finally, a long sigh. Then his back broke.

Afterwards in the delirium of two nights, he would swear a thousand and one times that he was not dying from the whipping the blue-eyed man gave him.

"No it wasn't the lashes, but the damn scorpions," he insisted.

Chapter XII

Altagracia left the big house under the pretext of doing some shopping, but she headed towards Malambo to visit Tomasón. She found him with Jaci. The old men were smoking in front of one of the walls. They were looking attentively at a painting. She saw Tomasón point to something she could not see, and she heard him mention a person who had drowned in the sea. She was startled.

"Have you heard anything about Pancha and Venancio?" was her greeting. "They should have been back by now."

Tomasón clears his throat, rubs his hands, and, waving aside the smoke sees her pregnant silhouette. It takes him several seconds to recognize her. Jaci addresses her first.

"Altagracia Maravillas! Girl, what good winds brought you here?" He offers her a seat in a small, battered chair. It was obtained, along with a new cot, in exchange for a painting of the

Last Supper, and another of Saint Peter with the keys to heaven in his hand.

"I'm worried about the two of them. Have you heard anything?"

"No, but I'm not worried. It's not that I have a good feeling about it or anything, but bad news is the first to arrive." Tomasón steadies his gaze. She doesn't resemble Venancio at all, in spite of them being half brother and sister.

"Tell me, how's your arm progressing?"

Jaci begins to nail a frame for the image of Christ.

"It's all right. Looks like it's finally getting better. I hope they're back for the procession. I regret making Pancha go look for Venancio. I was the one who should have escaped from master's house to go look for him. Of course I'm a coward for those types of things."

"Don't be sorry, everything is going to turn out fine. Anyway, it was Pancha who wanted to see what's beyond the clouds of dust of Malambo's streets," Tomasón consoles her.

"Yes, and it's about time that she knew all that life has to offer," adds Jaci. "She's already old enough to learn the virtue that few have: how to go to any unknown place and then find without hesitation the road back home."

Tomasón mentally notes that all of Altagracia's features have become more rounded with the pregnancy.

Despite her bad arm and her sadness, she appears healthy. She seems secure in a way that is new to her.

"Each day she's getting prettier," he thinks out loud.

"It's the hens." Jaci quickly clarifies.

"This girl must have been drinking a black hen's blood."

They laugh loudly.

"What's going on with Doña Catalina Ronceros?"

Altagracia continues to laugh. She tilts her shaved head,

adorned with a ribbon of multicolored glass. Without accepting or denying the comment, she says:

"She's okay. Now, nobody's moving her out of the big house. Master doesn't dare tell her to go. Well, he's not like how he used to be, either. Ever since he whipped Guararé to death he's been edgy. Nazario is also restless. I don't know . . . those two, for a while now they seem like souls pursued by the devil."

"Remorse, probably."

"Who knows. Master even sent for Father José and the two of them talked behind closed doors."

"The Jesuit? Hummm. It must have been to confess his sins, then. He must be regretting all the bad things he's done. He's going to die."

"Or he's going to get married," Tomasón remarks.

"Not one or the other. There's something going on between master and that bearded Father. Some business maybe. As far as marrying the widow, Nazario's right. Master isn't going to let her twist his arm and she knows it. That's why she moved into the big house. She makes life impossible for him, and in the process she doesn't let me sleep in peace either."

"If he puts up with her, it must be for something. It's his house and he can do with her what he wants."

Altagracia's words criticizing the widow have irritated Jaci. He puts his work to one side. "After you slept with him, being a married woman, you can't complain about her. But, I won't say anything more. Because in the end, you gave Tomasón ten pesos, and because of you, we have the Christ for the *cofradía*."

Jaci gives the impression that he is going to close his mouth and be quiet, but he soon gets worked up again.

"Of course those pesos also came out of De la Piedra's pocket." He hesitates for an instant: "What does Nazario say about your pregnancy?"

Altagracia pays him no attention and continues talking with Tomasón.

"Everything's a mess, and not because I'm expecting. It's those loose hens. There's no peace. Any day now the house is going to burst. I hope that Venancio buys my freedom papers before it happens. I'm not asking for anything more."

She makes a resigned pause and changes the topic. "Will you go with us to drop off the Christ for the Pachacamilla *cofradía*?"

"I don't know caraaá!!" He rubs his eyes. "Altagracia Maravillas, girl, you know good and well that I've never gone back and crossed that blessed Stone Bridge ever since I came to Malambo. But these last couple of days, I've felt more in the mood to go to the other side."

"You're not going to visit your master, are you?" intervenes Jaci.

"Nooooo, I have to settle a few matters with someone who has a debt with Pancha. But I don't know. Maybe I'll wait until she comes back. Or maybe I'll get my nerve back and do it before then and follow along with the procession. We'll see, there's still a few days between now and Sunday."

"Three, no more, and they'll fly by."

She says goodbye, with a hug for Tomasón, and without even looking towards Jaci.

"Once again you said the wrong thing. I don't think you'll ever get rid of the bad habit of picking on the person that least deserves it."

Tomasón watches Altagracia walk away with the shopping basket swaying in her hand.

〰〰〰

In the street market, the peasants from the adjoining haciendas sell vegetables in a Castilian tinged with Quechua and African languages. Even though it takes Altagracia twice as long to buy provisions there, she prefers to, in order to save a few reales. Caught up in the clientele, she learned to leave behind her timidness and give herself over to the improvised lingo of bargaining. In a give and take with the eagerness to acquire sales, sometimes she won, other times she gave in. If she obtained a discount, Catalina Ronceros never knew—she kept the difference in her bodice. She mentally added the reales, but the memory of Candelaria spoiled her joy.

She returned to the big house and entered the main hall, shooing away hens and chicks. The rocking chair was empty and the coach was not in the stable. She looked at the deteriorated dwelling, at the destruction caused by the birds: broken dishes, torn tapestry, and pecked-marked fine cedar.

But the ruin and plundering of the rooms no longer bothered her so much.

The yellow chicks, recently hatched, followed their mother. Clucking along, she was looking for food for them in the bookcase, in the cupboard. All of the big house was theirs.

Altagracia's feet felt light. She left the pantry, past the mangled sacks, past the two hens fighting for grains. She climbed the stairs two by two and on the second floor she said goodbye to the bedroom with the silk mosquito net and the immaculate sheets. She went downstairs and immediately organized her master's desk, but only on the surface. She wiped the intricate carvings with a rag, moistened with linseed. The weight of her belly slowed her as she removed some stains from the rug.

In the garden, the orange blossoms and the passion flowers were mangled, the geraniums grew with their stems twisted. She shooed away birds, removed crushed petals, tried to straighten stems. Lost in digging deeply into the earth, she did not realize that she was moving her bad arm until she felt the pecking of a hen protecting her brood.

She sat down on the ground and began to undo the wrapping of rags over rags, herbs over ointments and poultice, and more herbs and soaked leaves that Pancha had prescribed.

At twelve noon, the roosters sang. The skin showed bruises, it was very dry and flaky, but the swelling had gone down and she could move her arm. She raised up to her face. It obeyed her wishes, stretching or forming a fist. She lowered her hand and pinched herself with it. She was incredulous at feeling once again the tickling of soft hairs in her armpit. She marveled at the roundness of her shoulder, the point of her elbow, and her broken fingernails.

Only her skin continued to be foreign. She rubbed it gently, very slowly, as if caressing a child who had known no tenderness. Little by little she learned to be kind to herself. She learned to love herself.

〜〜〜

"I'm not from here. I come looking for my friend, Venancio. He's two quarters bigger than I am, and more or less my color," as Pancha described him to the woman with grey hair who, seated under an awning, was stringing together necklaces made of seashells. She was looking at the sea. From far away Pancha would have confused her with the sand hills, for the dark grey of her clothes and of her skin.

"Venancio," as if recollecting. "No, no, I've never heard that name and I couldn't tell you if I've seen him because my eyes don't distinguish well. It could be that he's around here. A lot of people come here because we have a little of everything, except fish." She showed her the basin. "Every once in a while the sea sends scallops, conchs, shells."

"Who would be able to help me?"

The woman shrugged her shoulders and shook her head. A

beautiful pair of filigree trinkets moved, vigorously bumping against her sand cheeks.

"My son made them for me. I don't know who could help you. We're not ones to talk a lot. You've probably noticed that some don't even greet you."

Indeed, Pancha had observed in this desolate place that people did not stop to answer. Perhaps the blowing sand made them hurry home.

"The fishermen may have seen him, but they've left. Tonight there's a full moon and I'm sure that they will come do their dances for the carnival celebration. Stay, and you can ask them."

It seemed to Pancha that she had left Malambo an eternity ago. She had walked entire days through ports, meeting people she never would have imagined existed. Perhaps Venancio was no longer in any of these coves and had returned to Lima, and had even bought Altagracia's freedom. She would return tomorrow. She said this to herself each day. But upon waking, her feet carried her in the opposite direction.

"Is Venancio your husband?"

"No, not yet. But I'm going to marry him."

"You love him?"

"I feel good when he's by my side. I miss him when I don't see him."

"That's not enough. If he's here for you to take him back, you have to love him very, very much. You must be willing to give your life for him." She reached for a pot containing food. "Or if not, the same thing could happen to you that happened to the woman that drowned." She continued looking distractedly at the horizon.

"Who is the woman that drowned?"

"A woman. Nobody knows her, and it seems like she even forgot why she came here. She drowned a short time ago."

"That has nothing to do with me."

"I don't know. You're not the first to go to the trouble of coming down this way. A lot of people come looking for relatives and friends. I'm one of them. I came for a man that I still haven't found. But sooner or later he will come. I have a debt with him, and like you, I miss him."

"How long have you been in this place?"

"I don't even know that any more. In this port they don't keep track of the days. Ever since the fish left, the days are all the same. And for those that are used to waiting, it's all the same, today as tomorrow."

"Not for me. No. I have a sick grandfather and they're going to cut off Altagracia's arm."

"If you're in such a hurry, you shouldn't have come. That same thing happened to the other woman. Because she didn't know how to wait, she drowned. But don't worry. I'll take you to the fishermen so you can ask them about your Venancio. What's your name?"

"My name is Pancha and you don't need to go with me. Show me the way, and I'll go alone."

"I'm Ángela and I have to go with you. If not, you'll get lost. You don't know the fishermen's wicked ways. They used to not be like that, but idleness changes people. Rest, it's still early."

She continued stringing together the necklaces while looking at the horizon.

Tomorrow I'm going back to Malambo, Pancha repeated to herself walking along the beach. At each port she would ask herself if Venancio could be among the fishermen, and she always doubted it. She stared at the islands, threatening giants of stone, emerging from the fog. The water was not the calm and silent kind, like that from the springs. In front of the islands, the surf was hungrier than normal. The fine sand she walked on drew her out to the sea. Pancha accepted the invitation. She shed her skirts and swam for a long time, though with some apprehension. Afterwards, on the shore, she tasted the salt on her lips and wished that, wherever Venancio was, he too might see the beautiful light that began to glow and shine on one of the islands.

Ángela did not hurry when she walked. She gathered little sea shells and conches. She touched them, examining the form that her eyes could not distinguish, and then put them in her bag.

"I use them to make necklaces. I'll make one for you too."

Pancha thanked her, and because she did not know what else to talk about, she asked how the woman had drowned.

"If I tell you, you won't believe me."

She turned some sea shells over and over in her hands.

They approached a group of people forming a closed circle around a bundle.

All of them were women. Some, younger. Others were the same undefined age as Ángela. They also had the same sand-colored clothes and skin. They all moved with a certain awkwardness.

"Well, what are we going to do?" They were discussing this when Ángela interrupted and asked about the fishermen. Without opening the circle, they turned to look at her. One of the younger ones responded: "They still haven't come."

They had watery eyes. They gave the impression of looking at Pancha without seeing her, until they touched her and convinced themselves that she was not an apparition from the water.

"You bring someone. Who is it?"

"Pancha. She just arrived, looking for a fisherman. What did you tell me his name was?"

"Venancio, and he comes from Malambo."

The women approached very closely and examined her skirts and her red scarf.

"Your eyes see well?"

"Of course they see well. She's not from here. She's passing through and I'm making her a necklace so that she finds Venancio. I collected them for her."

Ángela opened her fist with the seashells.

"Well, it could be that tonight she'll be lucky," added another of the women, and the distrust was broken. Pancha didn't know why they were laughing, but she laughed with them. She tried not to think any more about their eyes, their eyes that looked at her without seeing her.

"Maybe he's here. There's a lot of people that pass through. They come and go, but ask the fishermen. They know everything." And they turned their backs on her once again.

"Well, what are we going to do?"

"What happened?" Ángela made an opening in the circle and exclaimed shaken: "We shouldn't get involved in this. Let the fishermen decide, it's their problem."

Pancha focused her attention on the bundles and wrappings of nets at their feet. In one of them, the biggest one, the moss was turning green and partially covered a cadaver.

"What if we bury her without them knowing?"

"No. It's already the third time that the sea has brought her back."

"Yes, yes. Let's bury her with white flowers like a bride."

"Where are we going to get flowers from? Don't be silly."

"The fishermen from La Magdalena grow flowers, too." Pancha said. "I know one of them. He'll give them to me if I ask. It's not very far."

"She's right. It's not a bad idea."

They thought about it indecisively.

The drowned woman smelled like rotten fish. Pancha imagined that if she touched the rough and porous body after having been submerged so long, it would split open. It would give way in the manner of a soaked sponge. Her naked body could have been molded from opaque sand; her hair was indistinguishable from the seaweed that surrounded her head, from the necklace of iridescent seashells she wore. As with the other women, she did not provoke sadness, nor did Pancha feel afflicted that she was dead. On the contrary, her face bothered her somewhat.

After observing her a long time, as they discussed whether or not to organize a burial with flowers, Pancha studied the woman's mouth.

Yes, it was the mouth, with its meaty, obscene lips, that irritated Pancha. Yes, that's what it was. In spite of being dead, it was wide open and showed her blue tongue in an indecent scandalous laugh.

Pancha would have preferred that the drowned woman had a desperate expression, maybe one of anguish at the fight with the waves or one of conformity with her death. Or at least a vacant look.

They did not feel his steps in the sand. They did not know how long the fisherman had listened to their discussion about the burial with white flowers. But as soon as their eyes noticed the blurred, long shadow extending itself over the drowned woman, they became quiet.

He tied a rusty anchor to her ankles, grabbed the dead woman under her armpits and pulled her onto his boat. He rowed out to sea. Who knows if he reached the islands? He was swallowed by the fog. They lost sight of him as he went to submerge her in the deepest part of the sea, where the stars that might guide if you are lost, and your eyes see only water.

"This time she definitely isn't coming back," lamented Ángela as she continued stringing together the necklace.

The others paid no attention to her. They forgot about the episode with the drowned woman and began to untie the other bundles at their feet. Talking excitedly, they took out pots full of spicy stews, fruits, and *chicha* matés, and took out oil lamps with animal fat that they would light when the twilight began to set in.

In the midst of these women, Pancha saw that her face was smiling as if taking part in a silent joke. The power to observe herself from afar in a form so clear and precise made her doubt she was living that moment. Perhaps this all was nothing more than a dream, she dared to think. For brief spells, she had the same capsizing feeling she had during the long nights of her travels, when she was full of memories and stories of Tomasón and Jaci Mina.

Seated face to face, they smoked the empty pipe, thinking deeply. Whoever was in the mood would start. The other would correct or add details until they arrived at the end of the story. Then they would start another one.

She would hear them from her room. She always felt like she was about to fall deeply asleep. In this half-dreaming state, Tomasón and Jaci's voices floated towards her in a whisper, as if brought by the waters of the Talking River. She was sure that they were there without being there and that they had the ability to transport her to other places without her needing to abandon her four walls. Maybe one day she'd learn to do it too, she would think to herself, and at some point in time she would submerge into unconsciousness.

"Pancha, I hear the fishermen coming. Over there, look!" Ángela was pointing into the darkness along the beach.

Pancha strained to make out what looked like a group of dancers.

"A group of musicians is coming."

"That's them, the fishermen."

In a moment the beach was a celebration. The fishermen drank and tuned their *vihuelas* and shawms, while others arranged their costumes, hanging bells and little mirrors on the red material.

She asked them about Venancio. Some said that, yes, he was among them. Others said that he had already left.

"He's wearing a mask." They laughed and passed from hand to hand the thick maté, made from peanuts.

Pancha had a good time. She counted the devils in the group: eight peons and two overseers.

"No. There's eleven of us. It shouldn't be long before Casimiro, the High Devil, arrives."

"Wait for him." said Ángela. "Maybe he can help you with Venancio."

Pancha learned that only the first shot of fermented chicha tasted bitter. Afterwards it became sweet and tasty, just like the coca leaves that they chewed. The devils in the group danced around her switching their masks and singing.

No one saw Venancio. Nooo.

No one saw Venancio. Nooo.

Nooo, noooo, noooo.

She was amused to see so many tall devils, short devils, skinny devils, fat devils, devil devils, all dressed in red, all shaking their bells and little mirrors.

When Ángela hung the seashell necklace on her, Pancha was already dancing with the High Devil. The rhythm inundated her like a wave. Following the music with a tambourine, she sang with the sand women:

Achere rere iya milateo

Yemanyá asaybikolokun ibutagana

dedegua otolokun okobayireo

ibula omi. Kofiedenu Iya mia. Ago.

The scarf tied in her hair came undone in the breeze, slid down her shoulders, and fell to the damp sand.

"Your ponytail is so beautiful when it's down! You're so beautiful!" Casimiro's flattery made Pancha happy, and she laughed as she spun around in his arms. His salty breath enveloped her.

Her eyes began to water from the spinning, she could hardly see. But then everything came abruptly to an end: a woman came out of the night, pulled the tambourine from her hands, and took her place.

"Were you at least able to find out where Venancio is?" she heard Ángela say angrily.

"No" she responded.

Pancha had the music deep in her body, and she wanted to return to the swaying arms of the High Devil. She forgot about Venancio.

She was jealous of the woman dancing with Casimiro. The moon made the woman's white skirt glow as she laughed.

The devil ceased turning around and around. For a moment he was still, and Pancha recognized him. It was the same fisherman who had carried the drowned woman back to the sea. This time he wore a scarlet red cape, shook silver bells. She wanted to leave the fiesta and continue looking for Venancio, but the group began to sing and play with more vigor. She gave in.

The water asks and the water gives. Gives, gives, gives.
Give the water what he gives you. Give, give, give.
And if you don't give to him? And if you don't give to him?
He turns fierce and comes out and drenches.

Casimiro spoke softly to the woman with the tambourine. He danced with her and talked with her. With her beautiful sash, he stoked her face bathed in the moonlight. He said something in her ear. She looked at him, incredulous. She stopped playing her tambourine and dancing. But the devil kept whispering sweet nothings and turning pirouettes. He danced. He sang. He draped his cape around her. He enchanted her once again, and her gaiety broke out over the sound of the waves. She let out a guttural laugh.

All of the women envied that pleasant, long, greedy laugh. It was an entire ear of sweet corn.

The fishermen continued with their music. Casimiro captured her laughter in his arms, covered her in his brilliant red cape and surrendered her to the sea.

〰〰〰

Manuel De la Piedra tossed and turned in his bed. The hens would not let him take his siesta. Tired of trying to fall asleep and not feeling the least bit drowsy, he went down to the parlor and called for Nazario to keep him company.

"Serve me some wine."

He shooed a rooster with a slap and created a trail of floating feathers.

"Yes sir. As you wish."

"Have you heard anything about Venancio? I want to know how many pesos I can count on for Altagracia."

"We don't know anything about him, sir. Venancio still has not been seen."

"Damn it! And you, who begged me so much because you wanted a woman to marry, you don't care if I sell her? What kind of husband are you, Nazario?"

Standing, Nazario looked down on him. He spoke with his raspy voice, almost without moving his lips. "Altagracia is not Nazario's woman."

"She's going to have your son!"

"No. It's not mine. The seed of Nazario Briche has never borne fruit, sir."

"Hummm. Then whose is it?" De la Piedra tried to sound ignorant.

"Another man's."

"That I know. Now that you mention another man—I never asked you because I didn't want to get involved in any problems. And because in the end, it's a thing between niggers, you told me. And you were right, because no one else has made any complaints about me like the ones made because of Guararé. Once I saw you arguing with a man here, in this house. You attacked him in the garden. Was he Altagracia's lover?"

Nazario hesitated. He was surprised that his master knew of the incident. He considered his response carefully, and measured his words:

"No. It was the late Candelaria's nephew. He knew that you have a hiding place under the fulling mill stone. He came to take what you're keeping there."

With shaking hands, De la Piedra served himself a glass of wine and drank it in one gulp. He looked through the railing at the Lima streets. They were dirty with waste. Some stray dogs nibbled at orange peels. He had seen gloved hands throw them from a coach with squeaking wheels. The din of the city hurt his ears. If it were not for his daily wine, he would be crazy and deaf. If it were not for the loyalty of Nazario, he would be almost as poor as he was that first day.

"Tell me, besides that cursed old woman and her nephew, the two of us and Guararé, who else knows about the hiding place that I have?"

"Guararé didn't know about it. That man didn't come here to steal, the way you think. He came in looking for Chema." Nazario pronounced each word with great calm.

"Are you sure? Are you sure?" He pressed him for an answer.

"Yes."

"Then the poor wretch wasn't lying." He let loose the laugh of a drunk. "If you knew, why didn't you tell me?"

Nazario raised his shoulders, indifferent and calm.

"Go! Get out! I want to be alone." He shouted. He felt depressed at the revelation and bloated from the wine. Nevertheless, he continued drinking.

That morning, he had realized that colors had been erased

from his memory. Red, blue, and yellow were there, but some-how they meant nothing. Also Pancha's skirts were no longer important to him. He could count only on the nostalgia of sea-sonings, on the cumin and garlic flavor that Altagracia exuded. If it weren't for the hissing fan and the clucking hens, he would be happily close to that aroma, resting at her side like a newborn, sleeping the siesta beneath the blue silk mosquito net.

"Of course, there's still a solution to all this, Catalina. Catali-naaa."

"Catalinaaa, Catalinaaa," repeated the waters of the Talking River.

"What do you want? But please, lower your voice. You're drunk again."

"Only on wine, only on wine, Catalina. Tell me, when are you and your cursed hens going back to your farm?"

"Why should we? You promised to marry me. Besides, you sold the farm." Once again she felt blotches and blushes cover her face. "Or did you forget?"

"No, I remember that I sold it. As for the promise, I have a proposition: I'll buy you another farm, bigger than the first one."

"No. I'm staying by your side. We'll grow old together, Manuel."

"But why?"

"Do you want me to remind you?"

He did not answer her. Accustomed to negotiating prices at auctions, he cried out in his best voice: "A farm and an income of two thousand pesos a year for the rest of your days, Catalina Ronceros, if you get out of my life tomorrow."

" . . . "

"A farm and two thousand pesos if you leave today."

" . . . "

"If you don't accept, from now on you'll sleep in the store-house with your hens."

" . . ." Catalina began to fan herself.

"Don't shake your fan, the noise is breaking my eardrums, Catalina!"

"I accept." She lets her fan fall. "But Altagracia Maravillas goes with me."

"No. She's mine."

"Then forget it. I'm not moving from here."

Chapter XIII

"If you can have faith in what they say around here, Melgarejo and the priest José were crossing the old wood bridge when the miller lost his balance and fell into the river. The current gave him a couple of tumbles, Tomasón, and if the priest didn't dive in the water to save him, the Rímac would have carried him away," says Jaci.

"Hummm. And when was this?"

"After he came to pay you for that little golden bull that you sold him. I just found out about it yesterday."

"I didn't sell him anything, because it wasn't for sale." He gestures angrily and swatted his hands as if scaring away flies. "That's why I didn't accept the peso that he wanted to give me. What's more, if I were Melgarejo, I wouldn't get close to the river or any other spring or well, because sooner or later the bull is going to pull him in. I warned him and I asked him over and over again that he give it back. Tears even fell from my eyes. He never gave it back."

"Don't worry. God doesn't punish with sticks or stones. He'll get what he deserves!"

Tomasón regained his composure. He took a paintbrush and approached one of the walls. Momentarily he stopped with the brush in the air. "How's Pancha doing?" He exchanges glances with Jaci. "Shouldn't she have returned by now? For her first time, that's enough. It's not appropriate that she stays away so long. She still doesn't know the trails back to Malambo well enough. Don't you think?"

"Nothing bad is going to happen. Pancha isn't going to lose her way so easily, and she doesn't need anyone to direct her steps. You'll see."

"I hope you're right. At least up to now things have turned out as we might have hoped: Altagracia's arm has finished healing, and the widow Ronceros' hens aren't killing her anymore. It still bothers me that she still has to live in the house with that master."

"Yes, but she hardly sees him. He and Nazario leave together every day to go to the port. A new loaded ship has arrived. Speaking of the port, yesterday they saw someone who could be Venancio."

"And you're just telling me now, Jaci!"

"Yes, I wanted to make sure first. If it's him, it shouldn't be long before he arrives here."

"I hope so. I'm anxious to see him together with Pancha." He heard the six o'clock bells and felt the need to rest. "Want to sit down here beside me, *cumpa* Jaci? Come, come, close your eyes too."

"Go meet the four winds," Ángela advised her as she said goodbye to Pancha. "Ask them about Venancio; maybe they know. You see he's not here. Anyway, this beach isn't like the others. The sea clouds the eyes. When there's fish again, it will be different. Don't you want to take a necklace with you?"

"No, it will bring back memories of what happened last night."

"Last night. What are you talking about?"

"You know exactly what I'm talking about."

"If you're thinking about the woman who drowned, that happened a long time ago, girl."

"A long time?"

"Days, weeks. I'm not sure." She resumed collecting conches.

Whirlpools lifting the fine grains of sand announced the location of the four winds. At her first stop, Pancha thought she had found Venancio among the fishermen who salted and strung fish together on a line. But it was not he.

"What brings you here, girl?" An old, shrunken man approached to greet her, dragging his tired feet.

She had a huge desire to hug him. He was identical to Tomasón.

The old man grabbed her by the hand and took her to a group of people removing fish from the nets and cleaning the boats.

"Listen, look at this girl." He shouted to them. "Looks like she escaped from the beach where so many people drown. Look at her. She still has that thing in her eyes that doesn't let you see well."

"Give her three mouthfuls of water to get rid of the fright, and rub her face with a sponge. Let's see if it gets rid of that drowned-person smell," advised a man who could easily have been Jaci himself.

"You look exactly like my grandfather and my friend," replied Pancha still in amazement.

"No, girl, you can't be serious! That's just your eyes."

"Or could it be that you've seen one of those mischievous devils?" they joked.

"Yes. All of them. I even danced with Casimiro."

The women abandoned what they were doing to listen to her. They were surprised, yet not convinced that it was true. They took here to a corner away from the others. "Come on, come on! Tell us about Casimiro!" they urged her.

The men, surprised, wondered if her story could be true.

"Nooooo! How could she have danced with Casimiro himself!"

"How the devil should I know! Could it be that times have changed?"

"Nooo. If she had danced with Casimiro, we would be taking her out of the nets and throwing salt right now," they said at last, chuckling.

It took Pancha a long time to make them understand that she had seen Casimiro with her own eyes. But as they began to believe her, she began to loose the certainty of what she had lived. Doubt invaded her. She wanted to stop talking. It was better for her to be quiet.

"And why did you go there?"

"To look for Venancio."

"He didn't want to come back with you?"

"No. That's not it. I didn't find him."

"Ah, well who is Venancio?"

"A friend. No, boyfriend. I'm going to marry him."

"No one's come around here. Not long ago, an Indian happened to pass through. He had jumped off a ship and swam here. But Venancio's not here either."

"I can't understand how they let you travel alone! It's very dangerous around here. You don't have somebody to go with you?" asked the one that looked like Jaci.

"No. I only have a grandfather who's very sick. They killed my *taita*. They found him dead in the river. At first I didn't believe it because I hadn't seen it with my own eyes. But that's how it happened."

"Girl," interrupted the old man who resembled Tomasón, "forget that thing about 'seeing is believing.' Anyway, the eyes that you have still haven't learned to distinguish between what's real and what's not real. Just a little while ago you mistook me for your grandfather."

"And you confused me with your friend! Those two big eyes are pretty, but they still aren't doing you much good. It's like that. It takes a while to learn to see what's at the bottom of things. It takes time to be able to see far without having to tire your feet in the process. Go ahead, ask the four winds about Venancio, and afterwards find your path home. What you're looking for isn't here."

Pancha thought that they were right. The more she looked at them, the more her eyes saw Jaci and Tomasón in them: attentive, studying her, guiding her with gentle words, showing her the way home to Malambo.

〰〰〰

In the big house, Chema was packing his belongings in a trunk when De la Piedra knocked on his door.

"May I?" He asked and entered. It was the first time that he visited the room. He had always imagined that it would be stuffed with books and manuscripts, and that is how he found it. De la Piedra didn't just take a seat, he collapsed on the platform that Chema slept on. It was hard and narrow, the bed of an unmarried man. "As I'm sure you've noticed, things have changed a lot since you left on your trip, Chema my friend."

"Yes, the house has been converted into a farm."

"But what's going on? Are you packing again? You just got here and you're already leaving? Well, I understand. I imagine that you're looking for another lodging."

"No, I'm leaving in two days. This time I'm going to Europe. I don't know when I'll come back. A year, maybe two."

"Then this will be our goodbye. Because at the rate things are going with Catalina and the birds, when you return to the big house there won't be anything but dust and feathers."

Chema thinks about what he said without responding. He sits down in front of him and he resolves to listen to a De la Piedra frustrated at not being able to sleep the siesta with Altagracia Maravillas. Furthermore, De la Piedra was drunk.

"You ask yourself why I let Catalina do it," he comments with bitterness. "If I tell you that I don't really know why, would you believe me, Chema my friend? Never mind! I've lived intensely—I imagine that you already know that—and I've not always lived honestly. The issue of my last name De la Piedra . . . my origins . . ." he prolongs his speech with silences. He cleared his throat, stroked his hair. "I would tell you the incredible story of my life, but it's irrelevant."

"Why not? Please do so. After what I've seen on this trip, I'm inclined to believe anything. Tell it to me."

"Nooo, no. Better you tell yours. How did it go?"

"Very well. I explored five islands. They're not too far from the coast. Actually, they're islets, groupings of rocks that stick out of the sea. To my surprise, on one of them I found two shipwrecked men, an Englishman, and you won't believe who the other one was: Venancio."

"Altagracia's brother?"

"The same. He was fishing and his boat sank. When I returned from the island, I brought him with me to El Callao. I don't think that he'll stay there. His adventure cured him of any desire to ever return to sea. He'll probably soon arrive in Malambo."

"Venancio shipwrecked? How absurd! And the Englishman, who is he?"

"He said his name is Sterling. I looked into it and in El Callao he's known. They figured he was dead. They told me that the aforementioned Sterling is crazy, but they exaggerated. He's a little disturbed, but he hasn't completely lost his mind. And he knows what he's talking about when he says that the island is worth gold."

"Why do you say that?"

"The manure from the birds on the islands enriches the soil. The European fields would double their yield fertilizing with this manure. The guano accumulated for centuries on those islands is worth a fortune. Sterling's only insanity is that he doesn't realize that that island or any of the others are not English, much less his."

"Do you think that it's worth the trouble to exploit them?"

"Of course, Manuel, but wait. Before I continue talking about my discovery, let me tell you something very important. Do you remember the wine that you gave me for this trip?"

"Yes, it's the same muscatel that I drink every day. Why?"

"Recently, haven't you felt as if you're going out of your mind? Like you were losing your memory?"

"Well, yes, I forget things more often. Of course, I have my good days and bad days. I work too much, I don't sleep enough and I can't deny that I indulge in drink more than I should."

"Your memory loss has nothing to do with what you've mentioned. During the trip I did the same thing, but I can tell the difference between the effects of alcohol and the effects of a narcotic. Let lightening strike me if I'm wrong, but I'm sure that the wine you drink has *paico*."

"*Paico . . . paico*, what's *paico*?"

"A plant that grows in the Sierra, and I think I'm also not wrong in daring to say its flowers can cause irreversible damage. Don't drink the wine. You'll completely lose your memory and it may even cause your death. Someone is poisoning you. Stop drinking it if you want to go on living."

De la Piedra shuddered, livid.

"Damn it. Thank you for warning me. Keep it in mind if I die suddenly."

"If that happens I won't be here. I've already told you I'm returning to Spain. In two days a ship leaves for Seville. I can't waste time. I have to get there as soon as possible and find a way to handle that guano. I don't want the Englishman to beat me. I'm sorry. Excuse my lack of tact. Getting back to you, you should report it today. I'll support you. I'll be a witness."

"I won't do it."

"Why?"

"Because I suspect that it might have been Altagracia and I prefer not to see her involved in problems."

Chema remained pensive. "Or Nazario, the one who has plenty of motives."

"Nazario, no. He's a brute. He would have killed me violently, once and for all. But now that you mention it . . ." Sneering, he adds: "There's the storekeeper—anyone could have done it. Allowing me to drink that poison slowly so as to not raise suspicions and then take over my slave routes and my businesses. So they don't have to settle their debts with me. But what a story, Chema! Doesn't it seem amazing to you? Write all this in a book. I'll finance it, whatever it costs."

"You would really do that?"

Upon realizing his interest, De la Piedra changes his mind, and negotiates.

"Of course—when and if you find those two women who

marked your face and present them to me. Then I'd turn over the cost of the edition to you. After sleeping siesta with each of them, I would pay them the remaining balance, in bars of gold. What women!"

Chema shook his head. He would never betray them. "Always thinking about women. Are you still obsessed with Pancha's skirts?"

"No. I've forgotten them. Truthfully, I'm too old for adventures. I think the time has come for me to retire from commerce. I feel tired, weak. Sick, probably from dejection."

"It's the wine, I'm telling you."

"Noooo. A little poison every day doesn't do anybody any harm. On the contrary, it makes you strong."

"You don't believe me. That's fine. It's your health. As for retiring , if you can live on your income, do it. I recommend it."

"I'll follow your advice. Now let me tell you something that happened while you weren't here. Altagracia ceased being a *maravilla*. She's very pregnant. Oh! You already knew. Her infected wound has healed. Now it shines like a new arm, white. Nazario carries on as if she no longer existed. I'm ready to sell both of them. But I came in to ask you about a certain Guararé. Do you know him?"

"The silversmith's assistant?"

"The same."

"Yes, why?"

"Guararé isn't alive anymore. He died and it's not important how. It was an unfortunate accident. There's not a person in Lima who doesn't know all the details, and they could tell you better than me. Or if not, ask the river. But as to whether or not he's dead, he's dead. What relationship did you have with him, Chema? If you wouldn't mind telling me, I would appreciate it."

"Not much of one. I didn't have time to know him. We barely

talked, but I'm sure that we would have been friends. I saw him only once, and I promised to help him. Afterwards, I was busy trying to heal my face. I left for the trip... Would it surprise you if I told you that Guararé was a mulatto?" And without waiting for an answer, he continued, "His dark skin didn't give him away, but according to him, he was. He was looking for his relatives. Spaniards maybe. Possibly they live in Lima."

"I didn't even suspect it. See there, my associates who send me shipments of niggers from Portobelo and Cartagena are completely undependable. Did he mention his family's surname?"

"No. He didn't know it, and the information he shared with me was vague. A very difficult case to solve. A common bastard, understand? I explained this to him, but I promised to look into it anyway. Now that I know about his death, I realize that I didn't try hard enough. It was stuck in his head that his father was a merchant. I mentioned this to Nazario Briche and gave him a kind of talisman in a leather bag. Guararé had entrusted it to me. It was the only clue I had to look for his father. I thought that Nazario could help me, but it wasn't to be."

"You wasted your time. Nazario isn't good for anything but driving coaches. In regards to the talisman, I know that the niggers carry seeds from certain plants with 'magical powers,' and sometimes even part of their own umbilical cords to bring them luck. If you had shown it to me, I doubt that I would've have been able to make any sense out of it."

"It wasn't a charm, per se, but rather a memento. A delicate piece. Very fine, old silk, that Guararé said was a gift from his father to the woman who raised him. I asked Nazario to find out if they still sell it in any of the stores."

"Did you say it was silk?"

"Indeed."

"Was it blue?"

"Uh huh. I see that Nazario showed it to you."

"Yes."

De la Piedra preferred to lie rather than explain his guess. That way Chema would not dwell on the story already begun. De la Piedra wanted to avoid having to make the effort to remember, to think deeply, and to explain his urgent need to know the color of the silk.

"Two or three nights later, Nazario knocked on my door. I was reading. I got up to open the door for him. I'd never seen him so upset. He could hardly express himself sensibly. He gave me back the remnant. He tried to tell me something, but I only understood about half of what he was saying. Afterwards I preferred not to know the details. You'll understand me when I tell you that on that very night, after curfew, Nazario escaped. Before I went to bed, I went to the kitchen for fresh water and I found Altagracia. 'I'm expecting a child,' she told me. She was less cheerful than usual, but still happy as a clam. Then she went up to your room. I was happy, but I also felt sorry for her and for Nazario. I thought about the double exploitation they had fallen into, about the injustice and abuse of the system. As you can see, in passing I've taken advantage of our conversation to give you my opinion about the matter."

He paused, as if organizing his ideas.

"Nazario was desperate, and didn't stop pointing to your lit window. I made him come into my room. He sat on the bed the same way that you're doing now. I tried to calm him. To give you two time to finish making love. I asked him a thousand questions. Where did he go when he went out at night? I asked a thousand things about Malambo. If he had found out anything about the silk remnant. All in all, he insisted on going up to your room with me.

"'A child by him.'

"He stammered unconnected phrases, and dragged out words. I realize that he wanted me to understand that Altagracia was expecting your child, De la Piedra. The scene that would have taken place if he saw the two of you in bed, destroyed me. I was scared. I don't deny it. I acted like an idiot. I tried to give him some reales so that he would flee from the house and from the disgrace. He didn't accept them. Little by little, he began to recover his composure. Soon he was distant, cold, and once again mute. Almost without opening his mouth, he asked me to keep secret what had happened.

"'I've thought about it more, Don Chema. I have to leave things the way they are. I'll know what to do.'

"He left. I went out after him and saw him disappear into another courtyard. I don't know—maybe he resigned himself to Altagracia's infidelity. That his master took the right to sleep with her. To raising the child of another man—in this case his master's—I don't know. I followed him. I saw him jump the garden wall and escape. I came back, went to bed, and fell asleep immediately.

"The next day I looked for him in the stable and he greeted me as if nothing special had occurred the previous night. That's why I didn't say anything to you. I no longer thought that Nazario would commit a crime."

"Do you still have that piece of silk?"

"Yes."

"Can I see it?"

"I'll give it to you. Guararé doesn't need it anymore."

He took out a box and handed the silk to him.

De la Piedra can feel it smooth and transparent between his fingers. It is the same fine silk of the mosquito net that hung above his bed. He slowly slid it from one hand to the other and did not notice that he shed a tear. He could touch and control the sky-blue color, but he could not quite grab hold of the memory that came to him upon seeing it and it filled him with a sudden sadness. He tried to console himself. Maybe it is another of the many stories that travelers scatter in their journeys. And in the end, who knew if it ever happened or if it was invented for the purpose of shortening a tedious and long chasm.

"What does it matter!" More than anything, he longed to hear the furious drumming of a downpour on the mud. Why didn't it ever rain in Lima? In other places it rained and the sun burned year round. Whoever carried a child in his arms took great care to shelter him under a shadow. He preferred not to remember.

"And what better than a glass of wine!" He wiped off his face.

"Do you feel okay, Manuel? You look pale. Are you crying?"

"No. It's the weariness in my eyes . . . in my arms . . . My body can't give anymore. I feel as if I've traveled fifty leagues by foot and just arrived home."

"Then rest."

They paused to listen to the church bells. It was exactly two o'clock in the afternoon.

"Yes, I'll rest. But before I take my siesta, let me tell you that it was I who killed that young man you met. Guararé was his name. I killed him with my own hands. I broke his back with the whip. I thought that he came to steal from me. Guararé was a simple slave and I mistook him for a thief."

"You didn't give him the chance to defend himself, to explain why he was here?"

"No. He couldn't talk. I thought that Nazario crammed the rag in his mouth so that the neighbors wouldn't hear his screams. Now I know better."

"I don't know what reasons Nazario had, but it's all the same. The crime was the brutal punishment you gave him. You killed him and in a horrendous way. Do you know what a despicable person you are, Manuel?"

De la Piedra let go a foolish laugh.

"You're not the only one with a bad opinion of me, Chema. Remember the poison that they're putting in the wine. But don't despise me. Have pity for me. I know why I'm saying this."

He opened the door. He went out into the destroyed yard. He noted, in turn, the nests that the birds had made in the entrance hall, the pile of broken shells, the trail of maize, the neglect in every corner. He entered the kitchen and, as always, found on the table a demijohn full of wine and a crystal glass on a tray. He drank directly from the spout and climbed the stairs, hoping the roads he had traveled buying slaves in Cartagena de Indias, the gallstones in Quito, the silks in New Granada, would soon fade away.

"All roads intertwine, they fork, and in the end they disappear."

He lay down to sleep the siesta, alone.

Chapter XIV

It was Sunday, and Malambo awoke at the crack of dawn. She got up early using a broom made from palm leaves to sweep the dust from the side streets. Then she adorned the trees with vines and garlands.

The devout women were the first to visit Tomasón and ponder the Crucified Christ, followed by the *cofradías* of Angolans, Congos, and a group of six musicians playing their shawms. The washerwomen entered next, then the fishermen, then the vendors. And finally, the rest of the neighborhood curious. The hut overflowed with people who were praising the Crucified Christ and the painted walls. They sang *panalivios*, sad songs that soothe the soul.

Tomasón rested his sickly feet in a corner. He promised himself not to dose. With a piece of coal, and little concentration, he drew in profile the musicians and Altagracia, who was serving *sango* to the visitors.

The steaming *mazamorra*—made of maize flour cooked with plenty of pig fat—and *chancaca* smelled like perfumed cloves. Jaci went about lighting the oil lamps with a sulphured wick. And Venancio, with his disheveled red hair, filled the incense burner. Then he lit the Malambo wood, the holy wood, and the lavender. Little by little, the smoke filled the hut. It rose undulating to the low-lying roof. It danced to each corner. Its spirals of smoke said softly: "Altagracia's free now. Venancio bought her."

"He bought her?"

"Ah!"

"And Pancha?"

"Where was Pancha?"

"They say that she left to travel."

"That she went to look for Venancio, but no one saw her leave."

"And where is she now?"

"Gathering herbs," answered Venancio. He had finished perfuming her room and was admiring the new cot.

"Are you going to get married?"

"Yes, we're getting married."

"Ah, how wonderful. They're getting married. They're getting married."

Although again he felt the shooting pains in his chest, Tomasón smiled, proud of Venancio.

The sea agreed with him. The dip in the water had made him mature. Yes, now I'll give Pancha away to be married, Tomasón thought. He lifted his gaze to better see the dark dust that bathed the entire dwelling. His eyes remained fixed on the opening of the window, and he confirmed what he had been waiting for; what sooner or later would happen. "It's faded. The bull's been erased. Caraaá!" he said in a low voice, almost without breathing. He let go of the piece of coal.

He began to organize the jars of paint. He carefully cleaned the brushes with a rag, rubbing away the residue of colors from the bristles with linseed oil. He returned them to the wooden box. He closed it well. He got up from the hard bench with enormous effort. He felt a spasm ripple through his back. He shook out his clothes, with both his hands, trying to put in order his crumpled garments. He could not.

He made his way slowly among the people, until he reached the center of the hut. He was dragging his tired arms. Heavy. Dangling. Like branches loaded with huge bundles of mature fruit. He was almost sweeping the floor with his fingertips. Finally he began to unite with the strident rhythms of the shawms. Moving one foot, then the other, he began to dance. With the melody dedicated to the "Maker of all things," he felt a little better. Once again the blood warmed in his veins. The oppressive knot in his chest was loosened. Slowly he and the rhythm began to form one swinging movement. He felt his worn old body suddenly begin to float in a halo of pink morning clouds of dawn. A moment later they were blue or orange, depending on the angle of light from the chiaroscuro of the hut. There he was now, mixed with dust, present in each breath, free to land wherever he wanted. Free to come and go forever. Tomasón gave thanks for his luck and sang with a new voice:

Iguere yéye, iguere yéye
Otú gua mí, Obbatalá
Otú gua mí, Olú gua mí
Obá orisham Iba i Babá
Ibá y yeyé, Ibá karo wó
Odda cho ma me wó

Omé akaguó adaché
Olomí osá, Olofí obá arayé.

The Talking River repeated Tomasón's tributes, and they were accepted by Obbatalá.

"White rice without salt." They sang the rounded songs to whomever would hear them.

"Two quarts of milk poured into a white plate, whipped egg whites with white sugar, separated from the cooked yokes and cotton flowers." Having formed the teams of the faithful to accompany the procession to the temple, Tomasón was ready to leave. But before he did, he exchanged his frayed sheepskin jacket for a new one of fine cotton thread.

While he painted the Christ, Pancha had been sewing it for him, stitch by stitch. Then she dyed it with indigo powder and scraps of dried, crushed, prickly pears. The color was vivid and intense, between blue and crimson.

Tomasón pulled on his pants, tying a cord at his waist. It required much effort for his feet to once again submit to the prison of his large leather shoes—he used to enjoy wearing them.

"Use my arm for support, *familia*," said Jaci, seeing him so frail.

"That's fine, but only as far as the bridge, no more. Because I'm not going to the temple. I'm going to the other side."

"And where are you going? If I may know."

"As far as my legs carry me. It's an urgent visit."

"But it has to be today?"

"Yes, today."

"In your state, you should rest."

"I know. But I can't yet."

As soon as they crossed the bridge, he slipped off into the noise and hustle and bustle of carts that was Lima. The braying mules raised such a cloud of dust that he was almost blinded, but nonetheless, he continued, without delay, until he arrived at

Manuel De la Piedra's big house. He entered through the main hall.

Inside, disorder ruled. His attention was caught by the crowing and a hissing sound, similar to the slithering of those innocuous snakes through corn set out to dry. He also thought he heard the muted swaying of a grinding stone. He poked his head into the great room and saw that the rug had been destroyed by pecking birds. The lamps with Venetian glass were broken and scattered. The great room was empty.

"Who are you looking for?"

A boy, dressed in dirty and stained livery that must have once been luxurious velvet, shouted to him from the garden. He carried a pot full of crushed maize in his hands.

"And you, who are you?" Tomasón was surprised to see the lad.

"Antón Cocolí. Who are you looking for? Don Manuel is sleeping and Doña Catalina is busy in the kitchen. I can't bother them."

"So early for the siesta and they're sleeping? Well, what's it to me! I came to talk with Nazario Briche and then I'm leaving. Does he still live here or did they sell him already?"

"I think he's in the stable," he managed to respond, concentrating on giving maize to the hens.

"Nazarioooo. Nazarioooo," called Tomasón, without raising his voice too much.

"Here I am. Who's looking for me?" The coachman came out to receive him.

"It's me. Tomasón Valleumbroso, the painter. You know exactly what brings me here. I come because Francisco Parra asked me to."

"Ah." The coachman smiles sadly. "I see that he finally spoke. How did you find me, since he didn't have eyes to see, or a tongue to speak?"

"I don't know how. Guararé must have known how to persuade him."

"Oh, so it was the silversmith's apprentice who carried the message." He seemed to think this over.

They walked to the stable. Nazario moved the horse aside and buried his hands in the straw looking for something. He stopped. He took out a long leather sack, and then, extending his arms, handed it to Tomasón.

Tomasón held Nazario's hands in his when he received the sack. He never forgot the form or the particular movements of each person's hands. He knew Nazario's. He could draw them from memory. He knew the size of his palms, the deep lines, the length of his fingers. He had admired the florid way that they had of talking. He had listened to them on numerous occasions, playing the drums. Looking at them well, they still maintained a hidden glimmer from that illuminated night around the fires of San Juan. These hands he had recorded in his memory. With open fingers, with his wrists placed one over the other, rubbing them together as if by accident. United and at the same time strangely alone.

"What's this, Nazario? What are you giving me?"

It made a sound when it shook. Could they be bones?

"Many pesos and a gold bar, part of what the silversmith smelted. It's Yáwar Inka's. I know that he's your friend. Don Manuel reported him. The pesos are Candelaria's savings. It's not all there. Ten are missing. Someone stole them."

"This is why Francisco Parra came? Was this what he was looking for?"

Nazario Briche shrugged his shoulders and looked down. "I suppose so. His aunt must have told him that she had the same hiding place as the master, under the fulling mill stone. Candelaria's was below, under a false floor. Master never noticed."

"And why didn't you give it to him? They were his."

"It's that he entered the house. I was blinded by rage. I thought that he, too, came to take possession of my Altagracia. I think that's why I stabbed him . . . or maybe because of this burning anger that consumes me . . . I don't know."

"You took vengeance on an innocent man. Francisco Parra didn't do anything bad to you. I didn't know him, but he gave me the impression of being a good person."

"I also wanted to be a good person. This time, I tried to be meek. I only wanted peacefulness. I wanted to have a woman, to marry and be happy. But see what happened! Once again my mouth is dry, full of ashes. I can't talk without feeling the pain of the sores on my palate. I don't hear anything else but the sound of steps, echoing across the pavement in the Plaza, as they go time and time again to see the gallows, and the chest scarred with wounds, the back crisscrossed with welts, the hands withered by the wind."

His yellow eyes stared at emptiness.

"You loved Altagracia?"

"At first yes, but I've had as many women as I've had masters. I don't blame her for what's happened. I know how the masters are. But this time I tried to be different. It was hard for me to tame my spirit, but I thought if I did, he would respect my woman."

Tomasón watched him, saddened. He would have liked to console Nazario, but did not know how.

"I have to go now. You don't want to come with me?"

"No, not yet. I still can't. Master will drink his wine when he wakes up."

"Then . . . we'll see each other later?" And without waiting for him to respond: "I was hoping to hear the drums with the six o'clock bells."

Nazario Briche did not answer.

Tomasón left the stable. He was walking hurriedly, taking long steps, when he heard Nazario mutter:

"You'll hear them."

~~~~~~

"And you, where did you go? Everybody is asking about you." Jaci Mina chides him as he waited for him to cross Stone Bridge, back to Malambo.

"To fulfill a promise." He handed him the long sack. "It's for Pancha."

"What's inside here that weighs so much?"

"The inheritance that the late Candelaria left to Francisco Parra, so he could buy their freedom papers. And there's another thing that's Inka's."

"Ahh. I'm beginning to understand. And what else did Francisco Parra tell you? Who did that to him?"

"Bernabé . . ." and he is interrupted. A coughing attack drowns him out.

He hesitates. Jaci is convinced that Tomasón's health has worsened. He waits until the cough calms down. They continue to walk.

"You're confused. When all that happened to Francisco Parra, Bernabé was already not among us." But Jaci does not pursue the conversation because Tomasón seems not to be paying attention to him but rather listening to the water's murmur.

"Let's go, let's go, *cumpa*. Pancha will give you a tisane made from those herbs that she knows so well. The one with ground beans or maybe plantains. Even today, I can't tell them apart. All the herbs taste like honey to me, you know."

"Nooo. Not all of them. Maté made with *yerbaluisa* tastes good. Coca is fine with me too.

"Hummm, you feel really bad. Isn't that right?"

"Almost the same as always, with the only difference being that, today, the years aren't weighing me down. It even feels like I can fly."

"Hurry, hurry faster then. It's getting late," Jaci grows impatient.

"You're right. I want to be in Malambo by six o'clock. That's the time I always lie down."

Nevertheless Tomasón barely quickens his step.

"Yes, and you shouldn't paint so much. That drains you. With the Christ that you made, that's enough. Now that it's in its place, in time we'll pray to it again." Jaci supports him firmly by the arm.

"Tell me what happened. The procession and all."

"People arrived from everywhere. Not only from Lima and Malambo, but also from the hills and the haciendas. Noooo! No, don't you believe it! That Christ doesn't just belong to the Angolas, Congos, and Lucumíes."

Tomasón watched how the cloudy waters swirled that evening. He thought that this time he would head towards Malambo at a walking pace. He was not in the same hurry to arrive as he was that first time, when he had escaped his master and crossed the bridge looking for Jaci. Now he was familiar with the way and he knew what awaited him.

"I see Venancio and a woman at your door. I can't make her out well, though by the skirts—it must be Pancha," commented Jaci with increased happiness.

Tomasón half closed his eyes and imagined painting her skirts in waves, like rays of a blinding sun.

"Then walk. Make yourself useful. Tell them to go into the house and wait for me. I'm coming." He let go of Jaci's arm. "I want to walk slowly, so I can smell the trees at my own pace." He made him leave.

〰〰〰

In the doorway of the slaughterhouse, the vendors were listening to the bells of Ángelus. They heard Tomasón say, "Caraaá. It's six o'clock again."

The old man stopped beneath the trees that were adorned with garlands. He wondered why they smelled so penetrating that day. As the drums began to beat in the distance, he felt his chest squeeze him.

"I'm dying, caraaá!" He uttered in a voice accustomed to conversing alone.

The vendors argued over whether the sound of the drum's skins came from San Cristóbal hill or whether the river carried them. They went away to better ascertain. In their inattention, they left the leaves of the entryway open. The bull stuck out its snout, sniffed the air and left.

Tomasón walked slowly but with precision. He tried to fix in his mind the shapes and lines of his own face. He rehearsed the delicate movement of his fingers, in order to draw his own likeness on other blank walls. Somewhere, they were waiting for him.

"I'm sure of security."

He imagined the dark dust, dancing, mischievous, covering everything. And then he saw, face to face, in flesh and blood, the red bull that he had painted on the hide that covered the window like a spell. The painful burning in his chest magically disappeared. The cough left him. With effort he breathed the charged aroma of the Malambo trees, he was filled with doubt.

"About what?"

He gathered himself, so as to continue. He advanced. His body decided to obey him. He continued to advance, and when he heard in the distance the hushed murmur of the rounded songs of the Talking River, he did not realize that he had no more time to think that he had fallen asleep once again.

Translator's Note

When Lucía Charún-Illescas and I first began our work together, almost three years ago, we had not anticipated the release of the first English edition of her novel coinciding with the
one hundred and fiftieth anniversary of the abolition of slavery in Peru (1854). Black people, as W.E.B. DuBois reminds us
in *The Souls of Black Folk*, have given their spirit, song, and sweat
to the Americas from the beginning of the slave trade to the
present day. These gifts are apparent in the tireless creativity
of Lucía Charún-Illescas and in her novel's compelling story.

People outside the Spanish-speaking world are often unaware
of those of African ancestry living in Peru and the contributions
of Afro-Hispanic people in Latin America history. *Malambo*
helps to correct this, bringing to life fictional events that are,
nonetheless, historically valid. Fernando Romero—in *Quimba,
Fa, Malambo, Ñeque*—describes Malambo as a barrio that once

existed on the outskirts of Lima. The town, inhabited by black and indigenous folk, was created on the bank of the Rímac River (169). Aldo Panfichi, in his contribution to *Lo africano en la cultura criolla*, characterizes Malambo as the most important black settlement in all of Lima. Originating in colonial times, and taking up mostly peaceful relations with Spanish authorities, the settlement consisted of slaves and freedmen who aspired to create and maintain their own prosperity and independence (141). Well into the twentieth century, Malambo was known for its religious and cultural practices expressed in the town's numerous ethnic celebrations and *cofradías* or brotherhoods (142).

〰〰〰

The Malambo depicted in the novel is that of the late sixteenth to mid-seventeenth century, a time when Peru remained the center of Spanish viceregal rule, and Lima played a leading role in the Spanish-American Inquisition. The character, Sir, helps us locate the novel in time when he mentions having accompanied Richard Hawkins on various expeditions. Richard Hawkins (1562-1622), son of John Hawkins, was an English pirate of international infamy who served under Francis Drake. In 1594 he was captured, and subsequently incarcerated in Peru for three years before being transferred to Spain. (Sir also makes reference to large guano deposits, fertilizer made of bird droppings—these would not become a substantial export resource until the mid-nineteenth century.)

Slavery was quite common during the period the novel takes place. The colonies of Peru, Mexico, and New Granada (modern day Colombia), along with Brazil, as Frederick P. Bowser notes in *The African Slave in Colonial Peru 1524-1650*, were "the most important centers of African Slavery in the Western Hemisphere during the sixteenth and seventeenth centuries" (vii). Indeed, the slave trade, along with the smaller influx of slaves who accompanied their masters to the colony, gave rise to an Afro-Peruvian population that by the mid-sixteenth century numbered an estimated three thousand people, half of whom resided in Lima. At that time, Bowser states, the number of Spaniards in the capital city would not have been much greater (11).

Cartagena served as the principle port of entry for Africans destined for South America. Those headed to Peru were shipped to Puerto Belo in Panama, where they had a relatively short but arduous trek across the isthmus to the city of Panama, and then eventually to Callao and Lima. The slave trade to Peru was different from the rest of the Americas. In Brazil and Central and North American countries, it was common practice to import large groups of slaves from the same African tribe. In contrast, small and geographically dispersed ethnic groups were brought to Peru, and this hindered communication and the possibility of rebellion (Bowser 62-63). Indigenous populations were also forced into slavery by the colonists.

The African-ancestored cultures and communities that arose from the Black Atlantic slave trade in Peru are linked with those in other parts of the Diaspora. While the novel certainly examines the lives and struggles of numerous oppressed peoples, at its core is the treatment of those of African descent. Lucía Charún-Illescas, an Afro-Peruvian woman who currently resides in Germany, develops *Malambo* as the setting for the powerful portrayal of this group—a group often marginalized, oppressed, or forgotten altogether. A black woman author, as Maryse Condé attests, can often lead to more insightful and complex depictions of the Negro experience (Pfaff, Françoise. *Entretiens avec Maryse Condé*, 33). Charún-Illescas expresses, emphasizes, and elevates the African and the Afro-Peruvian experience as it relates to her native land under colonial rule. Yet she does so in a manner that neither belittles nor demeans the cultures and ethnicities of the other groups represented.

The Latin America characterized by Manuel Zapata Olivella as a cultural, historical, and geographical *mestizaje*, is apparent throughout Charún-Illescas' novel. In *Malambo*, we observe the connections among the Spanish, the Portuguese, the blacks, mestizos and mulattos, the indigenous people, the Jews, the Christians, the rich, the poor. Edward Said sees this ability to depict the connection between the text and the national and international context as a key strength of novels, and it is a strength of this one:

[. . .] understanding that connection does not reduce or diminish the novels' value as works of art; on the contrary, because of their *worldliness*, because of the complex affiliations with their real setting, they are *more* interesting and *more* valuable as works of art. (*Culture and Imperialism*, 13)

I have tried to be faithful to the original Spanish text—at the same time, I understand that translation demands the authoring of a new literary work in a different language. One area where I allowed myself some creative latitude (with the author's blessing) was in relation to the Spanish word *negro*. In the original work, Charún-Illescas uses *negro* consistently, which is the historically accurate term for most of Latin America, Peru included. Yet, given the different connotations of *black* before and after the Civil Rights Movement, this literal usage seemed inappropriate to fully convey intent and meaning. Consequently, I have primarily used the word "Negro" and "nigger" in the translation, depending on the situation and speaker, nomenclature more reflective of language used during slavery in the United States.

The glossary that appears at the end of the novel is also translated from the Spanish original. I have added a few words—again with the author's permission—to better clarify the text.

Without the unwavering support of my editor, David Rade, the realization of this text would not have been possible. He believed in the importance of Lucía Charún-Illescas' novel and in my work, even when the translation was in its earliest stage. I also wish to thank Margaret Mahan for her editorial help. I am grateful to Tim Lensmire who provided invaluable insight and guidance throughout the project. The translation of *Malambo* is dedicated to my wife Teri Hernández and our son S. Kalani Harris.

WORKS REFERENCED:

Bowser, Frederick P. *The African Slave in Colonial Peru 1524-1650*. Stanford: Stanford UP, 1974.

Orrego, Juan Luis "La república oligárquica (1850-1950)" *Historia del Perú*. Barcelona: Lexus Editores 2000.

Panfichi, Aldo, "*Africanía*, barrios populares y cultura criolla a inicios del siglo XX." *Lo africano en la cultura criolla*. Aguirre et al. Lima: Congreso del Perú, 2000.

Pfaff, Françoise. *Entretiens avec Maryse Condé*. Paris: Éditions Karthala, 1993.

Romero, Fernando *Quimba, fa, Malambo, ñeque: afronegrismos en el Perú*. Lima: Instituto de Estudios Peruanos 1988.

Rout, Leslie B. Jr. *The African Experience in Spanish America:1502 to the Present Day*. London: Cambridge UP, 1976.

Said, Edward. *Culture and Imperialism*. New York: Vintage Books, 1993.

Zapata Olivella, Manuel. *La rebelión de los genes: El mestizaje americano en la sociedad futura*. Bogotá: Altamir, 1997.

Glossary

aché African term: word, power or breadth that also radiates from plants.

aguardiente Brandy, liquor.

Babalú Ayé In the Yoruba pantheon, oricha of plagues and infections of the skin.

fulling mill Smooth stone in which food is ground by hand in kitchens. In Spanish batán from Kikongo: batá or to strike.

cachimba Pipe used to smoke. In Bantu: cazimba.

Carabalíes Ethnic group originating from the Calabar region in the southwest of Nigeria.

caramanduca Pasta made from flour, sugar, cloves, and cinnamon.

Carcancha Quechua word, one of the manifestations of death.

Chalaco Native of the port of Callao.

chancaca Maize cake, wheat cake.

Changó In the Yoruba pantheon, the oricha of fire, thunder, and the drum.

chicha A strong Peruvian alcoholic drink made from fermented maize associated with ceremonial and ritual occasions.

cimarrón A runaway slave who hides in the mountains and elsewhere in search of liberty.

cofradía or ***cabildo*** A brotherhood established for mutual assistance among slaves.

Congos Ethnic group originating from the Congo basin, including the Mondongos or Mondungas, and Angolans in the south of the region.

cumpa Afro-Peruvianism: a beloved friend, comrade.

cunda Afro-Peruvianism: ingenious, skilled in mending things.

Eleguá In the Yoruba pantheon, the oricha of destiny and the beginning of the contradiction.

humitas Food made with sweet corn and wrapped in maize leaves.

Lucumíes One of the Yoruba ethnicities called Ulcumí, term transformed accordingly in Latin America.

Mandingas Ethnicity originating between Senegal and the Gulf of Benin.

mazamorra Maize mush, maize porridge.

mazamorreras Sellers of mazamorra, a dessert with a flour base.

Minas Ethnicity originating from the region between the Gold Coast and the so-called Slave Coast.

Obbatalá In the Yoruba pantheon, oricha creator of the Earth and human beings.

Ochún In the Yoruba pantheon, oricha of love, feminine attributes, and lord of the rivers.

Ogún In the Yoruba pantheon, oricha lord of metal and war.

oricha Natural force, vibration, light, spirit of the ancestors, gods of the Yoruba religion.

Pachamama From Quechua, the Mother Earth; Mother Nature.

Pachamanca From Quechua, seasoned meats that are baked in an open hole in the ground covered with hot rocks.

panalivios A type of Peruvian music, comparable to gospels or spirituals

quimba Afro-Peruvianism, person with elegance and with grace when they walk. In the Mayombe language, to be valiant.

quincha From Quechua, wall made of cane, rods, or another similar material.

sala malecú Form of greeting among Peruvian slaves of this era. Possibly derived from the Islam greeting "A salam aleikum" (peace be with you).

sango yucca and maize pudding.

taita Name used to designate one's parents and persons of respect.

tamal A type of corn bread wrapped in plantain leaves.

tentenelaire Mestizo. Offspring of a quadroon and a mulata or vice versa.

tsacuara Ear of thin cane.

vihuelas Early form of the guitar.

Yemayá In the Yoruba pantheon, mother of all oricha, represents the sea.

Swan Isle Press is a not-for-profit literary press
dedicated to publishing the works of exceptional
writers of poetry, fiction, and nonfiction.

Swan Isle Press, Chicago, 60640-8790
www.swanislepress.com

Malambo
Designed by Jill Shimabukuro
Typeset in Hoefler Text with Volgare display
Printed on 55# Glatfelter Natural